THE
OTHER
COUPLE

BOOKS BY TRÍONA WALSH

The Snowstorm

The Party

THE OTHER COUPLE

TRÍONA WALSH

bookouture

Published by Bookouture in 2024

An imprint of Storyfire Ltd.
Carmelite House
50 Victoria Embankment
London EC4Y 0DZ

www.bookouture.com

Storyfire Ltd's authorised representative in the EEA is Hachette Ireland
8 Castlecourt Centre
Castleknock Road
Castleknock
Dublin 15, D15 YF6A
Ireland

ISBN: 978-1-83618-107-1
eBook ISBN: 978-1-83618-106-4

For Harry, Charlie, Ruby and Lily – you will always be the best story I ever told

PROLOGUE

'Who... who *are* you?'

Finn, face ashen, so pale its white glow was visible even in the dark, stared at her with hollowed-out eyes. The wind wailed around him, shaking him, unsteadying him, toying with him as he stood still far too close to the cliff's edge, the waves beneath crying out for a sacrifice.

Alice looked at the other faces staring at her in the dark, the lighthouse beacon illuminating them in flashes, like secrets briefly whispered then concealed again.

'Finn, what are you talking about?' Alice stuttered, holding her hands out to him. 'You know exactly who I am. I'm your girlfriend, I love you.' She took a step towards him, her face crumpling in anguish. This was agony.

Finn recoiled, taking another step backwards, now so close to the edge that small loose rocks slipped under his foot and tumbled, falling, falling, falling into the deep, black ocean. Alice gasped. Her breath caught in her throat.

'Oh no you don't!' He held a hand up. 'Don't come near me.'

Alice could see the distress soaked deep in his eyes. Her own tears spilled down her face. Mac and Vivienne moved closer to Finn, like bodyguards, keeping him safe from her.

'Finn, please... please let me explain...'

ONE

At first, Alice thought she'd imagined it.

She stopped unpacking and stood still.

Listening.

'Alice, was that you?' Finn's disembodied voice floated down to her from the floor above. So he'd heard it too.

Finn, like a little boy, excited and eager, had gone to check out every room in this quirky and charming converted light-house. It sounded like he'd made it all the way to the lantern room at the top.

Alice hadn't missed the note of worry with his words.

Leaving her book down on a windowsill as deep as the thick lighthouse walls, Alice stepped out onto the narrow landing.

'Not me,' she called up to him.

A moment later, down the metal stairs that wound throughout the interior of the tower, Finn and his concerned face appeared. Alice smiled. Even after six months together, she was the full cliché, her tummy still doing flips every time she saw him. Alice reached up and touched his face, sweeping back a lock of his dark, nearly curly hair from his troubled brow. He had the merest hint of grey here and there, but she didn't care a jot that he was older than her. He smiled at her attention, but then the frown soon returned.

'You did hear something, though?'

Alice shrugged, then cocked her ear.

They both definitely heard it this time.

Three loud raps.

Someone was at the door.

'No one is meant to know we're here.' He looked at her, eyes narrowed. 'You didn't tell anyone? Did you?'

'Of course not.' Alice rolled her eyes. 'I'm not stupid.'

'Sorry, I know, I know.'

The knocking continued.

Rap. Rap. Rap.

Alice went into the bedroom and looked out the round porthole windows. But the angles were all wrong. All she could see were the angry rolling waves beyond the cliff edge. The only view the lighthouse, rising proudly from the rocky peninsula, was interested in. She craned her neck.

'I think maybe there's a red car out there?' She looked back at Finn out on the landing. 'Know anyone up here who drives a red car?'

'Nope.'

Alice went back out to him, took his hand and gave it a squeeze.

'I'll answer it,' she said.

'No. Maybe don't, Alice.'

'We're a million miles from Dublin, Finn. We're not getting caught. It'll just be a lost hiker or something.'

Finn frowned but didn't try to stop her. It had only been six months, but he knew better already.

Alice skipped down to the ground floor. Down there, the wall that had once divided the tower from the old keeper's cottage had been removed, making the ground floor one big room. She paused in the curved wooden kitchen that hugged the lighthouse wall.

Listening.

Across, in the low-ceilinged cottage half of the space – now a comfy living room – the door remained quiet. With relief, Alice turned to go back upstairs.

Rap. Rap. Rap.

'Drat,' she muttered.

With a twitch of nervous habit, she smoothed down her dark chestnut hair, took a deep breath and trotted over.

Alice peered through the windowpanes in the door. But decades of salty spray had scratched and dulled the glass, making anything beyond it a blurry confusion. Holding the door handle tight, mindful of the wind outside, she cracked it open.

No one was there.

Where had they gone? Stepping out, the wind instantly took hold of her hair, tossing it into Medusan tangles. The weather had turned when they'd been halfway here. But late autumn was like that. They hadn't cared too much; they weren't here for the sun. A weekend of snuggles by the fire in the lighthouse was what they were after. Just the two of them.

With trouble she pulled the door shut behind her. Alice circled the lighthouse, heading for the narrow driveway that connected them to the mainland.

An older woman was walking back to her car, weaving as the wind buffeted her about.

'Hello?' Alice cried, barely audible over the thieving wind.

The woman stopped and turned. She was white-haired and ruddy-cheeked.

'Can I help you?' asked Alice.

'Ach, and there you are,' the woman said, coming back. She held something out to Alice. 'I gave up thinking you were home. These are for you.'

'Oh?' said Alice, taking a small box from her.

'I'm Mary,' the woman said, smiling. 'I'm your nearest neighbour – though, it's not that near.' She twisted and pointed inland, over low stone walls and scrubby fields. 'If the chooks are laying well, I like to drop any extra into the lighthouse guests.'

'Ah,' said Alice, looking down at the offering. 'Eggs! That's so good of you.' She smiled, relief slipping through her. Just a friendly neighbour.

'Not at all.' The woman waved her away. 'My grandfather was the last lighthouse-keeper, so I like to pop by, keep the connection with the place. I think he'd be amused to know it's a B&B now.'

'It is a bit different,' said Alice, looking up at the tall building.

'I'm just glad it's still in use.' She smiled and turned back towards her car. 'Right, before this wind sweeps us both away, I'll leave you to it. If you need anything, you know where we are.'

A man in a flat cap was sitting in the driver's seat. He nodded and smiled, giving a brief tug on the peak of his cap. Alice waved back.

'Thank you!' she called out after them as they drove off.

Finn was at the cottage door when Alice hurried back. His face tight.

'Just the neighbours, relax.' Alice smiled, holding the eggs. 'With fresh, organic eggs for breakfast tomorrow!'

'I hope you're hungry in the morning, she's given you loads,' said Finn.

Alice counted a dozen.

'Well, we might well need a big breakfast, mmm? Replenish our energy?' Alice winked and Finn laughed from his belly.

'I'm shocked!' he gasped with a grin.

Giggling, Alice put the eggs down on the kitchen counter.

'Come here to me,' Finn cried, following her over. Alice let him gather her into his arms. He laid a gentle kiss on her lips, looking down at her with those big blue eyes of his. When he didn't think she was watching him, Alice thought those eyes held an inscrutable sadness. But this melancholy always slipped away whenever he looked at her. Replaced with a love that spilled like happy tears from them. A love that she was nearly uncomfortable with. But a love that had also been transformative. She would have passed herself in the street, she so didn't recognise herself these days. Everything was perfect.

Except for the secrecy. She was getting tired of that.

The turf from the shed must have been a little damp. It spat like a cornered cat when they topped up the fire.

'Oh!' Alice exclaimed, jumping back, avoiding a spark.

'Careful,' said Finn as he sank into the sofa, the last curtain closed against the squally night. He grabbed the neck of the wine bottle from the coffee table and topped up her drink. The turf settled and they were soon lulled by the crackle from the hearth and the moans from the banshee bluster outside.

Alice tucked her feet up under her and nestled into the crook of Finn's arm. The flames from the lazy fire lit up half his face with a warm amber glow.

'I don't think you'll get any diving done if the weather stays like this,' she said. The car outside was loaded with all his scuba gear. Away from work, diving was Finn's passion.

'It's meant to break for a while tomorrow. There might be a window.'

'How can diving on your own not be super dangerous? Even without storms to worry about?'

'You don't need to worry, Al, I'm a very experienced diver, I've been doing it for over twenty-five years.'

'Twenty-five years? That's as long as I've been alive,' Alice giggled. 'What am I thinking, dating such a dinosaur!'

'I'm only forty-three!' Finn laughed, mock-indignant.

Alice sat up, a grin on her face. 'What's that calculation you do? To see if your younger partner's age is socially acceptable?'

Bemused, Finn shrugged.

'Let me see... you halve your age... and add seven,' Alice said. 'That's it.'

'Okay, then...' said Finn counting it off on his fingers. 'I'm forty-three, so half that is roughly twenty-one, plus seven gives us... twenty-eight. Oh dear, we're going to have to break up!'

Alice laughed, then snuggled back into him. 'Don't worry, seeing as no one knows about us, we're the only ones who need to approve.'

Alice felt Finn stiffen next to her. Her grin faded as she looked up at him.

'I didn't mean that how it sounded. I'm not trying to open up the argument again.'

Finn shook his head. 'Alice, while I'm still your boss...'

'No, honestly, we don't have to rehash it again. I do understand. Sorry, I shouldn't have said anything.'

'It's oka—' Finn turned his head away from her. Towards the window. He screwed up his eyes. Then shook his head.

'What is it?'

He looked towards the window again. 'I thought I heard a noise outside. It was probably just the wind.'

'Isn't that what they say just before the masked guy with the knife shows up?'

Finn laughed. 'I don't think we need to worry about that up here. Donegal barely has people, let alone murdering psychopaths.'

'Yeah, I dunno, Finn. We're sitting ducks!' Alice chuckled then uncurled her legs from under her. She stood up.

'What are you doing?' Finn frowned, then laughed. 'The pretty girl going to investigate is never a good idea!'

Alice chuckled. 'I'm just going to pop upstairs. I want to

grab something. You can go check things if you want. Actually, you never locked the car earlier. Maybe you should do that while you're waiting?'

'But I'm comfy here. I'll do it when we get up to go to bed.'

'Just don't forget.'

'I won't.'

'Right, I'll be back in a tick. Don't get too lonely without me.'

'I'll try not to.'

In their room Alice grabbed her bag, rooted around inside and drew out a small navy gift-wrapped box with a gold shiny bow. Alice smoothed a slightly squished loop. It was a six-month anniversary present for Finn. Cufflinks, shaped like mini scuba oxygen tanks. She hoped he'd love them. Stopping in front of the mirror on the wooden chest of drawers, Alice reckoned she needed a freshening up. She tousled her hair and picked up her lipstick.

Then she stopped.

Had she just heard something? Like this morning, it sounded like a knocking on the door. This place was worse than Grand Central Station. But not again, surely? It had to be close to midnight and even in the countryside you didn't go calling uninvited at this hour. She stood still, listening. There was nothing more. It had probably been the wind howling outside. The same thing that had disturbed Finn a few minutes ago. With a shake of her head Alice cracked open her red lippy, Hot Berry, and applied a dash to her lips. She loved how it clashed with the amber tones in her hair. Pulling her wide-toothed comb through her long waves she was satisfied with her reflection, feeling presentable again. Alice surveyed their room. She wanted it to look nice when they came up later. Romantic. She went over to the bed and smoothed down the white embroidered bedspread, then turned on the small bedside lamps. Stepping back, Alice looked around. It was cosy and inviting. Her heartbeat skipped a little in anticipation.

She picked up the wrapped cufflinks and slipped out of the room.

Alice came to a swift halt.

There were voices. Downstairs. Seriously, what the heck? One of the voices was Finn's and he sounded very unhappy.

She hurried down. The candles on the mantelpiece had gone out. Some wax splattered on the wall behind them. One of the curtains was caught up on itself. The wind had clearly galloped through the room like a hooligan. But Alice wasn't looking at that.

Because beside Finn stood two strangers.

Everyone stared at her.

Finn, oddly pale, spoke.

'Hon, we have a bit of a problem.'

TWO

The strangers were a couple. Well wrapped up against the weather. The man was very tall. No, Alice corrected herself, he was *large*. Tall but also all brawn and beard like a ghost of lighthouse-keepers past. The woman was pale and willowy. She removed her woolly red hat, freeing a cascade of dry and brittle-looking loose blonde curls. Her face was pinched and strained in the dim warm light of the cottage. Neither of them was smiling.

Alice approached the trio. The man seemed even bigger under the low ceiling when she got close to him. It felt like she'd descended into her own disorientating Wonderland, only this guy was the one magically growing. She joined Finn near the sofa.

She smiled tentatively at the strangers. Had their car broken down? Perhaps they were lost hikers like she'd speculated this morning to Finn. They certainly looked the part.

'So, what's the problem?'

'We're still trying to work out what exactly is going on,' began Finn, his words slow and cautious. Then he didn't say any more.

'... and?' prompted Alice.

'Well,' Finn looked at the strangers, standing there unsmiling. 'Al, so, somehow, we're not sure how – it seems these people are also booked into the lighthouse. For this weekend.'

'Sorry, what?' Alice replied, eyes narrowed, looking from Finn to the dour couple. She couldn't have heard that right.

'It's got to be a computer glitch,' Finn babbled. Alice had never seen him so flustered.

Alice's welcoming smile faded from her lips.

'We've just been comparing booking emails,' he said.

'We booked here – months ago.' The woman spoke for the first time. Her voice as cold as the weather and as pinched as her visage. 'We booked it for a romantic getaway. Didn't we, Mac?' She looked at her companion. He made a guttural noise which Alice had to assume was assent.

'This is all... I don't know... Finn, talk to you in private, for a min?' Alice nodded towards the furthest part of the kitchen.

'What's happening?' Alice said in a low voice, huddled up against the counter. 'Who are these strangers in our cottage? They can't have booked it. We have.'

'She showed me their email, and it checks out,' Finn replied, his jaw taut. He dragged a free hand through his hair. His eyes were troubled.

A horrible feeling washed over Alice.

'Are *we* at fault? You sure we got the right date?'

'Totally, don't worry, I double- and triple-checked.'

'Are you definitely *definitely* sure? Because we did have to rebook this after we cancelled two weeks ago...' This weekend was their second attempt to get away. They were meant to have come here a fortnight ago, with all the same arrangements. It was going to be their first weekend away together, and there was a food festival in the next town over they were looking forward to. But a last-minute crisis at the office meant Finn had had to cancel. Alice had been crushed. In Dublin they snuck around like criminals to avoid being spotted. Donegal was where they were going to get to be a normal couple. Hold hands as they walked down the street. Get to go to restaurants or pubs. Things Finn wouldn't risk at home.

'That was my first thought too,' Finn said, taking her hand and rubbing her palm with his thumb. 'But that meant I checked even closer. And the dates are identical. As I said, it must be some sort of glitch that let us both book the place.'

'This is bloody awkward. What on earth are we going to do?' said Alice.

They heard a cough behind them. Alice and Finn looked around. The woman had crossed the room as they'd been whispering.

'Hi,' she said to Alice. 'I'm Vivienne. That's Macdara.' She cocked her head backwards at the big man, who'd stayed at the other end of the room.

Alice turned fully around expecting a proffered hand, but the offer of a handshake didn't materialise. This Vivienne woman just stood there, arms folded across her chest. Finn moved closer to Alice and put his arm around her waist, holding her tight. It felt protective, thought Alice, and she stole a quick glance up at his worried face.

'I'm sure there's an explanation for all this,' Alice said, putting some cheer in her voice. She could be polite even if this woman couldn't. 'It must be a mistake.'

'Clearly,' she said, unfolding her arms. She began pulling at the zip of her heavy winter coat. 'But it's not ours.'

'It isn't ours either,' said Alice, hackles rising. And what on earth was she doing taking off her coat as if she was staying?

'We could call the GetaGetaway.com helpline,' said Alice to Finn.

'I doubt it's open at this hour,' Vivienne replied even though Alice hadn't been speaking to her. She smiled a self-satisfied smirk at Alice. 'Anyway, even if they were open, we're not going anywhere.' Vivienne folded her coat over her arm as if demonstrating her point. 'We're not venturing out again on such a horrible night hoping to find alternate accommodation. Not when we're legitimately booked in here *and* there's a second bedroom that can accommodate us.'

'You want to stay? And share?' Alice was horrified. That wasn't going to happen – this wasn't some kind of casual hostel where you had to share with all walks of life. She looked again at Finn. He seemed to have been struck dumb.

'What about Milford, or Letterkenny?' Alice suggested desperately. 'They're bound to have something.'

'We've just as much right to be here as you two, even if you got here first.'

'I know but...' Alice stuttered.

'It's already nearly midnight, it'd take us at least half an hour to get to Milford. And they won't have anywhere there we can stay. It's not much bigger than a village. Letterkenny might but that's an hour away – an hour away and no guarantees. Anyway, our taxi is long gone by now. This place has a second bedroom, we're staying.'

'Right. Okay, could you excuse us a moment?' said Alice, staring pointedly at her, waiting for her to give them some space. Vivienne looked at her but said nothing and wandered back to her partner. Alice grabbed Finn's arm.

'Finn!' she hissed quietly.

'Christ,' he said, running his hands through his hair again.

'What are we going to do?' said Alice. 'I don't want to share a house with two total strangers. Like, they could be anyone. And she's not being very nice. Can you drive them somewhere?'

'I could, but do they strike you as people who are going anywhere?'

The two of them stared back at the other couple. They were warming themselves by the fire, also with heads close, having a whispered conversation.

'No.'

'We could just get in the car,' said Finn, his voice low. 'Just get in the car and go.'

'And where are we then supposed to stay? We're not going to find anything any easier than they would.'

'We could go back to Dublin?' he said.

'No! And ruin our lovely weekend? We had to cancel once already this month. Anyway, we were here first, that's got to count for something.'

Finn sighed. 'I know. But are you sure? We could put something together last minute, head somewhere warm, the Maldives?'

'And you've the time off to go that far at the drop of a hat, Mr CEO?'

Finn said nothing.

'This is our couple weekend, we got here first, you want to do some diving. I say they are the ones to go. They can get themselves a refund from GetaGetaway if they're not happy about it.'

'Yes, you're right. But, honestly? I don't think we're shifting them until the morning...'

'Finn...' Alice could hear the whine in her voice. This was a disaster.

'I don't want them here any more than you do.' Finn threw up his hands. 'We can call the booking agents first thing in the morning. Until then just try and pretend they're not here. Let's just keep our distance, okay?'

She glared at the other couple. This wasn't how tonight was meant to go. Alice wanted to be back by the fire, her and Finn, sipping wine. Just the two of them.

'You're too nice, Finn. That's your problem.'

'Alice, c'mon—'

'Fine. Fine,' Alice snapped. 'But first thing tomorrow. They're gone.'

'Of course. Don't worry.'

'I'm going to bed,' said Alice, fighting the urge to stomp off like a tantruming child. 'I'm not hanging around down here with them, making nice.'

'I'll come with you. Let me just... I don't know, sort them out for the night.'

'Sure,' said Alice, her voice dripping with disappointment. She took a step towards the stairs, then stopped. She looked back at Finn. 'Is the other room even made up? There was only meant to be one couple staying here this weekend.'

'That's a good point. I'll go and see what the state of the room is.'

'Be back in a moment,' he said to the other two, then skipped up the stairs, two at a time.

Alice suppressed a small whimper. She made to follow Finn. With one foot on the first step, she nodded goodnight at the strangers, irritated at herself for still being polite, despite everything. There was no nod in return. Instead, the woman stared at her. Her expression impenetrable, as if Alice was some kind of puzzle she couldn't work out. Alice felt a chill, as though the front door had been left open. She quickened her pace up the stairs but stopped on the last step, silently observing Finn through the open door as he moved about the first-floor bedroom. She was just about to call out to him when she heard the voices from below grow louder. They must have thought she was all the way gone upstairs and out of earshot. She couldn't make out what they were saying exactly, but the tone was clear. They didn't sound happy. Alice, keeping her feet light on the metal steps, slipped back down a couple of treads, keeping to the darkness.

'... I don't care...' she heard Vivienne snap. From the shadows she saw the large man throw his hands up, his face screwed up in frustration.

'You should care! I don't like this, Vivienne, it feels all wrong.'

I couldn't agree more, thought Alice. She was glad she wasn't alone in thinking this was an unhappy set-up. Maybe Finn wouldn't have to get rid of them tomorrow, the big guy would do it for them.

'Mac, of course you'd say that. This is what you're always like.'

'Let's go, Viv, let's go home. C'mon.'

'No. Not until—'

'Alice,' a voice came from behind her. She whipped her head around. Finn's frowning, puzzled face looked down at her. Alice threw a finger up to her lips. He hushed, but the moment was over, the voices below were muted and inaudible again. Alice suppressed a groan of frustration. What had Vivienne been about to say? Not until *what*?

'What are you doing?' whispered Finn.

Alice looked downstairs towards the fading voices.

'Nothing.' She stood and joined Finn on the first floor landing. Alice stopped, standing close to him, feeling his reassuring body heat, hints of his musky cologne lingering after a long day, a smell that like a spell helped calm her down. She looked back down the stairs, the light glowing up from below. Who had they let in?

THREE

Alice and Finn lay side by side in the bed. They'd pulled the curtains closed across the round, deep-set windows despite the countryside-black night outside. It felt defensive. Close the door, close the curtains. Keep everything out. The only light was from the lighthouse bulb that pulsed above them, creating a faint glow which snuck in under the curtains. It flared and dimmed with regularity, the heartbeat of the building.

The sound of the bathroom door opening and closing on the next floor down drifted up to them. Alice was only thankful that the bathroom was on the floor separating the two bedrooms. If those two, Vivienne and Mac, had been directly under them, she couldn't have stood it. As it was, the romantic night she and Finn had been so looking forward to was in tatters. The whole weekend looked in jeopardy. Now, they were lying here, no part of them touching. Alice couldn't speak for Finn but she was way too wound up for anything romantic. She'd be surprised if she even got to sleep. Yet one more reason to be annoyed at these people.

It was still bugging her that she'd missed whatever Vivienne had been about to say to Mac. In the dark, she rolled onto her elbow and sought out Finn's indistinct shape. A new, worrying thought occurred to her.

'Finn... they've not been sent by shareholders to spy on us, have they?'

'Alice... what?'

'On the stairs, I thought she was about to say something to him. That's why I shushed you. Maybe that was it? Think about it. We've had some near misses, like when your assistant nearly walked in on us in your office. And that time at the party... in the cloakroom, maybe we didn't get away with it? And they're on to us? You're always telling me how high stakes this is.'

'Alice, my paranoia is rubbing off on you.'

Alice sank back against her pillow. It had all started when she and Finn had gotten chatting at the company summer BBQ. She'd been tongue-tied when the handsome and brilliant Finn Tobin – founder and CEO of TobinTech – had stopped and chatted to her as she helped herself to warm potato salad from the buffet. So distracted she left with a small mountain of it on her plate. And then, they'd run into each other again. At a small art gallery in town. There'd been this exhibition her friend had dragged her to see. Alice had spotted him first, dressed down in battered jeans and an old navy sweater. A yellow scarf wrapped around his neck. Those curls not quite as contained as when he was in the office. You'd have never guessed he was a very rich man. He'd been on his own, and she hadn't planned to approach him. But he'd spotted her and smiled. Recognised her, remembered her name. She'd blushed but they'd got talking. Went for a coffee in the gallery's café. And just talked and talked. Alice's friend had gone home without her. Alice had thought Finn seemed a little bit lonely, and Alice would have to admit she was too. She'd closed herself off over the years, pushed people away. It had been easier that way. But Finn Tobin – not even really her boss; he was her boss's boss's boss – had found a chink in her armour.

'I'm the one who should be paranoid. I'd get fired if it came out. You own the company, you'll be fine.'

'I won't be fine. It's a bit frowned on, you know, for the boss to use the office as his dating app. Anyway, we've been over this... the board, shareholders... it would tank the shares if it looked like any sort of scandal was brewing. And dating a twenty-five-year-old junior analyst, against all our company policy against abuse of position and power. It wouldn't take much. In this day and age – quite rightly too.'

They'd been over this enough. Finn was only repeating what she already knew, what they'd talked about a million times.

'Alice, those two downstairs aren't from the board. It'd be Laura McIntyre, HR director, here if they knew, not those two randomers.'

'I suppose... but... I dunno... don't they seem a bit *off* to you? Like, isn't it odd how they claim to have booked the lighthouse for the weekend... but they've only got those small backpacks with them? They're barely big enough for a pair of pyjamas.'

'Some people pack light, Alice. I don't know.'

They slipped into silence again.

'I'm sorry.' Finn's voice floated softly out into the darkness. The others might be two floors down, they had no way to hear Alice and Finn from there, but their presence felt all-consuming.

'What are you apologising for?' said Alice, quiet too. She'd meant to sound conciliatory but notes of resentment got tangled in her words.

'I shouldn't have pushed you to let them stay. I should have driven them to Letterkenny. What's the worst they could have done? Called the Guards?'

'You can't say what might have happened. That Macdara guy is big...'

Finn sighed in the darkness. 'Alice...'

Alice waited for Finn to continue, but he didn't.

'What?'

She heard the deep breath he took in.

'There's something I should have done... something I should have told you about...'

Finn's words seemed to float above her like a night spirit. Alice switched the bedside light back on. She turned to him. He was staring at the ceiling, his half of the bed still shrouded in shadow.

'You're sounding very serious there.'

He still said nothing.

'Finn, you're worrying me. What is it?'

He rolled onto his side and looked at her. Even in the low light Alice felt herself pulled, as she always did, into his earnest blue eyes. She reached out a hand and smoothed away a curl that had fallen across his forehead.

Finn lay there, struggling to bring his words forth. Alice saw the moment when he released something and rolled away from her.

'Hey,' she said, touching his shoulder, 'it's okay, you can tell me, whatever it is.' She reached out. Alice wanted him to unburden himself, whatever it was.

Finn rolled back. Now with something in his hand. It was a parcel.

'It's this. I didn't get to give it to you, what with everything. I should have given it to you sooner. I wanted to tell you I was sorry the surprise was ruined. Happy six month anniversary.'

Alice took it, confused. That was it? The big burdensome reveal was he'd forgotten to give her a present? He knew she wasn't a fool. Whatever he'd wanted to say, that wasn't it. She really hoped it had nothing to do with them. Could he be getting tired of their secret relationship? She could kick herself for bringing it up, again. She didn't want him feeling he had to make any radical decisions. She knew the only way to avoid a scandal was her leaving TobinTech. Getting a job where she wasn't sleeping with the CEO. She'd just have to be careful to leave without that little addendum to her CV. Then there'd be no jobs to go to. But Alice knew what she was doing. She'd had a plan since she was a little girl and it hadn't failed her yet.

Of course, maybe he was going to tell her that they had to break up. And had chickened out of that.

Alice sat up a little in the bed. Well, whatever it had been, he'd just given her a present.

'Thank you, Finn. And don't be sorry. I have something for you too which I forgot about in the confusion.' Alice turned to get out of bed.

'No, stay. Tomorrow will be soon enough. I don't mind. Open your present, I want to see your face.'

Alice adjusted the pillow behind her and got comfortable. She shot a coy smile at Finn as she slipped her finger under the end of the paper. She opened the present. It was a book, from her favourite author.

'Hey, this isn't even out yet. How?'

'I have my ways,' said Finn, a tentative smile returning to his lips. 'I'd hoped to have it for your birthday, but even I couldn't quite pull that off.'

'Stop it. You got me plenty for that.' Alice thought of the considered and expensive presents he'd showered on her a few weeks ago for her birthday. She'd been overwhelmed at his generosity. 'This... aw, hon. Thank you.' She looked over at him.

'You like it?'

'I'm thrilled. This is so thoughtful. But are you sure you still want to date me knowing my favourite books are silly little romance novels? Shouldn't I be reading "serious" novels to be your girlfriend?'

'Oh now, don't do that. There's nothing wrong or silly about romance.' He reached up and rubbed her cheek.

'Thanks, love,' Alice replied, her heart full.

She turned the book over in her hands. Ran her palm over the smooth pastel cover then looked at the back of it, reading the enticing words there.

'Go on. Dive in. I know you want to,' Finn said, his voice tired but happier than it had been a couple of minutes ago. 'You're just not allowed to mention on the internet that you have it, okay?'

Alice chuckled. 'No signal, so no fear of that.'

She beamed at him and opened the book.

Downstairs, the faint clunk of a door opening, or maybe shutting – it was impossible to tell from here – stopped both of them. Each turned their head towards the bedroom door.

Finn sighed, the weary tone returned. 'I promise. Tomorrow they'll be gone. Leave it to me.'

'I hope so, Finn... it's just so... unsettling having them here.'

'Don't worry about them, okay?' He squeezed her hand. His eyelids looked heavy, a weariness had come over him. Despite his clear exhaustion, it took him some time to fall asleep. He didn't quite toss and turn, but he seemed to struggle to get comfortable. Eventually, as Alice read quietly, she heard his breath become more regular, shallower.

She waited, reading on, giving him time to fall deeply asleep, before closing the book.

She placed it on the locker, darting glances at his sleeping form all the time.

Then she slipped silently out of the bed.

FOUR

Alice stood beside the bed. Outside the feeble radius of her bedside lamp, the room was in utter darkness. The only relief from the ravenous night was the faint on–off ghost glow from the lighthouse beacon as it pulsed above them, its light leaking into the room, slipping beneath the curtains.

Alice took feather-gentle steps to the end of the bed, slipping fully into the cloak of dark. Her eyes never leaving the sleeping Finn. She rounded the end of the bed. She took a few more careful steps, reaching Finn's side.

His phone was on the bedside table. She was close enough to touch him as she reached out and picked it up. He snuffled and stirred as she loomed above him. Alice froze. The phone felt as cold in her hand as her heart now did in her chest. But his eyes didn't open. He didn't move again. Alice felt the blood start pumping through her body again.

As quickly as she dared, Alice retraced her steps. She slipped herself back into the bed, causing as little disturbance as she could manage. Then, tugging her pillow down, she lay flat. With a quick glance at Finn – still sound asleep – she unlocked his phone.

It flashed into life like a blast grenade. Alice slapped it to her chest. Her head snapped over to Finn. But, other than a quiet moan, he didn't wake. Turning down the brightness, Alice tried again. She opened the camera app. Holding the phone aloft she settled back and angled the lens. She checked the image on-screen. No, that wouldn't do. You could see part of her arm. It was clear it was a selfie. And she'd gotten some of Finn's shoulder in it too. She inched over a bit, away from Finn, and angled the phone more.

That was much better. If she closed her eyes she'd look asleep, and there'd be no sign of her holding the phone. And no sign of Finn. She'd planned on taking some practice pictures with her own phone. But she'd left it in her bag when they'd got here and she'd realised there was no signal in the cottage. In all the unpleasantness later she'd forgotten it. And she didn't fancy going downstairs to retrieve it in case she bumped into one of them. So, she was just going to have to wing it. Hope she got it right first time.

She set the timer, then closed her eyes.

One... two... three.

She gave it another moment then opened her eyes. She brought the phone to her and examined it. Yes. Perfect. Then she deleted it from his camera roll.

Sliding out of the bed, Alice tiptoed around in the darkness and put his phone back.

Returning to her side, her shoulder brushed open the curtain. She stopped a moment, looking out as a startlingly bright moon lit up the sea. Wild and raging, the waves were still parrying with the wind. She imagined the ships that had been wrecked here over the centuries, the lighthouse's warning too late. Finn had brought her here, telling her he loved its desolate beauty. He came here all the time. Alice could believe it. Its isolation, its starkness, its uncompromising 'me against the world' soul reminded her of Finn. And herself for that matter. Maybe that was why they clicked so well.

She began to turn away but a flash of something made her stop. Alice leaned back in, closer to the window at the end of the two-foot-deep sill. Her hands rested on the cool brick as she peered.

She saw what had caught her eye. There was someone out there. Standing further down the cliff edge. Storm-powered waves leapt and broke in front of the figure. Like white ghosts they framed the person who stood there, arms by their side.

It was the woman, Vivienne.

Her wavy blonde hair, caught and tossed by the wind, mimicked the salty spray. If she wasn't careful, the ghost waves would drag her off the cliff and into the sea. Alice recoiled from the window, a reflex propelling her to rush outside and drag Vivienne to safety. But she stopped. Vivienne had turned slightly. Alice could just make out her face. Vivienne was roaring, yelling into the tempest. Her face a contortion of furious emotion. Though a good distance away, the expression on her face was unmistakable.

Rage.

Alice felt the ocean chill flow through her. Vivienne didn't need saving from the sea, rather the sea needed protection from her. Awoken and enraged, she was like the kraken invading dry land.

Alice watched, transfixed, until whatever demon inhabited Vivienne loosened its grip, and she turned away from the cliff edge. Her body moved more loosely, diminished in some way, as she returned to the lighthouse. A few feet out, Vivienne stopped and looked up. Looking right in Alice's direction. Alice flinched back and froze. It was dark, Vivienne wouldn't be able to see her, but still she could feel her heart hammer. The woman's narrow, drawn face glared up at her, eyes unseeing. After what felt like forever, but could only have been moments, Vivienne walked on, out of sight. Alice spun around and hurried over to the bedroom door. She cracked it open an inch. It was pitch black out in the small corridor, but the light vacuum didn't soak up the sounds of the returning woman.

The front door closing, four floors down, was a faint whisper. Vivienne's feet, as she started up the metal stairs, were clearer. Alice could tell that she was taking them gently, keeping the clang of ascent as quiet as possible. Alice held her breath as Vivienne reached the second floor, where her bedroom was. Would she stop? The footsteps paused... and then began again. Alice trembled. The bathroom was between them – maybe that was all she was up to, where she was going.

The muffled clang was interrupted by the downstairs bedroom door opening. A distant male called out softly, 'Vivienne.' The footsteps paused again. A pleading, 'Come back here,' drifted out. When the footsteps receded, and the door shut below her, Alice sagged and released her held breath.

She closed her own door and fell back against the wall.

Alice had always been that kid who brought home every bird with a broken wing and shabby lost little kitten. But... it was the way they'd come across. There'd been no conciliatory words when the problem of the double-booking had emerged. It had been 'my way or the highway' from Vivienne. And now this disturbing and weird behaviour out there. Alice had a feeling they weren't as freaked out down there as she and Finn were up here.

Tomorrow morning Finn would remove them. Whether they liked it or not.

The chill she'd felt watching that woman scream out to the ocean hadn't eased. Still resting against the wall, behind her Alice's fingertips felt a path along it to the door. Like an escapologist in reverse she found the key in the lock and turned it, locking them in. Keeping them safe. Her eyes watched Finn's calm, sleeping figure as she did so. Only partly illuminated, most of him lost to her in the dark, unseen.

FIVE

Alice sat bolt upright in bed.

Confused and disorientated, she looked around. Morning light streamed in through the thin curtains. She rubbed still sleepy eyes. Without her phone she'd no idea what time it was, but it felt early. Beside her Finn slept on, his breathing soft and regular.

Something had woken her, torn her from her slumber. She slipped out from under the duvet and stood beside the bed. Listening. But she heard nothing. At least, nothing now anyway. Perhaps it was just anxiety that had prompted her sudden wakefulness. A need to be the first up, to get downstairs and call the booking website. She thought of the strangers sleeping downstairs. Of the rage-filled woman screaming into the sea last night. How she'd even gotten to sleep in the first place was beyond her.

Alice grabbed a sloppy cardigan and pulled it over her cream pyjamas. With a look of regret at the sleeping Finn, and a look of trepidation across the room, she grabbed her new book and headed for the door. She'd go downstairs and read with a coffee. She had woken herself up, that's all that had happened. She needed to relax, to calm down.

Alice turned the key as quietly as she could and stepped out onto the landing. Despite the talking-to she'd given herself, she paused and listened. Just to be sure. But only the stillness of early morning filled the air. Though that stillness had an eerie quality that nearly disturbed her more. She forced herself to exhale a breath she'd been keeping in.

Tiptoeing down the winding stairs, Alice slowed as she passed Vivienne and Mac's door. She didn't want to alert them to the fact that she was up and about. And in pole position to make that call. Even if it was a system glitch and neither she and Finn nor Vivienne and Mac had a greater right to the place, she wanted to at least be the first to plead their case.

In the kitchen, the gloom of overcast skies outside and the small round windows meant the ground floor was murky and cold. There were shadows and dark corners everywhere down here. Alice felt jumpy. Nervous. She turned 360 degrees, slowly. Scrutinising every nook and cranny. It was so quiet she could hear the waves beyond the cottage door. She took a step towards the living room. Again, examining her surrounds. Discerning innocent shapes lost in the shadows from imagination's worst tricks. A shriek from outside nearly stopped her heart. A panicked seagull all it was.

Despite the mood of sleepy menace, Alice was alone. Forcing herself to relax, she looked up at the kitchen clock. It was 6.50 a.m. According to the booking email the phone line wouldn't be open until eight. She'd an hour or so to kill. She'd read, have her coffee and hope those two slept in.

She put her book down on the counter and looked around for her handbag. She wanted a hair tie to pull her unbrushed tangle of hair into a messy bun. She was pretty sure she'd left it hanging from the back of a kitchen chair. But it wasn't there now. She circled the room. Only on the second pass did she see it wedged between a cushion and the end of the sofa. Had she actually left it there? She sat down, snatched it open and rifled through its contents. Everything was as it should be. With a snatched furtive glance back up the stairs, she reached into the bag, her fingers finding the opening to a hidden pocket. With a second glance to make sure she was definitely alone, she drew it open. A driver's licence and a brass key with a gate fob attached were nestled within. Undisturbed, as they should be. She quickly closed it up again. Alice took out a scrunchie and shut the bag. Perhaps she had taken the bag over with her to the sofa last night? Frowning, Alice returned slowly to the kitchen counter. Mulling it all distractedly, on autopilot she clicked on the kettle. She rooted around in the cupboards, finding a loaf of bread, and popped two slices in the toaster.

Her eyes kept darting to the kitchen clock. It was amazing how time slowed down just as you needed it to speed up. Grabbing her coffee and toast, she sat at the kitchen table. She read as she ate, trying to distract herself, willing the hour until the phone line opened to pass.

Alice left the book face down on the counter and switched on the kettle for another large mug of coffee. She wasn't sure if this was mug three or four. If she hadn't been jittery already, she certainly would be now. Over the bubble of the boiling water she didn't hear the sound of feet on the stairs until whoever was coming down was nearly upon her. The staircase was unenclosed as it reached the ground floor, and with a sinking heart, Alice could see enough to know it wasn't Finn.

Vivienne came fully into view. She bestowed a weak half-smile on Alice.

Alice flashed back to the wild woman on the cliff edge of last night. The rage that had contorted her face. There was no trace of it now. Other than her insincere smile she looked like a regular, non-crazy woman. Alice nodded at her. A smile would have been a step too far.

'Good morning,' Vivienne said. 'Hoping to catch the early worm... or should I say early phone call to the booking agent?'

Vivienne, unlike Alice, was fully dressed and presentable. Her hair tied back and tamed. She was dressed in running gear.

'Yes, I'm going to ring them. This situation needs to be sorted out.'

Vivienne stepped in close to Alice, who immediately stepped back. The kettle bubbled furiously to its crescendo. Vivienne reached over Alice, opening the cupboard behind her head.

'Lucky me, right first time,' Vivienne said, taking a mug out. She stepped back, grabbing the coffee jar Alice had left on the counter. Ignoring Alice's waiting mug, she filled her own with the just-boiled water. She noticed the book and picked it up, turned it over in her hand.

'I suppose someone has to read them,' she muttered to herself, putting it back down as if it smelled.

'Eh, no need to be such a snob. It's a good book.'

'If you say so.'

Alice's cheeks prickled pink at the judgement. This woman was the limit. She stole a quick glance at the clock.

'The phone line isn't open until eight,' said Vivienne, who must have spotted the look.

'I know.' Alice re-boiled the water and poured it into her mug.

Looking down at her coffee, Alice fought to keep the wobble out of her voice. She wanted these strange, unfriendly people gone. She'd been anticipating days spent in bed, or mad long rambles along the coast. Finding a pub with a turf fire where they'd order hot whiskeys to warm them up again. Instead she was clock-watching, with a stranger, waiting for it to be 8 a.m. and hoping she could get them sent packing.

Vivienne took her coffee to the kitchen table, but Alice stayed put. Keeping as much distance between them as possible.

'You and your boyfriend seem very happy.' Vivienne took a sip of her coffee. Alice raised an eyebrow at the comment, but said nothing.

'You been together long?'

'I'm sorry?' said Alice, growing irritated at this nosiness.

'How long—'

'I heard your question, but it's none of your business.'

Vivienne shrugged. 'He's quite rich, isn't he? Is that part of the attraction?' she said, undiscouraged. She took another sip of her coffee, looking at Alice over the rim of the mug, a twinkle of cruel amusement in her eye.

'That has nothing to do—' spat Alice, before she stopped herself. She cocked her head to one side. 'How do you know he's rich? Not that I'm saying he is...' she petered out, lamely.

'Nice recovery,' Vivienne laughed. 'It's no big mystery. He was on the cover of the *Irish Times Magazine*, end of last year. What was the headline? "Tech Star of the Year", something like that. The article made a lot out of how successful he is. I remember it. Recognised him from it. So, like half the country I'm aware of who Finn Tobin is and his vast wealth. It's hardly a state secret.'

Alice pressed her lips firmly together. Fine. That was true, he had been on the cover of the magazine. A framed copy hung behind reception in TobinTech. In fact, they'd been hanging it when she'd come in for her interview ten months ago. She knew now that he'd been embarrassed about the fuss around the profile. But he was a real success story. He'd been a foster kid, his mother dying young and his father completely absent from his life. He'd built the business up through sheer grit and determination. It was one of the things they'd bonded over. Alice had had a different but equally tough childhood. They both understood what it meant to succeed when everything was against you.

'Well, think whatever you want, I'm not with him for his money. He didn't have it easy as a kid. He deserves his success.'

'Does he now? There's a lot of that about. Everyone seems keen to blame their parents for everything these days.'

'Your kids not keen on you? Is that it?'

Vivienne looked like Alice had slapped her. Her cheeks flushed. It took a moment before Vivienne spoke again.

'No. No kids. Wretched things. Child-free by choice.'

'Right. Good for you.' Alice had hit a nerve. She should have felt bad but she was just glad that she'd found a way to shut Vivienne up.

This time Alice didn't bother even trying to hide the fact that she was checking the time: 7.58 a.m.

'Probably worth a try now,' said Vivienne. 'It's not as if we're the Royal Observatory at Greenwich, is it? The clock might be slow a couple of minutes.'

With a glare, Alice lifted the landline handset, reading the GetaGetaway number from the helpful sticker adhered to it. She pressed the green phone icon button and prepared to dial. With her finger poised to tap out the number, she stopped. There was no quiet hum of a dial tone coming from the phone. She hit the green phone button again, but nothing. She peered at the small phone screen. A line was running through a small mast symbol. She put it to her ear. There was no sound from the handset at all.

Alice looked at Vivienne.

'It's dead.'

SIX

'Dead?'

Vivienne didn't look particularly perturbed but Alice felt her stomach knot and her heartbeat hustle. She fumbled the handset back into its cradle. If the landline wasn't working, they had no way to contact the outside world. Between already patchy rural coverage and thick walls, the old keeper's cottage and lighthouse had no mobile signal. And the lighthouse didn't have any Wi-Fi they could use. It had been one of the selling points of the place. Finn was always so busy with work, the temptation was there to grab a few hours here and there even while they were away. And his employees had no compunction about calling him on the weekend. Somewhere like here meant a romantic weekend stayed a romantic weekend. Total switch-off time. But what had seemed like the perfect element for a romantic getaway was now a very annoying hindrance.

But Alice wasn't going to let that stop her. She sucked in a deep breath.

'I'm going to go to the end of the drive – when we arrived there was some signal up there,' she said.

'Sure,' said Vivienne, her eyes on Alice catlike, lazily sizing her up. Her smirk sat barely below the surface.

Alice stifled an irritated growl at how much Vivienne appeared to be enjoying this hiccup. She skirted the table, giving it as wide a berth as possible, and grabbed her bag from the sofa where she'd left it. She sifted among the bits and pieces within. Wallet, make-up, random receipts, all the things you picked up and tossed in without thinking. The one thing she couldn't see was her mobile. She'd only been concerned with checking the private pocket in the bag earlier, so she hadn't noticed it wasn't in there then.

Alice looked up. She scanned the room, her brows furrowed. She was pretty sure that once signal had died on the driveway down to the lighthouse, she'd only looked at her phone once more – at the cottage door to check the time – and then she'd put it in her bag and not taken it out again.

'Everything alright?' Vivienne asked from the kitchen table.

'It's just... I'm...' Alice stopped. Her eyes narrowed a little. She was looking at someone who would probably be quite happy for Alice's phone to have 'gone missing'. No phone, no ringing the website phone line first.

'After we went to bed last night,' Alice said, 'did you look in my bag?'

'Did I what?' Vivienne's sneering smile faltered. Quickly replaced by barely contained outrage. 'Of course I didn't. How dare you suggest such a thing?'

'How dare I?' snapped back Alice. 'I dare because my bag has been moved since last night and my mobile isn't in it any more.'

Vivienne laughed a sharp laugh. 'You're actually suggesting I stole your phone! Mac and I trekked here, to the furthest tip of Donegal, just to steal your phone as you slept. Right. Perhaps have a look around for it first before you start making wild accusations, hmm?'

With cheeks flaming, no longer able to look Vivienne in the eye, she started looking around for the phone. Maybe she had taken it out last night and had just forgotten? She looked under the sofa cushions, close to where her bag had been. Checked the living room and the kitchen. The space wasn't huge and the search didn't take long. No phone. She was pretty certain the phone had never gotten upstairs.

With a glower at the watchful Vivienne she gave up.

'No luck?' Vivienne said with a barely disguised grin.

Alice said nothing in reply. She'd won this round, but Alice wasn't defeated yet.

'I'll just go to the neighbours'. They said they were there to help if we needed anything.'

Vivienne shrugged. 'Fine.'

Alice might have been imagining it but she thought she saw a wariness creep into Vivienne's expression.

Alice went to the door, grabbed her coat and pulled it on over her cardigan and pyjamas. She then slipped her bare feet into her boots. She looked ridiculous but she wasn't going to waste any more time going upstairs to get dressed. And despite what she'd just said to Vivienne about going to the neighbours', Alice knew she wasn't actually going to have to interact with anyone to make her phone call. She just needed to get far enough away from the lighthouse so that she couldn't be spotted.

Alice opened the cottage door and was slapped by a blast of bracing sea air. She tasted salt on her lips. With a little gasp, she stepped out and pulled the door firmly behind her. She was thankful she'd tied up her hair. Even with last night's storm calming, the wind still felt like a naughty schoolboy racing up behind her and tugging at it.

She marched on, but, at the end wall of the house, Alice stopped. She saw a bundle of wires coming up from the ground and into the house... except that they weren't quite going into the house. The cottage had no television, so they had to be the phone wires. They were frayed and dislodged. Alice crouched down, her fingers touching the damage. She didn't have much clue about these things, and maybe this was wear and tear. And neither she nor Finn had actually made a phone call since they'd gotten here, so perhaps the wires were like this all along. But...

Alice straightened up. She looked back into the cottage, keeping herself to the side so that she was partially hidden. Mac was just coming down the stairs now. She watched as he flicked on the kettle and Vivienne sat sipping her mug, looking out the other window. They didn't talk to each other. There was no 'good morning' peck on the cheek. They were the ones acting as if they were strangers. So odd.

Alice looked down again at the damaged wires. She spun on her heels and hurried towards the end of the drive. She slipped her hand into her coat pocket, her hand nestling around a small, smooth, rectangular object there. Her fingers played along its edge, finding its buttons. As she made it to the end of the drive she pressed the longest button and the small, discreet phone vibrated into life. Soon, as it connected to the network, messages and notifications started to ping.

She was going to make that phone call. Get these people out of the lighthouse. She shot a glance back at the house as she got further away, thinking of the frayed wires, her moved bag and the missing phone. Once she'd found a shielded place to take out her secret phone and make the call unobserved, Alice wondered who exactly she should be calling. The website helpline... or maybe the police?

SEVEN

Alice tried to shake off her disquiet as she walked down the small road that led away from the lighthouse. She wouldn't be calling the police. That had been a bit of an extreme thought. What would she tell them? Two strange people had turned up on their doorstep, the woman had shouted at the sea and some telephone wires looked off, with no idea of when they were last working. And she'd misplaced her phone. Hardly compelling. They'd write her off as a time-waster. And, if she was honest, it would be better not to draw any extra attention to herself or the lighthouse this weekend.

She stopped and looked back down the peninsula. The lighthouse stood proud and faithful against the Atlantic back-drop. She took a deep breath. It would all be fine. It would all be fine. She and Finn would be sipping wine together by dinner-time without any unwanted companions.

Alice walked on for another minute, then slowed down. She was far enough away from the lighthouse now. Crossing the road, she slumped back against an orange lichen-speckled stone wall. It was damp but she sat anyway and took out the phone. Two feeble bars of signal. But two bars would be enough. The screen was filled with a riot of messages and alerts, but she'd look at them properly once she'd talked to the booking agent and sorted this mess out.

She swiped and tapped in the number. With relief, a strong ringtone trilled in her ear. Alice looked around as she waited for it to connect. A sheep bleated in the field behind her. She smiled at it. A smaller black sheep wandered by and they appeared to glare at each other.

'Unwanted guest?' Alice asked the animals. The first sheep bleated at her again. 'I feel your pain.'

The call connected.

'Welcome to GetaGetaway.com. Press one for bookings. Press two for informa—' Alice dropped her hand and brought her attention back to the call. She took the phone away from her ear and pressed the hash key. That usually bypassed the automation and took you to a human. And that's what she needed right now. Someone to explain the problem to.

'Welcome to GetaGetaway,' a voice with only a smidge more animation than the recording came on the line. 'This is Ronan speaking, how can I help you?'

'Hi, I need to talk to you about an apparent glitch in your system. We've booked into Fanad Lighthouse for the weekend and we've had two strangers turn up saying they're booked in here too.'

'I see,' said Ronan. 'What is your name and do you have your booking reference number there?'

Alice gave him the details.

'I see here,' he droned, 'that the booking wasn't made by an Alice Armstrong. I'm afraid I can't talk to you as I would be breaking GDPR rules.' He sounded happy to have an out.

Alice stifled a growl. With exaggerated patience she replied, 'I understand that, Ronan. But Mr Tobin – that's the name you're seeing – is my boyfriend and he booked for both of us.' A moment of doubt gripped Alice. Finn's name was the one the guy could see? 'Emm, it is Tobin, right?'

There was quiet from the other end. Alice felt close to exploding. If Vivienne or Mac's name was on the computer, she and Finn wouldn't have a leg to stand on. They'd be packing up and heading home.

'Please, you can tell me that much.'

'Emm, well, let's just say that I can speak to Mr Tobin on this matter. Get him to ring us here.'

Alice could hear the wind-up in his voice; she could picture his finger hovering over the disconnect button.

'Hold on. Please. Just a moment.'

'Sure...'

'Can I just ask, if I get Finn to call you, how quickly can you have a dispute sorted out? These people are in our B&B as we speak. It's really very awkward. And the mess-up is clearly your end, so like...'

'We would escalate this sort of issue to second tier support. They'd have to look into it.'

'And how long would that take?' Alice felt a knot in the pit of her tummy. She'd a feeling she wasn't going to like the answer to this.

'We like to have issues resolved within forty-eight hours,' he said proudly.

'But,' stammered Alice, 'but we're going home in forty-eight hours! That's no good!'

'You can have Mr Tobin take it up with my supervisor. I'm not obliged to deal with customers who raise their voice to me so I am going to disconnect now. Have a nice day.'

The line went dead.

Alice looked at the phone in disbelief. Feck. That was no good. Maybe Finn could get onto them and use his heft as an important CEO to get something done sooner, isn't that what rich and powerful people did? Not that that was Finn's style at all. She'd never seen him throw his weight around. Finn led with quiet persuasion and respect. It was why everyone loved him and worked hard for him. And it wasn't her style at all either, for that matter. There was nothing that bugged her more than someone abusing their privilege. She usually thought it was obnoxious. But maybe just this once, to save their first-ever weekend away together. She winced at her hypocrisy.

The phone buzzed again in her hand. Alice sighed. She knew without looking at it who it was. Alice felt a different sort of sinking feeling, one fed by weariness. She scrolled through the messages with her thumb; they whirled by like a one-armed bandit machine. Only here there were no prizes, no chance to win. She stopped on a random one.

Where are you, Alice? What if I need you? I'm not strong like you.

And another one.

Alice, I need your help. The pharmacist is trying to kill me again. She is. This isn't my proper prescription, I know it's not.

Why bother talking to me, I'm just your mam, why bother telling me where you're going and what you're doing. Alice? Answer me!

Alice fought the urge to reply. To calm her mam down. To reassure her. But she'd been careful not to let her know where she was going. To say nothing to her about this weekend. She was going to keep it that way. She shut the phone down and dropped it back in her pocket.

A frantic bleating made Alice turn around. In the field behind her, the sheep she'd commiserated with earlier appeared to have gotten itself caught on something. Alice leaned on the stone wall and peered closer. It looked like it was entangled in some barbed wire at the edge of the field. Alice looked up and down the road. There wasn't a car or house for miles. Who the hell knew what farmer was who owned these animals? She took a look back down at the lighthouse. Then back at the frantic animal.

'But I'm in my pyjamas!' she said to the animal's panicked eyes. Another anxious bleat. 'Oh God, alright, alright, hold on.' Alice looked up and down the road again, this time looking for a gate into the field.

'Typical!' yelled Alice to the wind. The gate was inaccessible, over on the far side of the field. She assessed the solidity of the stone wall then scrambled herself up and over it. What must she look like? Messy bun, pyjamas, overcoat and sockless feet in boots. She must look as crazy as Vivienne had last night.

She approached the sheep slowly. For all her good intentions, Alice was a city girl. This was the closest she'd gotten to a farm animal since she'd been to the petting zoo as a small child. Did sheep bite? This one certainly looked stressed enough to lash out.

Low and soft, Alice murmured, 'It's okay, it's okay.' She got as close as she dared. The sheep had gotten its back leg tangled in some old forgotten barbed wire. She circled around to the back of the animal and inched forward. With a panicked wriggle the animal flinched when Alice touched its trapped leg. The barbed wire only got more entangled.

'Feck,' Alice whispered. She reached out again to help the sheep, but this time the frightened animal did more than flinch. It kicked out and, avoiding the hoof, Alice stumbled backwards and fell.

'Ouch!' she yelled, landing on her backside.

With a mixture of relief and embarrassment, Alice heard an approaching car. She got to her feet and waved it down. She immediately recognised the car from yesterday's delivery of eggs. She smiled, the neighbours. They probably owned the poor, trapped creature.

'Hi!' she called out.

The man in the flat cap got out. She noticed he wasn't an older man as the flat cap had suggested, rather he was on the youthful end of middle age. He was also tall and looked strong. Just who she needed right now.

'Do you need help?' he asked, a faint smirk on his face. Alice knew she must look ridiculous. Dishevelled and in her pyjamas, only moments ago flat on her behind on the damp scraggy grass.

'Yeah, this sheep. She's caught. I think she's in pain.'

'Well, we can't be having that now.' The man put one hand on the wall and scooted himself across with far more finesse than Alice had managed. 'Let me have a look.'

He came over and examined the situation. Alice pulled her coat tighter around her.

'Yeah, poor creature. Hold on a moment. Go whisper calming words to her.'

Doing as she was told, Alice went to the head of the sheep and started talking to it as if it was a crying baby. The man straddled the animal, bracing it with his knees as he reached down and untangled the leg. It took only moments and then the freaked-out sheep bounded away, joining the rest of the animals in the field. She cast only one suspicious, backwards glance at her rescuers.

'Thanks for that, it was very upset.'

'No bother. I'll make sure she gets checked out properly. Glad you came along.'

'Ah, I was just trying to get some signal for my phone.'

'The lack of signal is a selling point of this place.'

'Ah yeah, yeah. I know. It's just...'

'Everything okay?'

'Yes. Definitely. Just addicted to my phone, I guess.' Alice forced a smile. She wasn't going to tell this man about the strangers in the lighthouse. She wasn't great at confiding in people at the best of times, so she certainly wasn't opening up to this guy. And anyway, she'd too many strangers involved in her business right now, she didn't need another. 'Right, I think I'll head back, I don't want to have to rescue any more animals in my pyjamas!'

'Good idea,' the man laughed. He took two steps away and then stopped. 'I'm Michael, by the way. Pleased to meet you properly.'

'Alice,' she said, extending her hand. He smiled, a real twinkle in his eye, as they shook.

'Oh, you forgot something,' the neighbour said when they started back toward the wall. Alice turned around. He was picking up her mobile from where it must have dropped in the grass when she fell. 'The whole reason you're out here, you wouldn't want to forget it. The sheep are quite good at cracking passwords.'

Alice laughed.

'Thank you. I'd have missed that.' She took it with a shy smile. She hoped – though she wasn't sure why – that the man hadn't seen all the unanswered messages and notifications. She slipped the phone back into her pocket without looking at it again. They clambered over the wall, the man holding Alice's hand to steady her. Once back on the road, Alice thanked him again for his help.

'I'm just glad I stopped by when I did.' He got into his car, indicated and pulled away. Alice watched him head off. Only when he was a red dot in the distance did she cross the road and start back down the long drive to the lighthouse. The sea crashing against the coast. Salt in the air. Unlike the distressed animal, no one was coming to help out her and Finn. No one was going to untangle them from this mess.

EIGHT

VIVIENNE

The girlfriend was a curveball.

How had they missed that very significant bit of information? They had done their homework, and there wasn't even the merest hint of a partner. He had kept that very quiet. Which set Vivienne's alarm bells ringing.

'Vivienne?'

She looked up. Mac, his coffee mug like a child's toy in his large, overgrown hands. It should have made her laugh, but she didn't seem to find much funny these days. Hadn't for a long time.

'What?' she snapped. He didn't flinch. Vivienne couldn't tell if it was pity or if he was just punch-drunk on her bitterness by now.

'Are we really doing this? No second thoughts this morning?'

They'd argued, in that circular bedroom last night, going round and round. Mac wanted to leave. Pack up and slip out. He reckoned it wasn't smart to continue with this surprise turn, and even if they wanted to, how could they? He wanted them to regroup. She'd accused him of not being committed, that he was just looking for an out.

In truth, Mac was probably a bit shaken. Vivienne knew she was. She hadn't been as prepared as she thought she was for coming face to face with Finn. It was a moment she'd imagined for months. Years even. She'd gone through every scenario she could imagine in her head. She'd had a tingle in her tummy, righteous excitement every time. But at the door last night, the sight of him, rage engulfed her: bubbling, boiling lava, punching at the crust, screaming to erupt. Just looking at that face of his.

It had taken him a moment. At first he hadn't realised who he was looking at. But as the recognition came, the colour in his face went. Beneath the layers of misfortune and pain he'd realised who they were.

Mac didn't come over and sit at the table. Vivienne's force field repelled even him.

'We're doing this alright. We've had one false start, and I've waited long enough, worked hard enough to make this happen.' The volume of her voice rising.

'I can't believe we've come here,' he muttered to himself. 'Of all places. Again.'

She could barely make out his words. But he was looking back at her now, raising his voice so she could hear him.

'Aren't we trying to get away, not get closer to the root of our misery? We should leave them alone. It's clear they're happy, no?'

Vivienne slammed the table with the palm of her hand. Her mug jumped, clattering against the wood, nearly toppling with the force. Mac flinched.

'Dammit, Mac!'

He glared at her, sullen, like a reprimanded child.

'We have a plan. Which we agreed upon. I'm seeing it through.'

He had to stop pushing her. That cliff out there wasn't the only edge she was close to.

'Have you seen either of them yet today?' Mac was quieter now. Tentative. He walked on eggshells around her, but a man that size couldn't tiptoe anywhere. Vivienne turned in her seat, looking out the end window.

'You just missed her.'

Mac followed Vivienne's gaze.

'We had all the fun. She accused me of stealing her phone and now she's gone off to the neighbours' to call GetaGetaway to get us turfed out of here.' They both watched her disappearing figure, looking ridiculous in her nightwear and coat and boots. *Silly girl. And so young, what was Finn thinking?*

'You see,' said Mac, 'that's what I'm talking about. What's going to happen when she gets through to them and she discovers we're not booked here at all? What then, Viv?'

That had been quick thinking last night on Finn's part. The double-booked story. It got them in the door and allowed them to stay. It was smart, but Mac was right, it hadn't aged well. Vivienne had been happy with how she'd held her nerve when the girl had picked up the phone to call the helpline; she'd made the right decision to mess with the phone wires last night. But that and the girl's missing mobile had only slowed her down a little. She'd be at the neighbours' soon enough. So, as Mac had asked, what then? Vivienne knew one thing for certain: Finn was going nowhere.

'What if she calls the Guards, Viv?'

'So what if she does? Nothing will happen! We haven't done anything wrong, have we? The Guards will tell her it's a civil matter and to leave them alone. By the time she gets anyone to take her seriously, we'll be done. And we'll be gone. Anyway, you saw the way Finn capitulated? When he realised we could spill the beans on him? This is very much a Finn problem, and he'll be very motivated to find a solution.'

'Vivienne... she's seen our faces. What if Finn tells her our full names?'

'He won't tell her anything. End of. The stakes for him are too high to do otherwise. You've been looking at this as if she's a problem. I think we're going to find her quite the asset. She's actually going to be very useful. Excellent leverage.'

Mac said nothing. Just sighed. He knew she had a point. When Finn had let them in last night he'd kept looking towards the stairs. Vivienne had spotted the two wine glasses. The extra coat by the door. He had company. And they were someone important enough to him that he was willing to do what they said. Just as long as they agreed to keep the real reason for their visit quiet.

'So, what's the next step then? Seeing as everything we talked about is out the window? And did you say something about you stealing her phone?'

'Don't worry about the phone. And as for the plan, I'm not sure yet. I need to think. There will definitely have to be a few... adjustments...'

Mac turned his head, hearing the footsteps first. Vivienne shifted around in her seat, so Finn would come face to face with them both as he rounded the stairs. She was shaking but hoped he wouldn't be able to tell.

'Good morning,' she sneered, all front.

Finn took the last steps down the clanking metal stairs and stepped into the kitchen.

He looked at her from under cautious eyes, hesitant.

'Coffee?' asked Mac.

'He can make his own damn coffee, for Christ's sake.'

'Thanks,' Finn muttered quietly, throwing a side-eye at Mac. That was something Vivienne needed to watch. Mac had such a kind heart. A stupid kind heart. But she didn't think he would waver. He had suffered too. So much.

'Your little plaything has gone to call the booking agent.'

Finn went over to the kettle and fixed himself a coffee. Mac moved out of his way and leaned against the other countertop. Finn grabbed the milk from the fridge and put the merest drop in. Just like he always had. Vivienne wondered why he bothered. That little milk in his coffee could hardly make it taste any different. But always that one, tiny drop, turning it only the very slightest bit lighter. She could see her hand vibrate and she grabbed her own coffee mug to hide it.

'Don't call her that. It's demeaning. Alice is smart and brilliant—'

'She's practically a child, Finn.'

'Don't be ridiculous. She's young, yes, but twenty-five is hardly a child.'

'Whatever helps you sleep at night.'

'Vivienne,' he lowered his voice. It was soft, but firm. 'Leave Alice out of this. Okay? That's the deal.'

'We'll see,' Vivienne said. 'By the way, your quick thinking bought us time last night, but if she gets through to the helpline now, then she's going to learn the truth. You're going to have to work on a few more convincing stories about why we have to stay. Okay?'

'Why don't we talk now, then? That's what you said you wanted to do, to talk. Let's get it over with before she gets back.' He looked out the window, checking for her. A mixture of relief and regret passed across his face when there was no sign. He stayed at his counter. They made up a Mexican standoff. Vivienne at the table, Mac at one counter, Finn at the other.

He was doing a much poorer job than her at hiding his emotions. She could hear the quaver in his voice. See the way he couldn't meet her eye.

'That doesn't give us nearly enough time,' she said. 'We've a lot to talk about.'

Finn's shoulders sagged. He wasn't getting away that easily. They needed time. It wasn't just a chat they were after.

'But... you can't just hang around here all weekend.'

'Why not?'

'Oh, for God's sake!' He raised his voice to her. 'That's impossible!'

Vivienne glared at him. 'You're resourceful, Finn. You'll think of something to say to her. I'm quite sure you don't want us to give her a little crash course in your history?'

With a visible effort to control himself, he backed down. Vivienne smiled.

'No, I'd rather you didn't say anything to her.' He was hesitant. 'Or anyone else. But, honestly, I can't see her agreeing to share the lighthouse for the weekend. She might not even want us to stay if she thinks you're not leaving.'

'Then you'll have to convince her otherwise.'

'Viv...'

If Vivienne wasn't so scared, she could get drunk on this power. But she wasn't stupid. She knew it was a delicate balance. This was a dangerous game she was playing, and there was a sword of Damocles hanging over each one of them.

'And don't think about the pair of you slipping off back to Dublin in the night. We know where you live, where you work. We'll have no trouble finding you. We came here for privacy, I think you appreciate that?'

'I do. And, look, I know you deserve answers. And apologies.' Finn took a few steps towards her. He looked at Mac and then turned those piercing blue irises on her. 'It's eaten me up inside every single day. I've wanted to make it right, but...' He dropped his eyes, couldn't hold her stare any more. 'But I know sometimes things can't be made right.'

'It's all a bit late for this kind of talk, isn't it?'

Finn hung his head, nodding. 'Yes, it is.'

'She's coming back,' said Mac.

They all turned and looked out of the window.

'That was quick,' said Vivienne. 'How'd she get there and

back, and talk to the helpline in that time? Maybe she wasn't
successful?'

Rogue gusts of wind were pushing Alice about. She was
struggling down the driveway. Her face didn't scream success.
Quite the opposite. It looked like things were going their way.
Maybe Finn wouldn't have to work too hard to keep them there.
Time left to do what they'd come here to do.

'Get working on what you're going to say to her,' Vivienne
told him.

'If I do, when do we talk? Tell me that.'

'I'm not sure yet. We didn't expect you to have company.'

Finn looked at her, said nothing.

'We did our homework, but you've managed to keep her
quite the secret,' Vivienne couldn't help prodding. 'Why? I
know you like secrets, but what else are you hiding? She's
young, but way off prison-young.'

She saw him flinch when she said the word 'prison'.

'I'm her boss,' Finn mumbled.

Vivienne laughed. Long and hard, a cackle so sharp it could
cut you. *Oh, Finn. That wasn't very smart, was it?* But it had
given Vivienne a nice little threat to hold over him. A gift. The
girl wouldn't realise it, but she'd help Mac and Vivienne get
what they wanted.

What a shame it would break her heart.

NINE

ALICE

Alice had taken the walk back down the driveway slowly. She wasn't in a hurry to meet trouble. The wind helped slow her progress, the first time she'd been happy with the weather since they'd left Dublin yesterday. Back when she and Finn were still thinking this was going to be a lovely weekend away together.

As she'd gotten closer to the cottage, the wind making the narrow driveway feel like a bustling platform, she'd looked in on the cottage and its inhabitants. Finn was up. They were talking to him. Perhaps he'd be able to do what the useless GetaGetaway Ronan was unwilling to do and unseat these interlopers. She wasn't ready to concede that the weekend she and Finn had been looking forward to was gone. Hopefully Finn would do a better job than she had with her phone call. As she'd gotten closer, still unobserved, she'd screwed up her eyes, puzzled. The body language was weird. The defensive way Finn was standing – at the bottom of the stairs – with one arm crossing his body, as if protecting himself, his hand gripping the bicep of the other arm that hung by his side. It was odd and unfamiliar. She'd seen him take down foolish developers and careless employees with a deftness that would leave them castigated before they even realised what had happened. Finn was fair and reasonable to a fault, but no pushover. The Finn she was seeing through the window... she'd never seen this guy before.

Alice darted her eyes away. Mac had spotted her. She felt, rather than saw, the eyes of the other two on her now as well. She didn't want to lock eyes with any of them. She didn't want them to know she'd been observing them all this time.

Alice stopped at the cottage door, her hand hovering over the handle. But she withdrew it and instead turned around, leaning against the outside wall. The sea roared just beyond her. Alice sagged a little. She didn't want to go back inside, not with whatever was going on in there. Even if he looked odd, ill at ease, Alice hoped Finn was making some progress with them. And when she thought about it, she didn't blame him for not looking himself. Those two, they'd give anyone the heebies.

She'd take a minute, wait out here. She'd watch and listen to the waning storm for a bit. It was cold and she was still in her pyjamas under her coat. But Alice didn't care. If she went in right now, it would be like at the office, when you accidentally opened the door to a high-level meeting you hadn't been invited to. You'd back out, awkward and embarrassed. Only here she'd have to stay. She couldn't wait too long though. They'd seen her and knew she was coming. But hopefully that would prompt them to wrap it up.

Alice looked out over the grey foamy sea as stray tendrils of hair tickled her face. Like Poe's reproachful heartbeat, she felt phantom vibrations from the phone in her pocket. She was beyond signal here, so there were no new messages coming in. She was only remembering the incessant alerts. With a furtive backwards glance she took out the phone and scrolled again through the messages from her mother. Letting the guilt roll over her like the angry waves just beyond the cliff edge. She scrolled. Then stopped. She'd missed a message from someone else. From the only other contact on this phone.

Evrthing in place my end

Alice stared at the words. Irritated at the bad spelling and lack of proper punctuation. She would have expected more from Ted, of all people. But she knew this was a deflection, poor grammar wasn't why she was annoyed.

Earlier this year, after all this time, The Plan had finally started coming together. She still called it that – *The Plan* – the childish name she'd come up with when she was a kid. She felt like a bargain-bin Bond villain whenever she called it that in her head. And it was true, The Plan wasn't big and it wasn't elaborate. But she reckoned it would be pretty effective all the same.

As part of The Plan she'd gotten her position at TobinTech. The next step had been identifying Ted, and getting him on board. But while excited that it was finally happening, after all this time, Alice couldn't dismiss a quiet, unsettled feeling. It was as if, out of nowhere, a quirky habit in her lover – which had always been endearing – suddenly became irritating. A surprise crack – just a hairline one, mind – had appeared in The Plan. The problem, which she'd never anticipated, was how happy she was. How happy Finn made her. The possibility had never crossed her mind.

Alice straightened up. Shook herself. She was just over-thinking things. Like a relationship, you don't walk away because there is one small niggle. No, you'd made a commitment. And Alice had made a commitment to this path the moment she'd been old enough to think for herself. Nothing had changed. She felt for a moment like copying Vivienne by going to the edge of the cliff and screaming. She hated this doubt. *No. No. No.* Just because she was overcome sometimes by these stupid sentimental feelings she'd never anticipated, it didn't mean she should be distracted. The only wrench in the spokes was those two in there. Not her stupid weak feelings. Both had to go. Her feelings and the strangers.

'No,' she whispered out loud this time. Fiercely to herself, through a gritted jaw. 'I am Alice Armstrong. I am unyielding. I am constant. I am in control.' With that she spun around and threw open the cottage door.

TEN

Alice closed the door behind her and got a close-up of the faces she'd observed from outside. Finn, pale and grim; Mac, distant and distracted. Vivienne, as if with another group, relaxed and happy-looking.

'Ah, you're back,' said Vivienne. 'Any luck?'

Vivienne smiled at her from the table, her coffee mug hugged to her. Finn stared at her from one side of the kitchen. Mac looked down at the floor, didn't turn to look at her, from the other side.

'They wouldn't speak to me 'cause it was Finn who made the booking. Data protection.'

'Oh dear, I'm sorry to hear that.'

'I'm sure you are,' Alice muttered to herself as she crossed the kitchen, heading for the sink. She turned on the tap and ran her hands under the cold, flowing water. Washing the muck and grass from her sheep rescue off her hands. 'They said they wouldn't have a dispute resolved until Monday.' *And so you should get out*, she wanted to add. *You should do the decent thing and leave Finn and me alone here.* But she said nothing more.

Finn came up behind her. Took one of her wet hands in his.

'What happened?' He kept his voice low, between the two of them. He frowned as he traced the graze on the back of her hand.

'I got distracted, rescued a sheep.'

His puzzled frown morphed into a wry grin. He took out a clean towel and dabbed her hand dry.

'A sheep?'

'Don't ask. Just call me Dr Do-Too-Much.'

His grin spread wide and with his free hand he brushed her cheek.

'Are you okay?' he whispered.

And Alice knew he meant not just about the cut on her hand. 'I'm fine. Except for a damp arse,' she whispered back. 'But I don't think it's fatal.'

'Oh, I don't know, I've heard a damp arse can get pretty serious.'

Despite everything, Alice couldn't suppress a giggle. Finn kissed the top of her head.

'So, how's it going in here? The energy is really weird. Is everything okay?'

'Well...' Finn looked over his shoulder back into the room. 'Let's go upstairs.'

'Sure,' said Alice, not liking the look in his eye.

They hurried up the stairs and into their room. Alice shut the bedroom door behind her. The daylight lit up the white-painted room, it was as bright now as it had been dark last night.

Finn tapped his foot and looked up at Alice from under his eyelashes. Forcing himself not to break her gaze.

'So,' said Alice, 'what's happening? Did you get anywhere while I was gone?'

'Don't hate me... but,' he began, 'I think they're going to have to stay.'

'What!' Alice exploded. Things had looked weird inside the

cottage, but how had they gone that wrong? 'No way, Finn, no way! Seriously. You promised me last night you'd get rid of them. What on earth happened while I was gone?'

Finn paced to the window. He spoke again, now with his back to her.

'I shouldn't have promised to get rid of them. I thought I could. I spoke to them, asked them nicely. Then I asked them less nicely. They don't want to budge. I hoped we might get somewhere with GetaGetaway and that would be us sorted.'

'Well, that's a no-go.' Alice threw her hands up. 'Even if you ring them yourself, it'll still be Monday before anything is sorted out.'

Finn turned to face her. 'That doesn't leave us with many options, does it?' he said. 'They're saying they've as much right to be here as us and are staying. We can hardly manhandle them out, not if they're determined to stay.'

'We could try.'

'Alice...' Finn looked displeased.

'I wasn't being serious.' She rolled her eyes.

Finn took a deep breath. He went over to Alice and reached for her hand.

'Al, let's not fight. I know this is a mess but we can't let it get between us.'

Alice let him take her hand.

'The way I see it,' he continued, 'if GetaGetaway won't help us, then we either go home, or we stay here with them.'

'Ugh!' said Alice. 'What a choice.'

'I know, I know.'

The pair of them were quiet, weighing it all up.

'Hear me out,' said Finn, drawing Alice closer to him. 'If we stay and share... would it be the absolute worst? We could still do all the things we planned. Walks, cosy pubs, you know? We keep out of their way and make sure we barely see them. A bit like if we were staying at a hotel. I don't want to go home, do you? This was meant to be our weekend where we can just be ourselves with no one running back to the board to report us. It can still be that.'

'Ah, Finn...' Alice heard the whine in her voice. She pulled away from him. 'I've been looking forward to this for ages. Even more after we had to cancel a couple weeks ago. And now this. I don't want to go home either. Dublin is so hush-bloody-hush. I'm sick of it. No cinema, no restaurants, no theatre. You know, Finn, in Dublin I feel like your mistress.'

At that Finn seemed to falter. He took a deep breath. 'Alice, I know it's hard.'

'There are only so many takeaways and Netflix at yours a girl can take. Donegal was meant to give us time to be a normal couple. The last thing I want to do is go back to Dublin and go back into hiding...'

'Good, then let's stay here.'

'... but staying here, Finn... with those two oddballs? Really?'

'It doesn't really have to be *with* those two. Just those two... adjacent.' Finn's face broke into his shy grin. Alice couldn't help but grin back. 'C'mon, let's salvage something from our time here, yeah?' said Finn, hopeful.

'I'm not sure,' said Alice, the flash of good humour brief. It wasn't just their romantic plans she was worried about, but her private one too. Could she still do what she wanted with that pair here?

'They're odd, Finn,' she said, scowling. Sharing this place would be a lot more palatable if those two were nice, normal people. They didn't seem like either.

'I know they're a bit peculiar, but as I said, we can keep out of their way.'

'I saw her last night, out there.' Alice pointed out the window. 'She was screaming into the sea. It was seriously strange.'

'Screaming?'

'Yeah. Middle of the night, standing on the edge of the cliff, screaming her head off.'

'Maybe she's just into some alternative Eastern spirituality? I think I heard about something like that once.'

'Eastern spirituality? And Mac is the Dalai Lama, is he?' Finn's shoulders slumped.

'What about the phone lines?' said Alice.

'What about them?'

'The landline wires have been cut.'

'Cut?' Finn's eyebrows raised at this bit of news.

'Well, they're detached.'

'Which is it – detached or cut?'

'It's hard to say exactly what's the origin of their issue but it looks seriously iffy.'

'"Never attribute to malice that which is adequately explained by stupidity"... or rather, in this case, wear and tear.'

'Fine, that's fair enough. But I think she stole my phone.'

'Stole your phone? What?'

'Yeah, it's gone missing. I can't find it anywhere. My bag wasn't on the chair where I left it last night, it had been moved to the sofa. And when I looked for my mobile after I discovered the landline was dead, I couldn't find it. It wasn't in my bag. Not anywhere.'

'That's quite the leap, Alice. Surely it's far more likely that it's just fallen down between sofa cushions or something. That you moved your bag and forgot. It was quite a night last night.'

'I've looked everywhere for it. And tell me, who benefits from me not being able to call GetaGetaway? Hmm?'

'I'm sure there's a reasonable explana—' Finn screwed up his eyes. 'Hang on. How'd you call them if your phone is missing?'

Alice turned to the bed and started tugging at the duvet cover, straightening it up. She replied, looking quickly back at him over her shoulder.

'I went over to the neighbours'. Used their phone.'

'Ah, okay.'

Alice turned and sat on the bed.

'Anyway, even if my phone turns up, they're not nice people and not who I want to share my weekend with.' She looked up to face Finn.

Finn ran his hands through his hair. Craning his head back, staring at the ceiling. Alice watched him close his eyes and sigh.

'Do you think we can have a good weekend, honestly?' said Alice.

Finn dropped his head and opened his eyes. He came over to Alice, sat beside her.

'I do, love, honestly. I know it's far from perfect... but we'll have fun, we'll make it good. I promise. And this time it's a promise I can keep.'

'Well, okay... for you, Finn. But perhaps we can keep going home in our back pocket?'

'Oh God, yes. It gets weird or miserable, we're out of here.'

Alice looked over Finn's shoulder, out of the window.

'It's clearing up. Just like you predicted.'

Finn turned and looked out. A patch of blue sky was gradually getting larger on the horizon. The low, late-autumn sun was making a valiant attempt to come out.

'It's a sign!' he said with a smile.

'I don't know about that,' said Alice. 'But do you want to go off for a dive? If we're going to try and carry on as if those two aren't here, that's what you'd be doing now.'

'And leave you on your own? No.' Finn shook his head. 'I don't think you've anything to worry about with them, but leaving you on your own would be a bad boyfriend move right there. I know that much.'

Alice smiled at him. He was always thoughtful.

'You getting a bit of diving in was one of the reasons we came here. I'll be fine. Honest. You should go.' Alice wasn't entirely sure she'd be fine. But if they were going to try to have a normal weekend, then they should try to have a normal weekend. There was no time like the present to start. And she'd been banking on having some time to herself... she had things she needed to do.

'Hmmm.' Finn cast a longing eye at the approaching blue.

'But only as long as it's safe to dive,' said Alice. 'I'm still not convinced.'

Finn gathered her into him.

'Look at you, always worried about me. I don't deserve you, Alice Armstrong. I'll take the steps down from the edge of the peninsula and have a quick dive in the waters around us. Nothing too crazy. I won't go far. It'll help clear my head too. I might come up with a solution to our little problem. But I promise I will take no risks.'

'Good.'

Finn hugged her closer. Alice circled his waist, hugging him tight too.

'Go on then if you're going. I doubt it'll stay clear for long.' She released him from her embrace.

'Probably not. Okay.' He stood and looked down at her. She was frowning again.

'Everything's going to be alright, yeah?' she asked.

'Absolutely.' He squeezed her hand. 'You have nothing to worry about.'

ELEVEN

VIVIENNE

Vivienne waited on the stairs. The temptation to follow them all the way up, to lean an ear in, listen at their door, was strong. But these blasted metal steps, each one echoed like a cannonball in an empty ship's hull. She'd gone as far as the floor above hers and was now stopped by the bathroom door. Thinking. And listening. She'd really wanted to hear what was going on inside their bedroom. She needed Finn to do his part and keep them here. Long enough for her to come up with a new plan and to execute it. She'd like to know he was doing his best to convince the girlfriend to stay. And to let the strangers stay too. He said he would, but she could hardly trust him. What if instead they were planning their escape?

She looked down at her side and patted the convex profile of her right fleece pocket. At her touch there was a little metallic rattle.

Finn's car keys.

As she said, she couldn't trust him. And now, even if he did think it was worth trying to make a break for it, he wouldn't be able to. Not quickly anyway. Good luck calling a taxi with no working phone. And hoping Vivienne or Mac wouldn't hear its approach.

She risked inching forward. Put one foot on the first step of the next flight. But it echoed its way up and down the tower, reverberating and ricocheting. So, again, she stopped.

Vivienne had the stupid girl to thank for the idea to pinch the keys. It came to her after that whole scene about the missing mobile. She should have thought to take the phone last night, like she'd been accused. That would have been smart. But, in the end, even if she had thought of it, stealing it would only have slowed Alice down a bit. The neighbours' phone she could do nothing about. Taking the car keys, on the other hand, wouldn't just slow them down, it would bring them to a juddering halt. Vivienne couldn't resist a sly smile.

A pop of noise came from above. Their door was opening. Vivienne spun around, but she wasn't quick enough with her retreat before a voice from above stopped her.

'Oh.'

Vivienne turned back. Alice was standing there with a towel over her shoulder. Her mouth still round with surprise.

'Bathroom's free,' Vivienne bluffed, unable to stop a sneer blossoming on her face.

Alice looked towards the bathroom. Then back at her. Vivienne knew she didn't believe that's where she'd been. Vivienne's hasty getaway was a bit of a giveaway.

'Eh, yeah, thanks,' the girl muttered.

Vivienne turned and continued her descent. She felt Alice's eyes locked on her back until she wound round out of sight. Vivienne pushed open the door to her room and stood in the centre of the bright white space, glowering at the ceiling until the sound of the shower hummed overhead. She relaxed then and sank onto the edge of the bed. She took a deep breath and closed her eyes. She released the breath slowly, shaking out her fingers, encouraging calm to her extremities. *I can do this. I can do this.* She whispered the mantra to herself. She'd had to improvise. But it was okay. Vivienne wasn't comfortable thinking on her feet. She liked to strategise, to research. To think. She didn't act on impulse. Acting on impulse was what stupid people did. And this was no time to change that. She wasn't going to rush anything. If she had to pivot, she'd do it properly. Take a look at it from every angle before she decided their next step.

She'd like to talk to Mac though. He was so wise, he saw the gaps, the cracks, the things others didn't. But he'd gone quiet after the chat with Finn. Was he getting cold feet? Being here, now. Doing this. It was suddenly very real. And real could feel a whole lot different to the idea. He'd given her one of his side-eye glances and sat down at the table without another word when Finn and Alice had hurried off upstairs.

Vivienne stood up. Beige and mauve-coloured dried flowers sat on the dresser. Vivienne grabbed the dusty blooms' stems, pulling them out of their vase. With a dull clunk, Finn's keys hit the bottom of the vase. She dunked the flowers back in. The keys would be safe there for now. She looked at her own mobile in its chunky black case, lying close to the flowers. She picked it up and checked the signal. Still the same as earlier. One bar. Wouldn't Alice have been jealous if she'd known? This is what careful planning got you – she'd dug up some local knowledge on which – if any – mobile networks had signal in the area. She'd then gone to the effort of picking up a SIM from them. That had killed two birds with one stone… a burner kept things a little cleaner. She didn't want to leave any traces. After this weekend she didn't want anyone coming looking for her or Mac.

She stared at the runty one bar of signal. Week and feeble, but hanging in there. She unlocked the phone and noticed she had a new email. The calm she had coaxed and cajoled into her body fled like insects deprived of their rock. With a hand that shook a little, she tapped her mail app. Despite the notification, it took the signal-deprived phone an age to download the new message. She felt like she was thrown back to her youth when you'd dial up using a modem, and text and images downloaded line by line.

She held her breath, but she knew it would be them.

When, finally, the steam-powered internet did its job, she saw that she was right. It was the same, familiar email address. She opened it.

Good luck. You've got this.

Vivienne hadn't been stupid enough to tell them what she was planning to do. You don't put that kind of info down anywhere. But she knew they both understood where this would all end.

'I've got this! Damn right I have!' Vivienne growled.

She spun around, like a child's toy that had been wound up and sent careering across the floor. She was a ball of nervous energy. She stomped over to the window. She hated that phrase 'you've got this' – one of a million so-American phrases that had crossed the Atlantic and entered the lexicon. Mac told her to lighten up, but she hated Americanisms. They reminded her too much of David. His big, brash Americanness, compromised for no one.

She rested her hand against the rough lighthouse wall and looked out the window. For a moment she was propelled back in time; the wall's gritty texture reminded her of how she'd run her hand through David's hair and there was always some sand caught up in it, nestled in there somewhere. He spent most of his life on the beach, out on the water, so it didn't surprise her. And she used to think his hair was always a little damp, that he was never on land long enough to let it dry.

He'd laughed at her when she'd told him that. Then he'd called her his beautiful nymph Calypso who'd trapped his shipwrecked Odysseus on her island. That she was a temptress on the seas who wouldn't let him go. He'd only laughed at her more when she'd protested, indignant, that he was free to go any time he liked. He'd just kissed her cross face over and over as she objected. That was David, infuriating and irresistible at the same time.

Vivienne turned away from the window. Turned her back on the sea. With some effort dragged herself back to the here and now.

She needed to focus on the task at hand. She needed to take back the initiative. The lighthouse was out as a location. She had to find them somewhere else with the same level of peace and quiet and isolation. She'd get out of here and do a scout around. It would need to be somewhere away from here, away from Alice.

A thought began to form. Vivienne grinned.

She might just know the perfect place.

TWELVE

ALICE

Alice came back into the room, towel-drying her hair.

'I thought you'd be gone by now?' she said.

Finn, barefoot and wearing his wetsuit, was rummaging around in his case.

He straightened up.

'Just grabbing these,' he said, holding up a pair of wetsuit gloves.

'You have everything now?'

'Yup. Everything else is in the boot of the car – which thankfully in all the fuss last night I never locked.'

'Why thankfully?'

''Cause the keys seem to have eloped with your mobile; couldn't put my hands on them.'

'That's odd—'

'No, stop, it's not. Stop with the conspiracy theories. I just didn't look very hard for them 'cause those two are downstairs and I don't fancy spending any more time in their company than you do.'

'Fine.'

He straightened up, his face darkening a little.

'What is it?' Alice asked.

Finn shook his head. 'Time to run the gauntlet, I suppose.'

'Good luck.'

He kissed her again, and with a brief, anxious glance, he left the room.

'Be careful!' Alice called after him.

'I will.' His voice floated up to her. She wasn't sure which she was wishing him luck about. The sea or the strangers in the kitchen.

She went over to the window. He emerged a minute later, shot a worried glance back at the cottage. He looked up then, spotting her in the window. His face transformed as he smiled and waved. He popped the boot of the car – turning again to give Alice a thumbs up – then hefted the gear onto his back and sloped off.

Through the succession of bedroom porthole windows Alice followed his progress from car to the top of the peninsula's vertiginous, cliff-side steps. Steps that brought you from the lighthouse right down to the water's edge. She lost sight of him as he began his descent.

Alice flopped down on the bed. Her long, troubled sigh harmonising with the expelling air of the mattress. She was on her own now, as she wanted. But, for some reason, she just couldn't settle. She'd wanted this quiet time partly to go over everything in her head, see if The Plan still held together with the new arrivals in situ. But she couldn't keep her thoughts corralled. She just couldn't focus, no matter how hard she tried. She swung her legs back over the edge of the bed and sat up again. Perhaps she should just do something simple and practical right now. She could go for a walk and then maybe afterwards her head would be clearer. She could ponder the bigger plan then.

She stood up and went over to the bedroom door. Finn's jacket was hanging on a hook there. Alice rifled through the pockets. She found a receipt for the petrol they'd purchased on the way up. Her face broke into a smile at that. Perfect. She slipped it into her pocket. Finn wouldn't miss it. Her coat hung next to Finn's jacket. She preferred to leave it downstairs, as far away from Finn as possible. But after her official mobile had gone missing, she was wary. She slipped a hand into the pocket and fished out her other phone. She crossed the room to the bed and sat down on Finn's side. She picked up his phone, left on the bedside table while he went off diving. She unlocked it and went straight for his email app. Went to settings. With the two phones side by side she copied his email details to a new profile on her own mail app. With a flurry of typing she composed a couple of emails on her phone. Once she hit signal again, the app would log in and send. With a satisfied smile, she put Finn's phone right back how it had been.

Maybe it was time for that walk now? Along the coast... where, coincidentally, there would be mobile signal.

Alice grabbed her trainers and pulled them on. She took her coat off the back of the door, slipping the small phone back into the pocket. She trotted down the stairs, every thump and clang a warning to those below that she was on her way.

She stepped into the kitchen, her chin set at an 'I dare you' angle. She wasn't as conciliatory as Finn, they wouldn't find her quite as amenable.

Mac, sitting at the table, mug in front of him and a slim book in his hand, looked up at her.

'Oh, hi,' he said. He put the book down and drew a hand through his beard.

'Erm. Hi,' Alice muttered as she kept going towards the door. But not before she snatched a quick look around for Vivienne. There was no one else there.

'She's upstairs. Don't worry.'

'Ah, right. It's not like that...'

'Oh, I think it very much is,' he said, then took a long drink of his coffee.

Alice held back. She looked at Mac. He smiled up at her.

'Vivienne's not actually as awful as she's coming across.'

Alice raised an eyebrow. 'Really? I think there's a good chance she's taken my phone.'

'What?' Mac screwed up his eyes. 'She wouldn't.'

'Even to stop me ringing the booking agents first?'

'No, not even to do that.'

'Well, perhaps we can agree to disagree on that. But she's not doing herself any favours.'

'Yeah, I know. It's just this pla—' Mac stopped himself. Dropping his gaze from Alice, he brought his mug to his mouth again, taking another big slug.

Alice crossed the kitchen and pulled out a chair opposite him. She sat and leaned forward, elbow on the table, her hand by her chin.

'This place?' She fanned her fingers, pointing to their surroundings. 'What about this place?'

Before he had a chance to answer, a sound that was quickly becoming familiar, of feet on metal, turned both their heads.

'Hmm?' She looked back, nudging him before Vivienne was all the way down.

'Nothing.' Mac waved away his words. 'I misspoke.'

Alice opened her mouth, ready to encourage him more. But Vivienne, bright yellow windcheater on and trainers in her hands, appeared.

'I'm off for a run. Along the headland,' she announced as she entered the kitchen.

Alice was unnerved by the bright and breezy tone she'd adopted. So at odds with everything else about her.

'Getting fresh air yourself, Mac?' She smiled at him, but it didn't soften her eyes. Alice wasn't sure if this fake smile was for her or Mac's benefit. 'It's clear out.'

'Perhaps in a while,' he mumbled, eyes never leaving the table. His index finger fussed at some crumbs.

'Suit yourself,' she said, the smile fixed. She turned her gaze to Alice. 'You look like you're heading out too. Do you run? Care to join me?'

Alice stared at her. Join her? Alice would rather toss herself off the cliff.

'No,' she finally blurted, feeling her cheeks flush with embarrassment. 'Not a runner.'

Not a runner... with both its meanings, thought Alice.

Vivienne's expression hardened again, the smile slipping.

'Suit yourself,' she repeated, in the same sing-song voice she'd used with Mac. Sing-song with an edge that was impossible to miss. By the door, she crouched down and pulled on her trainers.

Tying the laces, she looked up at Alice. 'Where is loverboy?'

Alice had to stop herself from rolling her eyes. What a ridiculous word. Loverboy.

'Finn?' she asked, playing the fool.

'Yes.' Vivienne stood up again. 'That's the one.'

'*Finn*,' she stressed his name, 'is out diving, in the bay.'

Vivienne looked out the window, as if she might catch sight of him out there.

'Well, good for him.'

Then, without another word, she opened the door and slipped out, pulling it shut behind her. Alice wouldn't have quite called it slamming, but it wasn't far off.

'So glad we had this chat,' she said to the shut door.

Alice turned and looked at Mac. 'So, what was that you were saying about her not being as awful as she comes across?'

Mac laughed a deep, rumbling belly laugh. The unexpected smile he allowed lit up his face. Alice couldn't help but return it. With that sparkle suddenly ignited, she saw, in years to come when his hair turned white, he'd make a great Santa Claus.

'So, what is she normally like, then?'

'What is she like? Let me see...' He spun his book around on the table, quietly repeating 'what is she like' to himself. He looked up at Alice. 'She feels things deeply. She's loyal. She's sensitive, hurts easily. She lashes out.' He took a deep breath. 'And I wouldn't be here if it wasn't for her.'

'What, she made you come?'

He laughed that deep belly laugh again.

'No. I wouldn't be here, *here*, without her.'

'Oh.'

'Bad drink problem. She helped me quit.'

'I'm sorry... I didn't mean to pry.'

'No, don't worry. I've no problem talking about it. It's important to talk about it, in fact. Look, she's doing herself no favours, I can see that. Life has been rough on both of us, and where it made me soft, it made her hard. But she is all bark and no bite.'

Alice looked at him, into his kind eyes. But she shrugged. She wasn't quite ready to concede. She'd seen the ferocity on Vivienne's face last night. She'd witnessed her less than friendly behaviour since they got here. Maybe she was only nice to those she cared about. Mac fidgeted with his book again, spinning it around on the shiny, smooth table. Alice looked down at it. The cover was of a painting. Of an albino peacock, bleached of all its glorious blues, cobalts and indigoes. No shimmering iridescent greens. The title of the book – *Braggart Heart* – was interwoven with the colourless feathers.

'Oh, Finn has this book,' she said, picking it up. She recognised it from his shelf at home. With Mac's hand reaching out, belatedly trying to stop her, she flipped it over. Next to the blurb was an author photo. Alice studied it for a while. And then looked up, eyes wide.

'Is this... is this you, Mac?'

The large man blushed. 'Long time ago. Looong time ago.'

Alice looked at the photo to the man and back again. Younger, slimmer and without the beard – if she hadn't been sitting across from him, comparing the old image to the man now, she wouldn't have made the connection. But it was definitely him. With a grin she flicked through the pages. Another surprise – it was poetry.

'You're a poet?'

'Don't look so surprised. Lumbering hulks can have a heart!'

'Oh, I'm sorry, I didn't mean...'

'You're okay. I'm not serious. It's been a long time since I was that guy.' He took the book from Alice's hands. Turned it over and back. 'I brought it along on this trip, thought I'd read over it, see if the spark could be relit...'

'I'm sure it can,' said Alice.

They were quiet for a moment. Alice looked out the window. The blue sky reminded her why she'd come down in the first place.

'Look, do you want to go for a walk? I'd prefer to go in the opposite direction to Vivienne... no offence. But it probably won't stay this nice for long and I think we could both use it.'

Mac put the book down. Looked out the window too. 'Feck it, sure, come on.'

'Great!' Alice said, and she and Mac stood.

'I'll just go get my jacket from my room.'

He headed for the stairs and with his long legs took two at a time. Alice gathered his coffee mug and brought it over to the sink while she awaited his return. She poured the dregs down the sink. She reached for the tap, to rinse it out. But she stopped. Raised the mug to her nose. And sniffed.

There'd been more than coffee in that mug. Alice turned and looked up the stairs. Quit, had he? With help from Vivienne? Her heart sank a little. She liked Mac. But he was a liar.

THIRTEEN

The sky might have been blue, but it was still cool. Autumn's last grasp on the weather was slipping. Alice tightened her scarf.

Mac rubbed his hands together.

'You can feel winter is on its way.'

'Definitely,' agreed Alice.

Walking along the coast road, no footpaths this far into the rural countryside, they kept parallel to the sea. The gulls who had fought the wind yesterday now bobbed, resting, on the water. Alice, a deft hand dipped into her pocket, turned her phone on. She gave it five minutes before, unseen, she turned it off again. Job done, she relaxed.

At intervals along the road Alice slowed down, reading tourist information notices attached to the stacked stone wall. She was getting a quick history lesson of the area. She stopped at the latest one and began to read. Mac looked over her shoulder.

25 January 1917. The SS Laurentic, en route to Nova Scotia carrying gold bars and silver coins to pay for arms in the US,

sank after it struck a floating mine 2 ½ miles north of Fanad
Head. 354 lives were lost in the frigid waters.

Underneath the writing was a black-and-white photograph of an old ship. Smoke billowed from its central funnel.

During the 1920s the British Navy launched an extended
salvage operation for the lost gold. Over seven years they
recovered 3,186 of the 3,211 gold bars on board. During the
1930s three more gold bars were recovered by independent
adventurers. The safe remains lost, at the bottom of the sea.

'The famous lost gold,' said Mac.

'I'd never heard of it.'

Mac nodded. 'They found the safe though. About ten years ago. Something like that.'

'They find the missing gold with it?'

'I can't remember whether they did or not.'

'That's the most interesting part!' said Alice. 'How could you not remember?'

'I don't remember a lot of the last twenty years,' said Mac, his voice muted.

'Ah. Oh right, sorry.'

They walked on from the sign, neither speaking. Mac had come back down from upstairs, his jacket on. At the sound of his return, Alice had rinsed the mug out. This wasn't her problem. Yet. But she was wary now.

There was an enthusiastic bleating from nearby. Alice stopped and turned around, searching the field opposite.

'Looking for something?' asked Mac.

'Just a friend I made this morning.'

Alice laughed at Mac's puzzled expression.

'I helped a sheep this morning. It was stuck.' She pointed to the scrape on her hand. 'Got this for my troubles.'

'That looks sore. You were good to help.'

'Ah, I could hardly leave it.' Alice failed to keep the sigh out of her voice.

'That sounded a bit loaded,' said Mac as Alice gave up searching for her sheep and began walking again. She looked at him, studied his face. His brown eyes were kind, open, though the lines around them and the entrenched bags underneath cried weariness.

'Did it? It's complicated.'

'I've found most things are,' Mac said with a wry smile. 'Though I'd have thought being good was one of the few things that is straightforward.'

Alice nodded. Maybe it was the kind eyes, or the fact that he was a stranger she wouldn't see again after the weekend, but Alice heard herself explaining. Not something she did often.

'It *is* complicated,' she repeated. 'For me anyway. I was... a carer, I guess you'd call it. For my mother. When I was far too young to be that responsible. It's left me with a... I dunno... a *difficult* relationship with "being good".'

Alice looked out to sea. Struggled to find the exact words.

'I mean... my world was a bit topsy-turvy. An eight-year-old should be selfish, not selfless. Don't you agree?'

Mac nodded. 'Absolutely.'

'I think as a consequence I sort of internalised being good, doing the right thing, as being overwhelming, too much. It's hard to shake childhood experience like that.'

'Yeah, no child should have to shoulder that alone. I take it your father wasn't on the scene.'

'No. It was just me and Mam from when I was little.' She shook her head. 'It wasn't bad from the beginning but Molly, my mam, she lost her job and then had a complete breakdown... God, why am I telling you all this?' Alice tried to laugh it out. She walked a little faster, trying to work the unease out of her bones.

Mac kept pace. 'Don't worry. I think it's because I'm a writer, it's a bit like being a priest. I have a manner, people say things to me.'

Alice managed a smile at that. She took a deep breath. She didn't talk much about her childhood. She'd learned young to keep her mouth shut. She covered up for Molly's problems, terrified she'd be sent away. She kept quiet and tried the impossible, to hide the cracks as they appeared. As the cracks widened, their life contracted.

'Look,' said Alice, as a gust of wind came in off the sea and animated her hair. She dragged strands out of her face. 'This isn't a pity party. I've dealt with it, lots of therapy. *Lots*. And it's not as if I'm unique. Finn... he was raised by a single mother too, she died and he ended up in foster care. He had a dreadful time of it. And his dad was knocking around and could have taken him. But refused to step up. Can you imagine? At least mine was just nowhere to be seen.' Alice shook her head, thinking of poor Finn as a child. 'It's why we clicked.'

'You deserve that, a good relationship.'

'Thanks,' said Alice, but still a bit gloomy.

'Is it not good?' Mac looked puzzled.

'It is, it is...' Alice hesitated, but there was a leak in the floodgates and she was hard-pressed to shore it up. But for all his gentle, open manner, she wouldn't be telling him anything about The Plan. She wasn't that stupid. He could hear the superficial secrets.

'He's my boss.'

'Ah,' said Mac.

'It's totally verboten, so we're a complete secret. It's such a pain. We can't do anything together. We can't even go out to the cinema in case someone spots us. It's getting a bit exhausting.'

'You can't go on like that, surely?' said Mac. 'It can't be good, for someone like yourself, with a history of secrets and all the damage they brought.'

Alice stopped and looked at Mac. The wind caught his hair too, tossing it back and forth. Unlike her, he left it, seemingly unbothered.

'I hadn't looked at it like that,' she said. 'You're wise. I bet you're a good writer.'

'Thank you... though I've found an intimate understanding of the human heart has been as much a curse as it's been a blessing.'

He turned and looked out to sea, leaning forward on the stone wall, his hair now blown out behind him. Alice stood beside him. She looked back in the direction of the lighthouse, wondering if she could spot Finn in the water, but knew they were too far away.

'And you're right, it can't go on,' she said, the sadness in her voice surprising her with its depth.

'I said it can't go on *like that*... Don't sound so sad.'

'Oh, I don't know. I'd have to leave TobinTech if we wanted to go public. That would be the only way we could... And that doesn't sound fair! I've worked very, very hard to get to where I am in life. After all I went through. Even for love, *especially* for love, such a flimsy, frail thing... no one has a full belly or a roof over their heads on love.'

'I'd call you cynical, but that wouldn't be fair.'

Alice shrugged. 'That was why this weekend was so important. Finn feels safe up here where no one knows us, this is where we can just be a normal couple.' Alice turned around, put two hands on the stone wall and popped herself up onto it. Sitting with her back to the sea.

Mac straightened up and looked at her. 'And then we came along and ruined that.'

'Well, it's not your fault the system messed up and let you book it too.'

'You were here first though.'

'That's a bit playground rules.'

'A bit.' He smiled. His face then went serious. 'I'll talk to Vivienne. See if I can convince her to go.'

Alice wasn't sure how to respond. This was exactly what she wanted to hear from him. But she didn't want to sound too eager.

'Thanks,' she said with a nod.

She searched around in her pocket for a hair tie. The wind was getting more insistent. She tugged her hair into a bun at the back of her head. She shivered, the temperature was dropping. Alice looked up. The blue sky was fighting a losing battle with dark, grey rain clouds. As if happy to have caught her attention, the clouds kept it, unleashing a couple of large, fat raindrops.

'Weather's turning,' she said.

Mac held out his hand, catching a few raindrops in his open palm. 'Yeah, let's get back.'

She hopped down from the wall.

They began back down the road they'd come. But with each step they seemed to goad the deteriorating weather, challenging it to get worse. The sheep in the fields were retreating into groups, huddling against walls. The gulls had taken flight, screeching their irritation at this turn of events. The sea was getting choppy.

Alice felt anxiety ignite in her belly. Finn would have noticed the change, right? Under the water? He'd have gotten out? Her pace quickened, powered by fear.

'Finn was diving...' she said to Mac, hoping to banish the building terror by saying it out loud. But it didn't help. And she saw a mirrored anxiety on Mac's face.

'Feck,' said Alice, hurrying even more.

They broke into a run. Feet pounding on the narrow tarmacked road. Alice cursed how far they'd gone. Finn had so much experience, she repeated to herself. He'd told her that so many times. He'd promised to be careful.

Finally they came to the bend in the road. From here you

could see the skinny drive down to the lighthouse and the cliffs and water, and the steps side of the peninsula.

The sea was whipped up, crashing against the rocks.

Alice stopped, panting. Eyes wide and searching. She looked to the steps first, to the land above beside the lighthouse and cottage. Hoping he'd gotten out of the water in time. But nothing.

'Oh God,' said Mac.

'What?' cried Alice, frantic.

'There.' Mac pointed.

Alice followed his finger.

Near to the bottom of the steps, but not near enough, with waves lashing around him.

Finn.

Clinging to a sharp outcrop. Barely clinging. The water grabbing and tugging at him. Pulling. Loosening his grip.

Finn was holding on, but was being tossed. One arm came away from his hold.

'FINN!' Alice screamed and ran.

FOURTEEN

VIVIENNE

The weather mirrored Vivienne's mood. She had tried to be pleasant with the girl this morning, but she saw the way Alice looked at her. Finn had found a good match in her, someone who clearly wanted to be nowhere near Vivienne either. She'd barely contained her laughter when Alice had rummaged for an excuse not to join her on her run. There was no polite way to say *over my dead body*. She hadn't actually wanted Alice to join her. She'd only asked to watch her squirm.

As she walked, Vivienne pondered if she might have pushed too much, asked too many questions and been too nosy. But Alice was such an enigma, such a surprise. She just wanted to know more about her, to figure out how much of a threat she was. Not that she learned all that much.

Vivienne stopped and looked at her phone. She was using an app to guide her to the house. It was Donegal, so not much had changed over time, but she still needed a map because *she* had changed. It felt like she had gotten old, though she was only forty-six. While the roads weren't familiar, there was still something recognisable about them. The spikey gorse, its drops of yellow a little sparse this time of year. The montbretia by the side of the road, its summer orange flowers long gone, now shrivelled up little knuckles, its abundant leaves brown. The supplicant pink bells of the fuchsia were hanging in there. Vivienne plucked some as she walked, rolling the flower in her fingers then pulling the petals apart. The goats and sheep in the blasted fields, as hardy-looking as the cliff edges, barely looked up as she passed. The entire scene was desaturated, the colour turned down, not the glorious wild rural riot of summer. She thought she liked it better this way.

She would bring Mac along later. What would he think, being here again? It might help remind him why they'd started this and get him back on track. Though it could backfire, even though he had come all this way with her. She knew that. His ambivalence was about the details she had shared with him. If only he could see the bottomless pit of fury burning inside her and what it made her want to do. He thought he understood the depth of her rage, but he didn't know a fraction of it.

The blue dot on the app led her around a bend, where the road narrowed into a small boreen with grass growing in the middle. It was just enough inland here that a few trees had managed to grow. Two large unkempt ash trees swamped the lane, their spindly branches bare, looming large and leering over her. She could feel a shiver run down her spine. It felt right this way. It should be sinister.

Vivienne checked her mobile for the time. It had been about thirty minutes since she left the lighthouse, maybe thirty-five. She had taken her time, meandering like the roads. You could get here quicker if you wanted. When they came back, it wouldn't take so long. If they came back, that was. So far, this was just an idea. She needed to see if it was the right place to bring Finn. It was exciting though, this place could end up being better. She'd read that it had been abandoned. That's what brought it to mind as a new location. There would have had to be some cleaning up at the lighthouse for future guests. Out here that was less of a problem.

At the end of the lane, she no longer needed the map on her phone. She put it back in her pocket. Vivienne knew where she was; wisps of memory took her hand and guided her.

The trees were larger, the low stone wall needed repair, but this was it. If she followed the boreen around, in the wall there would be a gate. Her heart was like a greyhound straining in the trap, ready to burst after the hare. Barely contained. She took a few deep breaths, steadying herself.

Coming back here, to this spot... it was a risk. But once the idea had come to her, not starting here felt wrong.

Walking again, a little bit of calm regained, Vivienne began looking out for the gate. Soon she saw it. Small and wrought iron, coming off its top hinge it lurched drunkenly at an angle. Its red paint was nearly completely gone. What little was left was flaking.

She reached it and looked over, down the pathway. There was the house. Her heart, racing only a moment ago, now felt like it had stopped. Stilled completely. The breath in her lungs sucked out like a blown window on a plane. She trembled.

The house was boarded up. There was a pale rectangle on the wall by the front porch where the sign had once been screwed on.

Teach na Gaoithe – Brú Óige /
House of the Wind – Youth Hostel

Plywood was nailed over the windows on the top and bottom floors. The slip-slated roof was a gap-riddled patchwork. The building was an abandoned wreck. Most days Vivienne felt like an abandoned wreck.

She pushed the gate open. A few red paint flecks stuck to the underside of her fingers. A larger fragment, like a stigmata –

the bloody representation of Christ's wounds – attached itself to the centre of her palm. She brushed it off, revolted, as if it were an insect. She wasn't a martyr. This was for no one but her. Not even for Hannah. Hannah, who knew nothing about this and never would, Vivienne presumed. Hannah, the lucky one who'd got out of this mess unscathed.

Inside the gate, Vivienne stopped, stood still. Taking it all in. She didn't usually let herself remember the happy times. When it was all good. She kept those memories locked away, in her very own Pandora's box deep inside of her. But it was harder here. And being back on this particular spot, she was powerless to stop them flooding back. David was there now; she could see him and his big, gorgeous grin. The infectious laugh that even the sourest misery-guts couldn't resist. It was as if he were real and here, coming out of the front door, a sausage speared on a fork, waving it at her...

'Come on, Vivi, breakfast is ready. I figured out how to get the hob working. I've made loads.'

'Brilliant!' she cried back at him, waving the orange juice she'd trekked a couple of miles to fetch. 'I'm starving!'

'You're always starving,' he laughed.

'How dare you!' She trotted down the path towards him. 'You're no gentleman, David Johnson!'

'Hey! A healthy appetite in a woman is a very attractive thing.'

'Well, if that's the case...' She sidled up close to him, then bit off the end of the sausage, a big grin on her face...

Vivienne touched her chin. She could still feel David's finger as he wiped away the grease that dripped down there. She shook her head, trying to dislodge the past and send it back to where it had come from. It was no good to her now. She wasn't that person any more. Too much had happened. She'd read that all the cells in your body were completely renewed every seven years. The philosophical question posed was: are we the same person if no original cells remain? It had been twenty-six years. That was just short of four times that her entire cellular make-up had broken down and been replaced since that day. Four times she had been renewed from the top of her head to the tips of her toes. And yet, the memories and pain remained. Perhaps they moved like fugitives through her neural pathways, outrunning their erasure. Clinging on, finding fresh new cells to hide in. Never letting her forget or let go.

Vivienne stepped through the gate and walked down the path.

FIFTEEN

ALICE

Alice ran.

Mac did too. His long legs taking him further, quicker. But Alice was fit and twenty years younger than him. The abuse Mac had spent the last few decades putting himself through also chipped away his advantage. By the time they made it to the lighthouse lane, arms pumping and feet pounding, Alice was leading the charge.

'Hold on, Finn!' she yelled, knowing it was futile, the wind was whipping away her words. If Finn hadn't spotted them, he had no idea help was on its way. She kept running, her lungs burning. Her eyes stinging from the wind. The ground underneath her uneven, rough. The rain was getting heavier. Alice felt it land on her, mix with the sweat on her brow.

She tripped. Skidding to the ground. She felt the gravel of the path cut up her knees, but she didn't feel any pain. Mac, coming up behind her, grabbed her under the arms and lifted her. Breathing heavily, he said nothing but ran on.

They got to the top of the steps. Mac grabbed Alice's arm, pulling her back from the edge. The rain and wind as frantic as they were.

'Let go of me!' she screamed, wrenching away her arm.

'Wait!' Mac yelled back. 'The steps are lethal! You need to slow down or you'll kill yourself! You can't help Finn then.'

They looked down, the view dizzy to the rocky water's edge. The steep descent made up of shallow, chipped concrete steps. The slightest misstep or slip and they would tumble, smashed and bashed against concrete or cliff outcrop, seriously injured or dead when they reached the water below.

Alice panted, sucked in air. Looked at Mac and then back at the steps.

'Come on!' she gasped. They began the descent. Fast, but slower than they'd run getting there. The rain was making the steps slippier. The wind trying to drag them off. Alice swayed out dangerously a few times. On each occasion Mac grabbed her. His size kept him grounded despite the weather's best attempts to dislodge him.

They couldn't see Finn at this angle. Alice had to pray he was still clinging on.

After what felt like forever, they were down. The waves spraying over the final steps. Alice was soaked to her skin in seconds. She saw Finn, wild-eyed, exhausted, clinging to a ridge further down from where he'd been when they'd spotted him.

'Oh God,' she gasped. Alice looked left and right. What were they going to do? Mac began climbing along the edge of the water, hands taking hold of any rocky protrusion. Feet finding creviced footholds among the rocks. Moving as quickly as possible. Spiteful waves crashed over him, soaking him too, trying to dislodge him. Alice followed his lead.

Inching along.

A slip, Alice's drenched trainer sole missed its spot. Her shoulder sockets shrieked, wrenched long as she held on, hoisted her feet back up.

'Hold on!' Mac's deep baritone bellowed out. 'We're nearly

there!' Alice didn't know if he was talking to her or Finn. Or both.

Rain was pelting down. Alice, no hands free to wipe her eyes, felt blinded. The cliff edge under her fingers, jagged and rough, was her only connection to the world. The slightest mistake and she could be lost to the waves. Dragged under.

Seeing through the rain for a moment, she realised Mac was close. He was crouching. Reaching out. Each time he seemed to have Finn within his grasp, a wave rocked Finn, moved him just out of reach.

Mac stretched, grunted, swiped his hand. Alice saw his giant fist of a hand grab at a strap of Finn's oxygen tank. He pulled.

But a gust of wind, a wave, the hold the sea had on Finn, something, was stronger. It fought back. Mac pitched forward, head first into the glacial sea.

'Nooo!' cried Alice. With salt in her eyes and terror in her heart she inched closer, closer.

Time seemed to stop.

Then, like Poseidon erupting from his kingdom below, Mac broke the surface, somehow propelling himself to the water's edge. There, he grabbed Finn's arm. Alice, finally close enough, reached, grabbed Finn's other arm, and pulled.

SIXTEEN

VIVIENNE

Vivienne headed for the back of the abandoned hostel. The gardens were overgrown, and she had to fight her way through brambles, her curls getting caught and her hands getting nicked. Scowling, she brought the cuts to her mouth. The old kitchen door gave with little resistance when she tested it. Inside, it was dark and damp. The air so saturated it felt like mist, but it couldn't be less refreshing. The odour was rancid. She imagined she could see mould spores floating like motes in the air.

The wall of what had once been the breakfast room was spray-painted with graffiti, clashing and illiterate daubs. All the kitchen cabinets were long gone. Wires hung lethal from the ceiling. The gas hob David had cooked those sausages on was nowhere to be seen. A few tables remained, their metal legs mottled with rust. The padding had been torn out of the one or two chairs that were left. The visible plywood seat bases were stained and warped.

Broken bottles, the tell-tale crumbs of illicit teen drinking, littered the floor. Vivienne guessed that even in the countryside, teenagers needed somewhere to misbehave.

She crossed the room, placing her feet carefully to avoid the glass shards on the floor. She grabbed one of the chairs and gave it a shake. Its basic frame was still sturdy. Someone could sit on it and it wouldn't collapse. And handily enough, it had armrests. She gave one a tug. It didn't move.

'Good,' she said out loud, the sound echoing around the room. She thought she heard a scurry behind her. She looked around but the creatures were well scared off. She lifted the intact chair and put it by the cracked kitchen window, making sure she'd know which one it was. She turned around, did a full 360, looking over the place again. 'Donal loves Ava' was half-scrawled, half-carved into the crumbling plaster by the door to the hall. She couldn't help but shake her head. Young love... just wait, Donal and Ava... you'll look back one day and wonder why you were ever so full of hope.

Through the half-open hall door, the banisters with mostly missing spindles caught Vivienne's eye. She could see David, conjured on the stairs, heading up to one of the small dorms. He is singing, a bit drunk. Someone is laughing at him, and someone else from another dorm is telling him to shut up. She hadn't liked it when he drank too much, but they were too young to embrace moderation, not sensible enough. That unbearable pain in her heart eased in. Standing there in that rotten, fetid house, the pain was an old friend who turned up when she thought about the past. Who lingered at the party after the memories got their coat and went.

Vivienne's phone buzzed in her pocket. Good to know there was signal around here. Taking it out, she saw she had another email. From them. Her mystery correspondent. Whoever they actually were. She'd never found out. She could have hired an expert who would dig at IP addresses and give her some idea who was sending the emails. But Vivienne had decided she'd rather not know. Plausible deniability was part of it. Keeping that separation when she realised what she was going to do. A bit of distance would keep her safe.

She'd trusted their information immediately. They'd told her enough that she knew they were genuine. They knew things only she knew. And knowing who they were wouldn't alter the cold, hard facts. Mac was less convinced: he thought she shouldn't be so blasé about who was sending them. But he agreed that everything they said made sense.

She opened this latest communication. But there must have been a glitch, probably the dodgy signal around here. It was just the same email from earlier, sent again.

Good luck. You've got this.

Those few drops of rain had picked up. More holes in the roof revealed themselves to her as the weather got in. The windows rattled like jailed convicts during a riot. It was time to go back to the lighthouse before it got too awful out there. One last thing needed to be done. Vivienne took off her backpack and unzipped it. She rummaged around inside, finding a few cable ties. She looked around the room, considering where to leave them. It seemed a good idea to stash a few here, as a precaution. But she didn't want them out on view. Those teenagers might be back and she wasn't sure when she'd be able to return. There was an old battered tin on the ground which had probably held tea in its day. She picked it up and teased open the rusted lid. She poured out the water that had found its way in and stashed the cable ties inside. Then she set it back down, shoving it aside with her foot, forgotten and useless, of no interest to anyone.

Vivienne turned. Headed for the back door. She stepped outside again.

Into the storm.

SEVENTEEN
ALICE

'Drink this.' Mac was handing Finn amber liquid in a glass as Alice came downstairs with a blanket. Finn, stripped of his wetsuit – discarded outside the cottage door with the rest of his scuba gear – was sitting by the fire in his jeans and hoodie, a couch throw pulled around his shoulders. Alice put the blanket over his knees. Despite the layers and the roaring fire – she felt its heat burning the side of her face as she bent over him – his skin was still ice-blue and his teeth were chattering so much he hadn't spoken properly beyond a few gasped thank yous.

'Are you okay?' asked Mac, looking at Alice. She nodded. She was. Physically, at least. She'd torn off her drenched clothes, desperate to get back downstairs to Finn with the extra coverings. She hadn't even wanted to waste a moment getting changed but Mac had insisted. He'd said she was looking after Finn by looking after herself.

He handed her a glass, like Finn's, half full of whiskey. She didn't ask where the whiskey had come from. She didn't care right now. Turning to face the fire, desperate for warmth, she tried to hold the glass steady. But her hands were shaking. Cupping the glass two-handed she managed to steady her grip enough to gulp a mouthful. She closed her eyes, feeling it burn her throat and warm her insides. She opened her eyes again. She looked at Finn. Pale. Probably in shock. Half-drowned. What would have happened if they hadn't turned back when they had? If they hadn't gotten there in time? She choked back a sudden sob. She felt a hand on her shoulder and looked up. Mac.

'It's okay. We got him,' he said, as if reading her mind. Alice managed a watery-eyed nod. Mac had a mug of steaming liquid in his hand. Coffee, by a cursory smell.

Unlike her and Finn, Mac was still in his wet clothes, the water saturating the fireside rug beneath him. He hadn't heeded his own advice.

'You need to get changed too,' said Alice.

'I was waiting, making sure you two were okay.'

'We are. Thank you. Now, go. Go on.'

He nodded. Looked quickly at Finn, then headed upstairs.

Alice sat down on the couch beside Finn. She got in right beside him, moulding herself to his contours, using her body heat to help bring him back.

'Th-thank-kks,' he tried again, still not in full control.

'Oh God, Finn... what if...' The last word caught in her throat, a bottleneck of distress.

'So-so-sorry...'

She slipped her hands in around Finn, hugging him. She stayed like that until she heard Mac coming back down the stairs.

Mac came over, examined Finn. He leaned down.

'How are you doing?' he asked softly. 'Warming up at all? Are we going to have to take you to Letterkenny hospital?'

'I'm... beg-beginning to...'

Mac straightened up. 'You look a little less pale.'

He looked at Alice, still holding Finn close.

'We'll keep an eye on him for the next twenty minutes. If

he's not improving by then, we might need to go to Letterkenny.'

'You seem to know what you're talking about?'

'Well. Another life... I knew some things.' He looked away, out the window, where the storm had taken hold again. Rain lashed against the glass. The wind howled.

Alice saw for the first time how pale Mac was. The gargantuan effort he had expended to save Finn, it must have taken its toll. He lifted his coffee mug off the mantel. Took a sip. It had cooled down.

'Let me make you a fresh one,' said Alice.

Mac put up his hand. 'No, stay there. You're doing the right thing for Finn. I'll make my own coffee.'

Mac went to the kitchen.

Alice turned back to Finn, touched his cheek. She sighed.

'Did you spot some of the missing gold, was that it?' She tried to summon a smile. Trying desperately to lighten the mood. To feel less terrified of what might have happened. 'Did its glitter distract you from the changing weather?'

'Gold?' Finn looked confused.

'You know, from the World War I ship?'

Mac came back with his coffee.

He did as she suggested and dragged the armchair closer to the fire.

'I was asking Finn if he got distracted by that ship's gold. That's what went wrong.' She kept the smile she wasn't quite feeling on her face.

Mac stared at her, not even a flicker. Alice decided to move on, her efforts at being light-hearted weren't landing.

'Mac, thank you again... I don't know what I would have done.'

'Yes, thank you,' said Finn, his voice still croaky and weak but – to Alice's relief – beginning to sound a little stronger.

Mac waved them away. Shook his head. His gaze kept

falling on the window at the end of the cottage, to the lane out to the mainland. The quiet man they'd met last night seemed to be returning. The openness that had appeared between him and Alice, the personal stories that had come out, felt like it was closing over again. Perhaps it had been the whiskey in Mac's morning coffee that had made him more human. Without it, he went back to the quiet, withdrawn half of an odd, antisocial pair. She turned to Finn. Finally he seemed to be reviving. His deathly pallor was beginning to recede.

'You gave us a horrible fright, Finn. And you broke your promise. You promised me you'd be safe.'

Finn coughed, his eyes screwed up in discomfort. 'I'm so sorry, Al.' Each word laboured. He pulled a hand through his damp dark hair. 'The stupid thing is I didn't even get much diving done.'

'You didn't? But you were out there a while before the weather went bad.'

He slowly shook his head

'I was snorkelling... for most of the time. Scoping out... potential dive sites.' Listening to him like this was like hearing him at half-speed on a voice message. He paused, exhausted by the effort of talking. He took a long sip of his whiskey. 'I only switched over to dive properly... five or ten minutes before the weather turned. I'd thought I had longer.'

He coughed again, his whole body shaking head to foot. His eyes again creasing in pain. Taking a breath, he forced himself to continue. 'Then the weather changed so quickly and I was a good way out...'

Mac, opposite them, suddenly sat ramrod straight. His eyes boring into the far distance.

Then he stood. Went right up to the window. Alice got off the sofa, looking to see what had grabbed his attention so violently. A good long way off, through the terrible weather, she could see a figure. Like a distress beacon, a yellow jacket glowing in the distance. Vivienne.

Mac swung around. Eyes wide. 'You can't mention what happened to Vivienne.'

'What?'

'You can't say anything about the difficulties Finn got into. Okay? Not a word.'

Alice looked from Mac to Finn, then back.

She pointed at Finn, pale and huddled on the sofa. Definitely improving, but clearly not right.

'Look at him,' said Alice. 'She's not blind, she'll be able to tell something bad happened in the hour and a half since she went out on her run.'

Mac looked out again, twitching. Went closer to the window. He turned and glanced at Finn.

'You can say he's not feeling well, you don't need to explain more than that.'

'Eh, I'm not sure I'm that good an actor. And...' Alice pointed to the puddles of water all around. 'And what, somehow it rained inside too?'

There was water everywhere. Where they'd stood when they got in. Where they'd pulled the wetsuit off Finn before they'd flung it out the door. The rug in front of the fire that had soaked up Mac's own cast-off water was still damp despite the fire's heat.

'Feck,' he bit, swinging round. He raced to the kitchen and grabbed a hand towel. Dropping to his knees by the door, by the largest deposit of water, he started mopping, his hands rubbing, frantic. Alice looked out the window: Vivienne was still a good way off. He had a chance of cleaning up, especially if she helped him. But why was he freaking out?

'Mac,' she said, her voice soft, gentle. 'What's going on? Why can't we tell Vivienne what happened?' She looked back at Finn, who was sitting up a little straighter. A tiny bit more colour in his cheeks. He returned Alice's look with concern. Alice felt the tension and anxiety in her rocket up again. These people. They were the gift that kept on giving. What further strangeness were they about to unleash?

Alice remembered what Mac had said earlier. Or rather what he'd nearly said. *Vivienne's not actually as awful as she's coming across... It's just this place.*

'It's something to do with here, with the lighthouse, isn't it? Have you some history with this place?' Alice went over to the kitchen, opened the press under the sink and retrieved tea towels. She started drying the kitchen tiles that led to the staircase. 'Come on, Mac, what is it? You can't just freak out like this and say nothing.'

With a heavy sigh, Mac stopped. He sank back on his heels. His head dipped.

'Alice,' said Finn, his voice still not quite itself, 'maybe we just leave Macdara alone...'

'No. No, it's alright.' The big man spoke, his words hushed and slow. 'It was all a very long time ago. Over twenty-five years ago now. We were just kids.' He shook his head.

'What happened, Mac?' whispered Alice. It felt like the lighthouse itself was holding its breath. The air around them seemed to still.

Mac looked up at her. His sad brown eyes boring into hers.

'There was an accident.'

EIGHTEEN

Alice said nothing. She sat frozen. Waiting for Mac to continue.
If he was going to. He ran his hands through his hair, sighed.

'It's not my story to tell...'

'If you tell us, we might understand her more. That can
only be a good thing. Right?'

Mac was quiet. Clearly debating if he should talk. Eventually, he started speaking again.

'There... there was an accident, in the water. Just a little up
the coast from here. But quite close really. Vivienne's partner,
David. He died. Vivienne never got over it. It shaped her whole
life.'

'Oh,' said Alice, shocked. 'I see. That's awful.'

Mac nodded. 'It was. It *is*.'

'You're a very understanding partner. To be this concerned
for her. I think I might be jealous of such a ghost.'

'Alice...' Finn's voice, weak, came from the sofa.

'What?' she said.

'I think, perhaps, that's not our business?'

Alice looked at Mac. Still kneeling, a faraway look in his
eyes.

She wanted to say, *I think it's my business if we're sharing a space with some traumatised madwoman and her enabling partner*, or, *I'd like to know exactly what kind of crazy I'm sleeping under the same roof as*, but she said neither.

'David was my friend too,' said Mac. He looked at Alice with a sad smile. 'So it's not hard to empathise with how Vivienne feels. He left a massive hole, in all our lives. He was one of those people, you know, larger than life, great fun to be around. God...' Mac laughed, his eyes both happy and sad. 'The messing he'd get up to. One time, he released a jar of frogs in a lecture hall. Created pandemonium. Like, where do you get that many frogs? I'd have been appalled if anyone else had done something that juvenile. But David would flash his stupid grin and we'd all forgive him. He loved that expression "live fast, die young and leave a beautiful corpse". He'd yell it as he cannonballed off a pier or chucked a water balloon at you from an upstairs window. But, unfortunately, that's pretty much what he did.'

'I'm so sorry, Mac...'

'He brought me out of my shell like no one else. I couldn't be jealous of such a ghost. I'd welcome it, truth be told.'

Alice said nothing, just nodded.

'So, I don't want to tell Vivienne about this,' he said, pointing to Finn. 'I don't want her to have to remember. Okay?'

Alice got up from the kitchen floor and went over to help Mac dry the doorway. She tried to look him directly in the eye, above his flushed red cheeks, through his hair that fell in front of his face as he leaned forward dabbing and rubbing. But he studiously avoided her gaze.

She gave in and blurted out a question she couldn't keep in.

'Mac... I won't say anything to Vivienne. I promise. But you have to answer me this... Why are you staying here if it's such a terrible place for her?'

Mac shook his head and dried the ground. He hemmed and hawed. Kept frantically drying. Alice looked over at Finn. She mouthed, *I told you they were odd!* Finn's brows furrowed. He shook his head and coughed.

'Why?' Mac muttered a few times. 'Why, why, why?'

Finally, he looked over at Alice. His eyes many shades darker.

'I think...' His low, rumbling voice filled Alice with a fear she didn't understand. 'One reason – closure.'

NINETEEN

Alice shut the cottage door behind her.

'I put the scuba gear in the boot, Finn. I wasn't sure what to do with everything so I just dumped everything in.'

'That's okay, I'll sort it out later when I'm feeling a bit better.'

Alice looked over at Mac.

'The wetsuit is hanging in the bathroom. We can tell her that Finn just stayed too long in the water and has gotten a chill.'

The tall man nodded, hints of panic still in his eyes. 'Sure. Okay.' Mac gathered up the towels and put them into the washing machine in the kitchen. They both looked out the window. Vivienne was walking down the path.

With a nod to Mac, Alice joined Finn on the sofa, popped his blanket over her knees too. Mac stayed where he was in the kitchen.

The cottage door flew open and a violent gust of wind came howling through before Vivienne did. The curtains convulsed and writhed before she shut the door behind her.

'Whoa!' Vivienne exclaimed as she shook off the storm. The

spot Mac and Alice had so frantically mopped up a few minutes ago was drenched again in seconds. They could have spared themselves the effort, she'd never have noticed.

Vivienne pulled down her bright yellow hood and looked around the room.

'It's wild out there again,' she cried loudly, as if she still needed to shout to be heard over the wind. Her blue eyes shone bright at the battle she'd fought against the elements getting back here. 'Wild.'

She zipped off her coat and hung it by the door, then kicked off her boots.

Side-stepping Mac, Vivienne headed for the kitchen and clicked on the kettle. She rubbed her hands together and stamped her feet, shivering violently as she waited for the water to boil.

'You've the right idea,' she said, looking over at Alice and Finn under the blanket by the fire. She made a beeline for the hearth. And Alice and Finn. She held out her hands to the flames, sighing quietly. She looked at Alice and Finn, regarding them properly for the first time. Finn in particular. Her lips pursed.

'You look *very* pale.'

Finn opened his mouth to speak, but a cough took hold of him instead.

'He went for a swim and stayed too long in the water,' said Alice, rubbing Finn's back. 'He got a bit chilled.'

'Oh, right. That wasn't very smart.' Vivienne turned around, now warming the back of her body. She looked down the room, back into the kitchen. Mac looming, standing silently there.

'And what's wrong with you? You seem extra sullen and silent.'

Mac's face was completely blank, no reaction blooming from the mild insults lobbed his way.

'I was worried about you, out in the storm,' he said, his voice barely audible.

'Really?' said Vivienne, smiling. 'How sweet of you.' She left the fireplace and went over to Mac. She put her arms around him. It took Mac a moment to unstiffen and accept the embrace. Alice watched the pair of them, still completely puzzled at their relationship. She knew couples could get complacent after many years together, but the interactions between these two... like everything else about them, they were just plain odd.

'How you doing?' Alice whispered to Finn.

He squeezed her hand under the blanket. 'Improving. I'll be okay, don't worry.'

'You really gave me a scare.'

'I know, I'm so sorry.'

'Anyone want a coffee?' Vivienne's voice called from the kitchen. She was smiling at the pair of them. But, as usual, it was the kind of smile that suggested she was thinking of something other than their welfare.

Alice looked at Finn, who shook his head.

'We're grand with these, thanks.' Alice lifted her glass of whiskey. Plastered an insincere smile on her face.

Vivienne's expression froze. She clearly hadn't noticed the glasses in their hands when warming herself at the fire. Her head snapped around to Mac.

'It's not mine.' Mac's muttered hiss just about made it to Alice's ear. He stalked further into the round of the kitchen, taking himself out of Alice and Finn's line of sight. Vivienne looked back to Alice and Finn and then to where Mac had gone. Alice could see the balled fists, the stiffened shoulders. A predator ready to pounce. But she wasn't going to do it in front of them. She followed Mac out of view. The white noise of strained low undertones escaped the kitchen. Alice and Finn looked at each other. Finn raised an eyebrow.

'Mac had,' Alice whispered to him, 'or maybe still has, a drinking problem.'

Finn looked at the glass of whiskey in his hand, he swirled the contents. Alice couldn't help but think his face looked suddenly very sad. He shook his head slowly.

'That's hard. I'm sorry to hear that.'

'He told me that Vivienne helped him get sober, but he's lying to someone, himself or her. There was whiskey in his coffee this morning, and this,' she waved her glass, 'didn't just materialise like some miracle. He didn't turn water into whiskey—'

'Christ, Viv!' Mac's voice cried out followed by the crash of a mug smashing and splintering in the ceramic sink. It reverberated about the space, splitting open the tense silence. Mac stormed by, stomping upstairs. Viv appeared, stopping at the bottom of the stairs. Her face stricken. More human and vulnerable than Alice had seen her. But when she saw the two of them watching her, the shutter slammed down again. The sneer returned. She followed Mac up the stairs.

A chill had entered the air, rousing Alice. The glow from the dying fire was the only light in the room, early evening darkness falling outside. Long shadows stretched their tentacles across the room. A tick of the kitchen clock was the only noise.

Alice straightened up. Rubbed her neck which had a crick in it. She shivered. She was still on the sofa, Finn asleep beside her. She checked the clock, it was after five p.m. They'd been sleeping for a few hours. A broken night last night, the upset of Finn's accident and two generous tumblers of whiskey had eased them off to sleep.

Alice extracted herself from under the blanket, careful not to disturb Finn. She picked a few lumps of turf and carefully built the fire up again. She straightened and stood still, listening. There wasn't a sound in the place, and no light streaming down from upstairs. Had the other two succumbed like they had? Were they asleep upstairs? Or – Alice's heart leapt momentarily – perhaps they'd gone. Come to their senses and packed up. They certainly both seemed on edge, perhaps after the whiskey incident earlier they decided they'd better go.

Checking that Finn was still sound asleep, Alice padded lightly across the cottage, stopping at the stairs. She cocked an ear again. Still nothing. Taking her time, Alice started up the steps. Mac and Vivienne were on the first floor, their room would be the first one she hit. Leaving the light off, she made her way up.

Their floor was in near darkness. A window on the landing wall let in what little light was left in the sky. Only the faintest hint of the bulb at the top of the lighthouse made it this far down. Every second beat the gloom illuminated a fraction more. But there was enough light for Alice to see that their door was slightly ajar. No light shone through the cracks. Alice put her ear to the door. No snuffles, no snores, nothing suggesting anyone was inside. Could they have left? She took a moment, standing there.

With two fingers, she pressed the door gently.

TWENTY

It moved a few inches, its hinges creaking slightly. She gave it another small push. It opened a little more. All it needed was one more little nudge and she'd be able to see inside.

Alice pushed.

The room was dark, but she could see that it was empty. Identical to her and Finn's room two floors up: double bed, two bedside lockers, wardrobe and chest of drawers. Alice's heart sank as she spotted the two small orange and black backpacks sitting on top of the drawer unit. Unless they'd forgotten the only things they'd brought with them, they had just gone for a walk, or something. Whatever it was, they'd be back.

Alice's brief dance with hope evaporated.

Oozing bitter disappointment, she surveyed the room. She felt like finding something of theirs and breaking it. Something less petulant occurred to her. This was an opportunity to search for her phone. Find where Vivienne had hidden it. It wouldn't be too hard. Other than their small backpacks, the room was devoid of possessions. It was so empty you'd hardly know anyone was staying in here. Something on the floor by the bed caught her eye. She stepped fully into the room. She left the light off – she didn't want them coming back and spotting light coming from their windows. So she was careful, took it easy crossing the room in the dark. By the bed she crouched down. What had she been looking at? It was a pillow and blanket. She rubbed the coarse wool blanket between her fingers. She'd seen one similar folded up on the shelf in their wardrobe. They hadn't needed it so she'd left it there. But in this room it seemed someone was sleeping on the floor.

So, things were not so rosy between those two. Sure enough they weren't acting like love's young dream in front of Alice and Finn. But to come away on a romantic weekend just to sleep separately? Was this one of those make-or-break trips? The pair of them certainly seemed unhappy enough. Maybe the spectre of that dead boyfriend was looming over them.

Alice stood up again. With great care she began looking for her phone. She ran her hand along the duvet. She felt under the mattress. It was hard in the darkness to be completely sure, but she'd dipped her hand so many times into her handbag to find that phone, she'd know the feel of it anywhere.

She peered into the gloom of the bedside lockers. Nothing. Then, the wardrobes. They were completely empty. Not even one item of clothing for Mac or Vivienne.

Next, she looked through the chest of drawers. Again, she came out empty-handed. She stood up straight. There, on top, were the two backpacks. So small, hardly adequate for one night away, let alone a whole weekend. So strange. It might have been too obvious a place to hide a stolen phone. But maybe it was a double bluff. She opened the first one. The contents suggested it was Mac's. Giant gloves, a bulky torch. A battered notebook with a pencil attached firmly to its front by a thin leather cord wrapped round it. There was no sign of her phone. She zipped it shut.

The second backpack, leaning against a vase of dried flowers, had to be Vivienne's bag. Alice zipped it open and peered inside. Even though it was getting darker by the minute, there was enough light for Alice to make out its contents. The hat Vivienne had worn last night. A water bottle. A book. A slim wallet. Nothing else. Alice checked and double-checked. No phone. She felt disappointed. But it had been a long shot. It would have been stupid to hide the phone there. For all she knew Vivienne had tossed the phone into the sea, had gotten rid of it completely. She really hoped that hadn't happened.

She let the bag rest back against the vase.

Was that it? There was nowhere else to look in the room. Her shoulders sagged. She'd been sure she was going to find her phone. She could have threatened them with the Guards then, and made them leave.

She turned to quit the room. But a hint of curiosity wormed its way to the fore. If she couldn't find her phone, at least this might be a chance to find out more about who they were? With a glance over her shoulder, and a listen for any noise, Alice opened Vivienne's bag again. She took out the wallet and flipped it open. Vivienne's driver's licence. Vivienne O'Brien. Date of birth 12/04/1978 – that would make her forty-six... Alice would have had her older. She scowled out from her photo on the licence. That was the sour woman Alice was reluctantly getting to know alright. Alice looked through the rest of the wallet. A few credit cards, a loyalty card with most holes punched for a coffee place Alice had never heard of. Some place that still used cardboard and not an app to track your free drink. Why did that feel very Vivienne? There were no notes or cash. Alice dropped it back into the bag and looked in again. There were two small dark objects at the very bottom of the bag she hadn't noticed initially. She reached in and drew them out. Alice turned them over in her hand. Just mints. *Le Lièvre Mort* was written across them in swirling lettering. Their paper wrappers a little creased and battered from sitting lost at the bottom of the bag. Alice screwed up her eyes – was that name familiar?

She shook her head, not sure. She dropped them back in and went to pull the zip back across when she stopped. She couldn't resist taking out the book. Vivienne had sneered at Alice's reading material, so what sort of thing did the serious Viv like to read? Alice examined the cover. She recognised the title as one of those difficult literary novels that had been shortlisted for some recent prize. Probably very worthy, but also hard going. Alice thumbed through the pages. She stopped at a page marked with a bookmark. Straining in the dark to read a line, she stopped, her eye drawn to the bookmark instead.

It was a photograph. Folded in half. But it was too dark to make out much. Alice moved over to the window. Making sure to keep a finger in the book at the marked page, Alice took out the bookmark.

Alice waited for the beam above to pulse. With the next flash she looked at what she had. It was an old photograph. Faded and creased. She waited another moment, another illumination. The photograph was of a baby. A very young baby, a newborn. It was held in a pair of arms. The top half of the photo was bent over in the middle, the head and shoulders of whoever was holding the child hidden. Alice flattened it, holding the image straight. The light flashed for only a moment and it took Alice a few looks to be sure. The photo was old and battered. But Alice would recognise those blonde waves anywhere. The young woman was definitely Vivienne. She looked very young. Alice flipped the image over.

Vivienne and Hannah, 23 Oct 1998.

All thoughts of her missing phone were forgotten.

Vivienne was a mother? She had a daughter called Hannah? Because that was unmistakably what this was a photo of. A new mother, in a hospital bed and gown, a new baby, wrapped in a regulation hospital blanket, in her arms. Each with an ID band around their wrists. She wasn't some visiting auntie. But Vivienne had specifically said earlier that she had no children. Had been quite clear about it. Alice turned the photo back over and examined the picture again. It was the strangest new baby photograph she'd ever seen. Even in this battered old photo, in this terrible light, it was clear that Vivienne wasn't full of the exhausted joys of new motherhood. She was distraught, eyes red and puffy. But even though it was such a sad photo, Alice added a new emotion to those Vivienne inspired in her. Along with annoyance, suspicion and worry there was now a hint of envy. Alice's mother's life had been so chaotic Alice didn't have anything like this, no mementos of herself as a baby. No photographs, no precious, much-loved teddy, no keepsake at all of her earliest years.

Then she heard the creak, followed by the whoosh of wind, of the front door being opened downstairs. They were back. Alice jammed the photo into the book. She had to get out of here before they discovered her. She hurried to the chest of drawers. She needed to put the book right back where she'd found it. Her heart thumped violently in her chest. She felt nearly dizzy with fear they'd find her in here. Her fingers fumbled with the bag's zip. It was as if she was trying to thread a needle wearing oven gloves. She heard the clang of footsteps on the stairs. Her heart nearly exploded in panic. Someone was coming. They were going to find her in here. Through some miracle she got the bag open. She shoved the book in and yanked the zip shut. Shaking, she slipped out of the room and pulled the door closed behind her. Headed for the stairs. But she stopped and went back. Opened the door again. Left it open just a tiny bit. Like she'd found it. She spun around just in time to come face to face with Mac.

TWENTY-ONE

Mac beamed at her. Alice reckoned she must look like she had a 104-degree fever she was sweating so much.

'Hi,' Alice croaked. He'd ask her now what she'd been doing in their room. The smile would morph into something much more sinister.

'I was coming looking for you,' he said. The smile still there.

'Ah,' she said. 'Oh... like, me too.' She turned and pointed at the door. Relief flooded through her. Of course that's all she'd been doing. She and Finn had fallen asleep, and when she'd woken up, they were gone. Any normal person might have gone to knock on their door. 'You weren't there when I woke up.'

Mac nodded. If he'd been suspicious about what she'd been doing, he seemed fine with this explanation.

'The pair of ye were out cold. We went to get food. I thought you'd appreciate it. After everything that happened today.' He lowered his voice for the last bit, looking over his shoulder, back down the stairs to where they could both hear Vivienne bustling about the kitchen.

'Thank you. That's so thoughtful.'

'Not at all,' he said, turning and leading the way back downstairs.

At the kitchen table Vivienne was taking food cartons from a plastic carrier bag. Delicious smells reached Alice's nostrils, and she realised how hungry she was.

'We walked to the nearest takeaway,' said Mac, taking a few of the cartons from Vivienne. 'We got enough for everyone.'

'Oh, that's very kind of you,' Alice reiterated, smiling at Mac.

'Don't get too excited now, it's fairly bog-standard Chinese fare.'

Alice looked over at Finn and raised an eyebrow. He was awake too now. He nodded his tired, but thankfully less pale, face.

'It's stone-cold,' sniped Vivienne, her face looking – to Alice's eye – even more disgruntled than usual. 'The nearest village with any decent facilities was five kilometres away. It took an hour to walk there and an hour to walk back.'

'We knew that, Viv,' said Mac. 'There's the microwave.'

'Oh, you should have woken us, we'd have driven you.'

'Would you?' Vivienne looked straight at her, eyes boring into her. Alice said nothing. Did Vivienne think that if they got into the car with Finn and her, that they'd keep going, kidnap them if you will, to remove them from here? Tempting as that would have been, the woman was paranoid. Alice shook her head.

'I'll heat you up two plates,' said Mac.

Alice smiled at him, then went over to Finn. 'Well, this is fun, cosy,' she whispered to him, grimacing.

'At least we get some takeaway?' Finn attempted some levity. Alice shook her head, not amused. Sounds of the radio came on from the kitchen. It was turned up just enough that the two couples could talk to each other and, if they didn't raise their voices too high, they wouldn't be overheard.

'Here,' said Alice, casting a quick glance towards the kitchen, keeping her voice hushed. 'Don't give out but I found something weird.'

Finn looked at her, wary. 'What?'

'So, I woke up about fifteen minutes ago and the place was deserted. I wondered if they'd fallen asleep like us, so I crept upstairs to check.' Alice checked the kitchen again, the pair of them were busy. 'But no, the room was empty...'

'Alice, what did you do?'

'I didn't do anything... really.'

'Alice...'

'I wanted to see if I could find my phone. No, don't,' she stopped him as he opened his mouth to give out. 'And anyway, Finn, like, who are these people? I don't think it's unreasonable to have a little check to see who they might be... no? That whole dead boyfriend Mac freaked out about earlier. That was intense... If that's how he was, I'd hate to see her actually triggered. I think it's perfectly logical to check these guys out.'

'Alice, you shouldn't...'

'Don't worry, I just looked around a bit.'

'Alice! You can't go rifling through people's stuff.'

'Shsssh!' Alice shot a glance at the kitchen, but thankfully neither of them turned around. 'I know, I know. Blah, blah, but she did it first!'

'You sound like a five-year-old.'

'She went through my things, she stole my phone! I can look through her bag if I want. Turnabout is fair play...'

Finn rolled his eyes. 'I really don't think she has your phone.'

'We'll agree to disagree there. But don't worry, I'm not in a hurry to do it again. Mac nearly caught me.'

'Learned your lesson.'

'Yes. Probably. But I haven't told you what I found. Wait till you hear this.'

Finn said nothing. Alice could see he was interested despite his disapproval.

'There was a book in Vivienne's bag. And it had a strange bookmark in it.'

Finn gave in. 'What about it?'

Alice dropped her voice another level. 'It was a photo. An old photo. It was of Vivienne. And she was holding a baby. *Her* baby.'

'Okay? So?' Finn looked confused. Alice realised he hadn't been there this morning.

'Earlier, she was asking me all kinds of questions about us. Being really nosy. I turned it back on her, asked her if she had kids and it was like I burned her. She was quite clear about not having any.'

'You sure then that the baby in the photo is hers?'

'Totally... right down to the matching hospital ID bands. I've no doubt.'

'Maybe something happened to the baby,' said Finn, his voice flat.

'Oh...' Alice felt a twinge of shame, Finn might be right. 'I guess.' If Vivienne had lost a partner *and* a child, that might also explain why she was so... difficult. People put up barriers. She felt sorry for the woman. But something about this, she couldn't let go, even though she could tell Finn felt she was skipping merrily over the acceptable line.

'Okay, but if that's the case, why did she say she wasn't a mother? Like, even if the worst happened, wouldn't you still be a mother?'

'Perhaps,' he looked at her pointedly, 'she doesn't like talking about it.'

'Maybe. And maybe it wasn't a worst-case scenario, the child could have been adopted? She's not smiling or looking happy at all in the picture, she looks miserable. Maybe that's why. She knows what's coming.'

'Alice, honestly...'

Alice decided it was time to drop it. Mac was coming in their direction with two full plates.

'I gave you a selection, I hope that's okay?' he said, holding them out.

'It's perfect, thank you,' said Alice, smiling up at him.

'Appreciate it,' agreed Finn.

They took the two warmed-up plates full of food. Both their tummies rumbled loudly. With all the drama and exhaustion from earlier, they hadn't eaten since breakfast. With a smile, Mac retreated to the table, where Vivienne was sitting down. They left the music on, keeping what little privacy the two couples had.

Alice and Finn tucked in, not talking as they hungrily scooped up spicy chicken and bit into deliciously crispy spring rolls. Alice sat back, shoulder touching Finn's, her thoughts still on the photograph as she ate. She knew that part of her surprise was reconciling the brittle angry woman across the room with anything maternal. With a sigh that garnered a side glance from Finn, she checked herself. Checked the bias that being a mother was one rigid thing. Everyone – who hadn't known them well – had thought her mam was a great mother. Bubbly, life and soul of the party. Molly was so friendly and nice. But the weight of the plate of food on Alice's lap right now took her back to the lightness of many empty ones she'd faced growing up. Things weren't always what they seemed.

'What are you thinking about? You've gone all sad-looking,' said Finn, concerned.

'I was thinking about mothers. Mine in particular.'

'Ah.'

Alice nodded. 'I shouldn't be judging Vivienne. We don't always have the full picture. But she doesn't have to inflict her trauma on us, right? We've got plenty of our own.'

Finn laughed at that. 'Yeah, that's for sure. Though, sometimes I think even that isn't the worst, you know?'

'What? Explain that to me, Professor Tobin?'

'Well, I just mean, our tough upbringings, they weren't all bad.'

'Speak for yourself.'

'I mean, they propelled us. Like, if I hadn't ended up in a succession of awful foster homes, I might never have gone to university so young. I was barely seventeen, still a child. I went to get away from foster care. And it was the going early that really made the difference. If I hadn't, I wouldn't have been taught by Prof Clarke because he retired after my first year,' Finn took a deep breath, 'and *then*, if I hadn't been taught by Prof Clarke, I wouldn't have gotten interested in heuristic algorithms, which were the very beginnings of TobinTech. A cosy life would have sent me down a very different path. I'd probably be a sad, lonely programmer now.'

'Interesting... Hang on, I thought you dropped out of university. Isn't that part of the Finn Tobin mythology? You and Bill Gates and all the others, university drop-out billionaires?'

'Well, not a billionaire. Just to say.'

'Yet.'

'Ha!' Finn laughed. 'But, yeah, I did drop out, in third year. I was offered some investment, seed capital for the software I developed from that original project in Prof Clarke's class. I couldn't say no. The rest is history.'

'I suppose,' said Alice, pondering the fates that had guided both their lives, 'that is a good way to look at it all. No regrets. What happened is what made us.'

'Yeah, no regrets,' said Finn, quietly. He frowned, then forced a smile. 'And look at you, you always say it was the drive not to be poor and at the mercy of fate which drove you to do so well. I know your mother didn't have that in mind, she wasn't putting you through some reverse psychology experiment. But you have been driven to succeed by it.'

Alice shrugged and raised her eyebrows in acknowledgement. That was true. She had been driven by what she had lived through. And it had fuelled The Plan as well... not that Finn realised that, how close to the bone he was getting.

'And I know she didn't plan to pass away and leave you alone to fend for yourself so young, but it made you self-reliant. Resourceful.'

'True,' said Alice, not looking Finn in the eye. She became very interested in her plate of food. 'You're right.'

Finn, happy with his little thesis, speared a piece of chicken and popped it in his mouth. Alice looked over at Vivienne. Mac was keeping a watchful eye over her. They were out of chat and Vivienne was quietly eating her food. Alice thought again of the sad photo of Vivienne and the baby. What trauma changeling had taken the place of her child in her mind? What effect had the shadow of motherhood had on her?

Alice shivered – what had it driven her to do?

TWENTY-TWO

They'd slipped upstairs not long after dinner. Both of them exhausted even after falling asleep on the sofa earlier. Alice had suggested they turn in, keen to get away from the other two. She was sick of having to keep their voices low in the hope of having any kind of private conversation. Sick of the unrelenting uncomfortable atmosphere. If Finn hadn't been feeling so wretched after the incident this morning – Alice couldn't bear to even think of the word drowning – they could have gone out. Found that promised cosy pub with its turf fire and trad music. But no, they had been stuck, sharing lukewarm food and red-hot tension, both couples trying to pretend the other wasn't there. It was actually worse than being in Dublin now. And while Finn had perked up and been chatty when the food had arrived, that hadn't lasted long. He hadn't needed much persuasion to retire for the evening.

Alice adjusted the pillow behind her back and picked up her book. Finn was the next floor down, in the bathroom, getting ready for bed. She stared at the page in front of her. But she couldn't manage to read more than a line or too. So much had happened today she wasn't surprised she was struggling to concentrate. And there was too much space, in the quiet still-ness of the evening, to stop her mind from wandering back over what had happened. For the full gravity of events to finally land. As she stared at the pages in her book, all she kept seeing was Finn clinging to those razor-sharp rocks, his head dipping under the waves. She could feel a sickness in her gut just thinking about how she and Mac had battled to save him.

'Stop it,' she admonished herself out loud. Hoping her voice would chase away her thoughts. 'He's fine. He's fine.'

To distract herself she forced herself to think about the photo she'd found in Vivienne's book. For a simple photo it had made a huge impression on Alice. And something she should have realised earlier came to her. Mac had said Vivienne's partner had died about twenty-five years ago. The photo was from 1998, about the same amount of time ago. This David guy must have been the father. No wonder she looked so sad. No wonder she'd had such a strong reaction to Alice's question about kids. Alice could feel her hostility towards Vivienne waver, just for a moment. It was hard to completely resent someone who'd suffered so much. But Alice didn't really want to feel that way about Vivienne. It was much easier to dislike her.

The door to the room opened and a tired and subdued Finn came in, a towel over his shoulder and a freshly washed and scrubbed gleam to him. He smiled a crooked smile at her. He yawned and stretched. The hem of his T-shirt rode up and Alice caught sight of the mottled edge of a dark purple bruise. A painful reminder of what had happened that morning. She'd seen more like it all over his body as he'd changed for bed. She'd had to look away.

'You okay? Like, relatively speaking?' she asked him.

He climbed into bed beside her.

'I've had better days. Not gonna lie.'

'Yes, sounds a fair assessment.'

He turned off his bedside lamp and snuggled down into the bed, not even attempting to open a book or look at his phone.

'I was thinking about that photo again. Vivienne's one.'

'The one you shouldn't have found? When you were snooping through her things without her permission?'

'Yeah, that one. Well remembered. Glad you were paying attention.'

'I hang on your every word.' He grinned sleepily up at her. His eyes were already drooping.

'That David guy, the boyfriend Mac mentioned. Do you think he was the father?'

Finn frowned. One shoulder shrugged under the duvet. 'I don't know. And probably, like her stuff, none of our business.'

'So long ago and she still seems so affected by it all.'

'Love will do that to you,' Finn murmured. His words sleepy-slow. He yawned. With heavy lids, he looked at her. 'Thank you, Al... for saving me.'

Alice reached out and brushed his cheek. 'Mac really was the one—'

He shook his head. 'Nope. You save me... all the time...'

Alice didn't trust herself to speak. She just nodded her head and smiled back at him.

'Love you,' he mumbled, sleep gently coaxing him away.

'Sleep,' Alice finally said, reaching out, rubbing his head and letting a curl wrap around her finger. As she listened to his gentle, rhythmic breaths telling her that he had slipped off to sleep, she whispered, 'Love you too.'

And she meant it. Completely. She slipped her hand carefully from his hair, which had air-dried by the fire, the curls more pronounced for it. Her eye then found the shape of his cheekbone and followed his face's contours down to his jawline. She loved every last inch of him. A truth she'd never fully allowed herself to acknowledge so simply before. She loved him. Nearly losing him today... Alice felt dizzy at the thought. But just imagining a world without Finn was forcing herself to be honest. Dating him had been central to The Plan, but it had never been on her radar that she might actually fall for him. Or that he would fall quite so hard for her. And, having never known what it was like to be loved without complication, Alice had been completely and utterly unprepared for it. She wondered if this... being loved by Finn, loving him in return... had it fixed her? And what more could she want? What else was the point?

She picked up her book again. Tried to read. To distract herself from the growing surge of emotion she didn't want to feel. She read one word over and over. But tears pressed at the corners of her eyes. Checking to be sure Finn was asleep, she finally gave in and let them fall.

Alice rubbed the back of her hand across her eyes. Tried to stem up the trail of tears. Her chin dipped to her chest, the tears falling onto the cover of the book on her lap. This silly little story. This enemies-to-lovers romance. Too close to home. Too close to the bone.

If only Finn knew. If he only knew that in their story, their fairy-tale romance... he was the enemy.

TWENTY-THREE

Alice's tears wouldn't stop. Building now into sobs. If she wasn't careful, her distress would wake up Finn. With mini-gasps Alice tried to suck in some air in between sobs, but it was a struggle. She forced herself out of the bed. She needed space. She needed to get away from Finn, to get control of herself.

On the dark landing the tears kept flowing. She did her best to muffle the sobs. She thought she'd go downstairs, ride out the engulfing waves of emotions down there, in private. Get control of herself. But she heard movement. A chair scraping on the tiled kitchen floor. Those two were still awake.

Alice turned for the stairs upwards. Towards the lantern room. She dragged herself as fast as she could upstairs. With each step away from the sleeping Finn she let the tears flow a little freer. Until she reached the lantern room and threw herself in, slamming the door shut behind her.

Her whole body shook.

Above her the lantern slowly turned, lighting the way for lost ships. She stood speckled by its dissipated glow, shining like a disco ball through latticed metal treads. She took the last few steps up, tucking her head into the crook of her arm at the brightest revolutions of the bulb. With the light rotating behind her, she grabbed at the lock on the hatch out to the gallery balcony. She needed to get outside, to get air. Finally it swung open and she stumbled out, assaulted instantly by the howling, gasping, glacial air. Flung against the railings. Feeling, rather than seeing, each of the seventy feet to the ground. Invisible in the dark. She gripped the rail. Gusts shook her. Her hair tore skyward, seized by the storm. Her flimsy pyjamas no protection against the icy chill. She shivered, shook, cried. Her hands gripped the railing tighter. All around her, the wind, the wild sea, the glittering bitter stars above her.

She'd nearly lost Finn. Forever. Every fibre of her being was grateful that he was downstairs now, sleeping. Safe. And she loved him. *I love him.* Admitting that felt dangerous. It felt like it was going to change everything.

'Dammit!' Alice roared. She released her grip on the railings and hugged herself, shivering violently. She let the wind rock her like a mother with a baby.

This was a crossroads she'd never expected to be at. Since she was a little girl she'd worked on a meticulous plan that had brought her to this point.

The Plan.

Its sole aim to destroy Finn Tobin's life.

Her life had been entirely centred around destroying his. Even before she'd known his name. Before she'd known what he looked like. She'd gone to bed each night dreaming of his demise.

But no one but herself was making her do this. She had originated The Plan and, a small voice whispered to her, she could abandon it too, if she chose to. Alice felt the air sucked out of her at that thought. Could she abandon it? She'd no idea of who she was without it. At this stage it had been her companion so long, it *was* her.

Alice, tentative, allowed a little light to shine on this radical idea.

What would happen if she left her life's work behind?

What would that look like? It wasn't as if she'd adopted a whole new persona to snag Finn. Calling off The Plan wouldn't be like *Scooby-Doo* where he'd pull off her mask to reveal someone different entirely. Nope. The Alice that Finn loved was really who she was. It's why The Plan had worked so well and so quickly. She hadn't had to get to know him and mould herself to his tastes, turn herself into his perfect girl. Because she already was. They'd had such similar upbringings, they understood each other. They were built from the same blocks. Both had been left with a drive to leave that life behind. They were both smart, dedicated, hardworking people. If they'd been on a dating app they'd have matched one hundred per cent. The Plan had blossomed, and was now threatening to wilt, in the face of such compatibility. Of such happiness. Such simplicity. They worked. They clicked. For the first time in her life Alice was happy. Really, really happy. No strings attached.

Alice noticed that her tears were slowing as she thought about this. Her breathing gradually going back to normal. Her body calming.

A stupid grin spread across her face imagining just being with him. No hidden agenda. No secret plan. But such a path forward felt as hidden as the dark waters around her and she had no lighthouse to guide her. Who was she without The Plan? It was all well and good to try and do this, but who was Alice Armstrong without it?

Alice turned. She'd go back down to Finn. Go back to bed and snuggle up close to him, test out how it felt to do that with no other intention than to love him and be loved in return.

She clambered back in through the hatch, down the steps, nearly giggling as she went. Though she was shivering from the cold she was shivering from hope and excitement too. She stopped at the door to their room. Her hand on the door handle. Her head was running through everything that might change. She could quit her job at TobinTech, she and Finn could go public... well, after waiting just a little bit. Didn't want it to look too soon. Alice's excitement tempered a little. She took her hand off the handle. Okay, it wouldn't be enough just to decide to abandon The Plan. There'd be practicalities. She'd need to dismantle it too. Ted would have to be called off. And soon. A little fear gripped Alice. The photographer. He was due tomorrow or Monday, Ted hadn't told her which. He'd definitely have to be cancelled.

Alice opened the door as quietly as she could. In the soft light of her bedside lamp, she looked at Finn sleeping. Watched his chest rise and fall. Just the sight of him, it was a reassurance that this could be the right decision. That she could do it.

By the end of the bed she hesitated. Listening to his breathing. She could pack up The Plan and put it away. It would take some work but she could do it. Harder though would be making sure Finn never found out what she'd been planning to do. She would have to live a life forever where he never found out. Could she do that? Because being honest with him would make it very hard to hide why – why she had started on this path to ruin him in the first place. The *why* was the key. With it he'd unlock all the secrets of The Plan. And it wouldn't matter how much she loved him then. If that happened, he'd be lost to her forever.

TWENTY-FOUR

Alice slowly woke up. A burning pain behind her breastbone rousing her. Heartburn. The greasy takeaway food exacting its revenge. How long had she been asleep? She leaned over Finn and looked at the time on his phone: 3 a.m. Alice yawned. It had taken her ages just to get to sleep. The excitement at the new vista in front of her, this possible new life, had kept her awake. Eventually though, the weight of everything that had happened was too much and she'd slipped into a grateful slumber.

Alice hoisted herself up into a sitting position, yawning again. Sitting up was meant to be better for heartburn. The Chinese food for dinner had felt like a nice treat but she'd probably gotten used to a higher standard of takeaway since dating Finn. Since they couldn't go out and about in the city, Finn arranged for all the finest restaurants to deliver to them. Very fancy takeaways. He always looked a little embarrassed, flaunting the power of his cash in this way – or any way, for that matter – but it was far outweighed by the pleasure it gave him to treat her. Alice smiled to herself despite the discomfort – maybe they'd be eating in those restaurants soon? No longer confined to the shadows.

The smile was short-lived as she grimaced at the discomfort. She should pop downstairs and grab a glass of milk, or see if there was anything she could take. She wasn't getting back to sleep anytime soon if she didn't do something.

She slipped out of bed and padded to the door. But, opening it, she could hear some noises from below. Good grief. Those two were still up. It took all her strength not to slam the door in frustration. She wasn't going down there, heartburn or no. She'd manage somehow. Maybe she had an antacid here somewhere. She took out her toiletries bag and rooted around. Nothing. She grabbed her gilet and searched its pockets. With a quiet cheer of triumph, Alice pulled out a roll of pills, two remaining. She popped them in her mouth and got back into bed, hoping they'd work soon. She wanted to go back to sleep. She yawned and stretched while still sitting upright, giving it as long as she could. Despite her efforts not to think about it, her thoughts strayed back to stepping away from The Plan. She didn't want to think about it because it had taken her long enough to get to sleep already. But it was irresistible. A whole new world opening up for her. All she had to do was choose it.

Alice felt a niggle of worry tap her on the shoulder, interrupting her happy thoughts. Something among all the excitement was bothering her. A quiet whisper of worry at the back of her mind. What was it? Ted? Having to keep secrets forever? These weren't trivial concerns, but no, it was something else. She just couldn't quite put her finger on it. She tried to quieten her mind. What was her subconscious trying to tell her?

Right, what had she just been thinking about when this little voice piped up?

What had she been thinking about that had stirred a deep part of her brain? She scrolled back over her thoughts.

Finn. Ted. The Plan and Finn. Heartburn. Food. Fancy

restaurants. Alice stopped. Food and fancy restaurants? Was this what pinged an uncomfortable feeling in her gut? Alice shook her head, really? But when she sat with it, this was when her anxiety shot up. Considering the stiff competition, why was thinking about food and restaurants the thought that had kicked off her subconscious? She retraced her mental steps again, just to be sure... Abandoning The Plan, dealing with Ted, heartburn, takeaways, happy Finn and fancy restaurants delivering...

Fancy restaurants. That was definitely it.

Oh.

Alice realised what it was.

Her mind's eye rushed back to earlier, in Vivienne's room, when she'd been rooting around in her bag. The two mints she'd found and dismissed. The photo of Vivienne and the baby had completely distracted her. That hadn't been what was so important at all. It was a complete red herring.

Alice closed her eyes and tried to remember. What had been the name on the mints? Le Lièvre Mort. The Dead Hare. Yeah, that had been it. And that had rung a bell. Which she'd ignored in favour of the much more immediately interesting photograph of Vivienne and her baby.

Alice grabbed Finn's phone from the nightstand. There might not be any signal here, but she could search old emails, they'd still be accessible. And she had a feeling she'd find what she was looking for there. She typed Le Lièvre Mort into the search bar of his mail app. It threw up one email. Sent to her from Finn, dated a month ago.

She clicked the email open.

And gasped.

TWENTY-FIVE

Alice read the email a few times. Checked the dates. And all the details. She could hear the blood rushing in her ears. Her brain ran over every scenario, searching for an innocent explanation. But she couldn't find any.

This was no accident.

Those two down below.

Alice could feel her heart pick up speed, her belly drop. All awareness of her heartburn gone.

She'd no idea how they'd managed to swing the double-booking, but it was no unintentional computer glitch. Vivienne and Mac had intended to be here, now, while she and Finn were. She was convinced of it.

Le Lièvre Mort.

One of Finn's favourite restaurants. She should have remembered it immediately with its odd name. Who names a restaurant The Dead Hare? A pretentious three-star Michelin restaurant, that's who. A restaurant that Finn only got to infrequently because it was located in New York. But who, for one weekend only, had opened a pop-up restaurant about ten miles down the road from here as part of an international food festival. Finn had been so excited. It was partly why they'd picked that weekend to visit. The weekend they'd had to cancel at the very last minute.

And now she'd discovered Vivienne and Mac had been there.

What were the chances? The very place Finn had wanted to take her. Had made a booking for. And it was the same Le Lièvre Mort, not another place with the same name. The logo on the mint wrapper matched the one on the sample menu Finn had attached to the email. Might they have visited Le Lièvre Mort in New York? Sure, it was possible. But was it *likely*? Jet-setting to New York and eating at a ridiculously expensive restaurant? They definitely didn't seem the type. What seemed far more believable was they'd been up here a couple of weeks ago. The same weekend she and Finn had meant to be here. They'd been about the area, gone to places Finn had intended going. Had they been planning to do the same as they had on Friday night? Rock up on the doorstep pretending the place was double-booked? They just hadn't got the memo that the weekend was cancelled.

Alice was utterly certain that's what had happened. What she couldn't fathom was *why*.

Alice got out of bed. She stopped at the end of the bed, steadying herself. Her whole body was beginning to shake.

Why were they following them? What were they up to?

Were they dangerous?

Vivienne had admitted to knowing who Finn was, yesterday morning when she'd accused Alice of being with Finn for his money. She'd claimed it was because of the profile in the news-paper. But perhaps she'd been projecting... was it she, not Alice, who was interested in Finn's money? Was that at the root of all of this?

Alice shook her head. Only Vivienne and Mac knew what they were up to. All Alice knew was that she and Finn had let two people under their roof who were up to no good. And she had no idea what level of no good that was.

Alice went to Finn's side of the bed.

She sat down beside him. Shook his shoulder.

'Finn. Finny. Wake up,' she whispered, knowing they couldn't hear her all the way up here, but not able to help her caution.

An exhausted eye half-opened.

'Hmmm?'

'Finn. I've got something I need to tell you.'

'Alice, what is it?' Finn struggled awake. Bleary-eyed, looking at her, concerned. He hoisted himself up on one elbow and dragged his hand through his hair.

Alice grabbed his free hand.

'I didn't tell you earlier. I found something else in Vivienne's bag.'

'Oh right?' Finn squinted.

'I didn't mention it 'cause I didn't think it was important. But I just realised that it is!'

'What are you talking about, Al?'

'She had mints from Le Lièvre Mort.'

Finn looked at her blankly. 'And?'

'Do you really think she's been flying to NYC anytime recently for a spot of fine dining?'

'Well...'

'Yeah, well, no, Finn, I don't really think she has. But do you know where I think she might have gone?'

Finn said nothing. He was waking up fully as he realised where this was going.

'I bet if you rang Le Lièvre Mort, asked them if we turned up for our booking after all, I wonder what they'd say? That we did and that you've grown quite tall and hairy since they saw you last. Okay, maybe they didn't go that far and just picked the mints up at the festival, but either way, Finn, you can bet your

New York minute and Irish country mile that Vivienne and Mac were here in Donegal a couple of weeks ago, when we were meant to be here. And now they're back again. Why is that, Finn? They're up to no good. I'm scared.'

Finn pulled himself fully up in the bed. He stared at Alice. Ran his hand again through his hair. Shook his head.

'Hey, don't worry.' He took her hand and stroked it. 'They might just like it up here? I come here all the time. I'm not stalking anyone, or whatever it is you think they're doing.'

'Ah, come on, Finn!' Alice withdrew her hand. 'I know you think the best of people, but seriously? They just happened to be up here the weekend we were meant to be here? And then out of all the restaurants that were taking part in the festival they went to your favourite? They could have gone anywhere. And then, coincidentally, they're back, again, on the weekend when we do make it here? And coincidentally *again*, they've double-booked into our very accommodation? Of all places? And no one, just no one normal, would then insist on sharing. No one does that. Lob in that she's weirdly hostile all the time, the phone lines look tampered with, all the super personal questions she's asked me about the two of us, and this is one very suspicious, scary situation!'

'Alice...'

Her mind was made up. They had to get out of here. And that was all she needed now to make her other decision. To let herself love this man and put The Plan in the past – because if she didn't need The Plan, then she didn't need to be here. They could walk out the door right now.

'No, Finn, no! Don't "Alice" me. We're going home. We're not safe and I don't care if you believe me or not.'

TWENTY-SIX

'It'll be okay if we leave, now.'

'It's the middle of the night, hon.'

'All the better, we can just sneak out and they won't know we've gone for hours.'

'Will that even work? If you're right, and they've deliberately targeted me, then they'll know where I live and work in Dublin.'

'Yeah, but at least we're surrounded by people there and we have phone signal to call for help. Let's not serve ourselves up on a platter here!'

Alice had no time for his strange reluctance. She was packing and getting dressed. And leaving. She knew he'd follow her, despite any misgivings he had.

In a flurry of anxious energy, Alice flew about the room, packing her things, then Finn's, as he sat on the bed watching her, his mouth a grim straight line.

'Alice, what if I go and talk to them? What if I do that? Might that not be safer?'

Alice paused over his case, a pair of his jeans in her hands.

'The only safe thing to do is to get out of here. So, if you're feeling up to it, pull on some clothes before I pack everything away. We're leaving. Now.'

Finn shook his head but stood and started to get dressed.

It didn't take Alice long to get their things together. She smiled at Finn, despite the seriousness of the situation. She tried not to smile too broadly. For the first time she could see a future stretching out in front of them. No little voice at the back of her head reminding her that this was just temporary. The cracks that had been there, in the lead-lined vessel that had encased her heart for so long, were widening and beginning to crumble.

But this new life didn't start until they got away from the pair below them.

'Right, come on.' Alice, a bag in each hand, crossed to the door and ever so slowly unlocked it.

Finn came up behind her and took the bags. 'I can manage them, don't worry.'

'You feeling well enough?'

Finn nodded. 'I'm okay, feeling much more myself.'

'Good.'

She cracked open the door. The pair stepped out into the dark. Alice shivered in the chilly air. But instead of the hoped for quiet of the night, she heard noise from below. Vivienne and Mac still hadn't come up from the kitchen. Alice rolled her eyes. *Why couldn't they be in bed like normal people at this hour?*

Then a splintering wooden crack reverberated up the stairs to them. A plaintive admonishment of 'Mac!', clearly Vivienne's voice, echoed up after it. Alice shot a look over her shoulder at Finn.

'What is that?' she whispered. Finn frowned. Alice crept forward, towards the top of the stairs. The light from the bottom floor was a faint, faraway shimmer, like an anglerfish's lure, guiding her into deep, murky waters. She descended the first step.

Finn reached out for her shoulder, stopping her.

'Alice, what are you doing?'

'I'm going to see what the hell is going on down there.'

'That's a bad idea!'

'I don't care, I want to leave and they're in our way. I want to know what's happening.' She shook off Finn's hand and took another step down.

'Fine. But you're not going on your own,' he replied. He put their bags down and followed her. Gripping the rough rope banisters, feeling the way in the dark, they kept light on their feet. They passed Mac and Vivienne's room. The door was open, the room empty.

Things were getting louder downstairs. They paused where the staircase opened up as it rounded the wall into the kitchen. In the shadows they crouched down. Putting their heads to one side they could see Mac and Vivienne.

Mac was swaying, a small bottle of whiskey in his hands. One of the kitchen chairs was on the floor, a leg broken. Vivienne was holding both hands up, and Alice could hear her soft repetition of his name. Gentle and coaxing. 'Mac, it's okay. Mac, don't worry.' He was steadying.

'I see him, Viv... I see David. I don't want to but he doesn't go away.' Mac's voice, the words loud but slurred. 'He's haunting me.'

'Oh, Macdara.' Vivienne reached out a hand, but Mac pulled back. 'He haunts us all.'

'Why are we here, Viv?' he cried, and she hushed him. 'I hate it here.'

'Mac, you shouldn't be drinking, hon. You've worked so hard...'

A gulp and the big man's face dissolved, sobs and tears a blur of misery from him. He grabbed the damaged chair and held it above his head, swinging it.

'I need to make it stop! Stop!' he yelled and Vivienne cowered. Alice felt Finn move behind her.

'What are you doing?' Alice hissed, grabbing his arm to stop him chasing down the stairs.

'He's going to hurt her, Alice!' He shook himself free.

'You can't—'

Mac had dropped the chair on the floor. A second leg breaking. The big man followed it, sinking to the ground himself. Finn stopped.

'I drank the whiskey. So sorry, Viv, so sorry...' Mac, a crumpled mess, held the near empty bottle aloft for Vivienne to take. He sat there and sobbed. She snatched it and poured it down the sink. The bottle empty, she went back to Mac. Standing behind him, she leaned over and hugged his broad shoulders. She kissed the top of his head then rested her chin there.

'There are ghosts, Mac, you're right. This place is full of them. That's why we're here... to get rid of them. Just hang in there.'

Alice stared at Vivienne. Her belly was a ball of ice. Getting rid of anything sounded ominous. She turned and looked at Finn, inclined her head, indicating they needed to retreat. They would have to wait till these two went to bed before they could make their escape. And right now Alice felt exposed in their hiding place. With Mac on the ground and Vivienne leaning over him, their line of sight was lower, meaning if either of them looked up, there was a chance they would see them in the dark. She inched her right foot backwards as Finn did the same, feeling their way back up the steps without turning around. Holding tight to the banister, they were quickly engulfed by the near total darkness on the first landing.

The sounds from below receded the higher they got. Finn grabbed their bags, and they were quickly back in their room.

Alice shut the door behind them, and locked it.

'We'll go once they head to bed.'

Finn said nothing, just sat down on the bed. Alice sat on the ground next to the door.

'Come back to bed, Alice. If they were going to kill us in our beds, they'd have done it by now, no? We can go first thing in the morning. I don't think Macdara will be waking up anytime early.'

'We need to go while they're both asleep so they won't know we're off. You rest there, and when I hear them come up, I'll wake you. Okay?'

Finn looked at her for the longest time, but then just nodded. 'I'll wait up with you.'

'No, love, don't worry, you need your rest.'

'I'll be fine.'

Finn came over and sat down beside her on the floor. He took her hand in his. They huddled in close, leaning back against the door and each other, listening for movement from below. Alice felt the warmth of Finn beside her.

They'd leave just as soon as those two downstairs went to bed. Away from here their future together could start. Alice felt a bubble of excitement. They were getting out of here any minute now. And then everything would be perfect.

TWENTY-SEVEN

Alice woke with dull, diffused light slipping in under the curtains. She rubbed her eyes, momentarily confused about where she was. Her bones were sore and she looked around. Fully dressed, she was sitting on the floor. Finn was beside her, though he was lying flat on the ground, still asleep. She picked up his phone which was on the floor between them. It was 6.15 a.m.

Last night's drama came back to her. The revelation of what they were up to. The scene in the kitchen with the drunken Mac. They hadn't meant to fall asleep here, by the door. But it had been quite the day yesterday, she wasn't surprised they hadn't been able to stay awake. Alice frowned. It did cause a problem: had they missed their window to get out of here? Maybe it would be okay. As Finn had suggested last night, Mac in particular would be needing a lot of sleep after his binge. Hopefully Vivienne would be worn out too.

There was something she wanted to do before they left. Something that would be harder to do once she was on the road with Finn. Calling off Ted. She stood, grimacing at the stiffness from sleeping on the ground, and grabbed the duvet off the bed.

She carefully laid it across Finn. She felt that new sensation, the tingle of happiness in her belly, as she looked at him. That stupid smile on her face was back. It was hard but she just stopped herself reaching out to touch him. But he could get more sleep – which he needed – while she took care of business.

Quietly, with eyes on Finn, she got up.

Turning the key in the door slowly, she slipped out of the bedroom. She tiptoed down the stairs. She paused briefly at Vivienne and Mac's door. Loud snores reverberated from within. She kept going.

She was annoyed at the prospect of the trek to the end of the road again just to make the call. But at least this time it was for better reasons. Ted wouldn't be happy, but she didn't care – she was. Finally, after all these years, Alice was happy. It was a glorious feeling. It was like a first sip of wine. The smell of cut grass in spring. A baby's smile. Something pure. She thought she might float away; she felt so light and free.

At the front door she pulled on her boots and her coat and slipped out of the cottage. The sky was that murky mid-light of pre-dawn. It was cold. Alice shivered and watched her breath as she exhaled. Stillness filled the air. It was as if the world was waiting, knew everything was changing, changing for the better, and was holding its breath in anticipation. The sheep in the fields remained huddled together, the gulls were nowhere to be seen, presumably asleep in their nests. Everything was a sleepy calm, the promise of a new day waiting at the edges. Alice strode down the driveway, keeping her steps light and quiet, leaving the lighthouse's residents undisturbed.

She repeated the process from the morning before. As she walked, her hand dipping into her pocket, turning the phone on just using touch, keeping it hidden until she got to her spot on the grey stone wall. She felt the inevitable vibrations of alerts and messages ping as they came in.

She pondered where she might dispose of the phone when

she got back to Dublin. Perhaps she'd toss it in the Grand Canal, that would be good enough for it. She'd enjoy doing that. Alice crossed the road, pulling her coat tightly around her. Her eye was caught by the sight of someone in the distance, in one of the fields. A figure with a dog next to them. Alice reckoned it looked like Michael, the neighbour, from up the way. A farmer, up and about his business already. Alice yawned. It wouldn't be the life for her.

Happy she'd chosen well yesterday and certain she couldn't be seen, she stopped. She reached out and felt the dampness of the dew against the cool stone wall and, deciding it wasn't too wet, she sat. Alice took out the phone. And stopped. The screen was smashed. Shattered. What the hell? The phone itself seemed to be still working – she'd felt the pings, and through the few shards on the screen that were hanging in, she could see the edge of messages. But she couldn't see how she could use it to make a call. She tried tapping the screen to see if it would respond. Nothing. Then she held the home button down, to see if she could use the voice-activated assistant. There was a brief robotic enquiry, then a squeak and it stopped. She tried a few more times, but nothing. Dammit. Maybe the phone had smashed against the rocks when they were saving Finn yesterday. She could imagine that might have happened. Though water damage felt more likely under those circumstances. Not that it mattered. There was no way she was calling Ted on this phone. And with her other phone still missing, how was she going to call off the dogs? Sure, she could probably come up with some reason to borrow Finn's phone and come out here yet again. But she didn't know Ted's number. Who remembered such things these days? They got put in the phone contacts and that was that. Back in Dublin she had it written down, but that wasn't much help right now.

She looked around. Head snapping left, then right. Searching the fields and winding roads for the glint of a photographer's long lens. The happy knot in her belly handed the baton to fear. Fear took off at a sprint. Alice moaned. Oh God. How had this happened? If Ted got a photo of her and Finn together, up here on a romantic weekend away, he wouldn't need her cooperation to get his story. He could ruin Finn without her. The Plan could spiral out of her control. Beyond her ability to stop it.

A footstep crunched near her. Alice swung around.

'Jesus,' she gasped, wide-eyed.

'Just me!' Michael held his hands up, walking up the road towards her. 'Sorry to frighten you.'

A black-and-white sheepdog leapt the low wall from a nearby field. Alice realised Michael must have come from the fields behind her, masking the sound of his approach. The dog came bounding up, smiling, tail wagging furiously. Alice put her hand to her chest, feeling the rapid beating of her heart. She shook her head, trying to recover herself.

'Sorry... sorry, I was just... miles away.'

'No worries. I thought I was being loud enough, but I guess I'm used to treading softly at this hour.'

Alice nodded.

'Speaking of which, you're up early.'

'Oh, yeah. I em, I had to make a phone call. Again.'

'Very early for a phone call.'

'Eh. Yes. It is... but it's to my brother. In Australia. It's his birthday, so I don't want to miss him. It's the right time there now... I think?'

Michael laughed. 'Well, I won't interrupt you then.'

'Ah, don't worry,' Alice said. She held up the phone for him to see. 'I wasn't getting very far.'

'Oh dear,' said Michael, taking the phone out of her hand and examining it. 'What happened?'

'Not sure actually. But it's pretty useless now.'

'Yeah, looks like it. Your brother will have to wait for his birthday greetings.'

'Yeah, poor... John. He won't mind though. I'm a bit of a flake in general, always forgetting something.' *Chill your boots, Alice*, she thought to herself. *No need to over-elaborate.*

'You're free to come up to the house and use the landline if you like? Mary might appreciate a few bob if it's a call to Australia though.'

'You're so kind, thank you. But can't do that either. Number is on the phone.' She held it up again and pointed at the splinters.

'Ah,' Michael laughed. 'That is a problem. Well, best of luck, sorry not to be more help.'

'Thanks.'

Michael clicked the corner of his mouth and the dog got up, excited to be on its way again. With a backwards wave, Michael walked off in the direction of the farmhouse. Alice waited a moment, let him get a good distance away, then started back. Eyes constantly watching, looking for something, anything, out of place. Not that she appeared very good at that kind of thing, the way Michael had managed to surprise her.

Back by the cottage door, Alice paused for a moment. Maybe she didn't need to worry, they'd be out of here soon, so the photographer wouldn't get a chance to catch them. And then she'd call Ted when she was back in Dublin. That would work. It would be fine. She watched calmer waves roll in. On the horizon, a streak of light signalled the sun was clambering out of bed. The brightening sky looked like it would be a clear-blue one. Despite this hiccup, Alice couldn't help but smile. Everything was going to be alright. Wasn't it?

She opened the cottage door, turning the handle slowly, careful to be as silent as she could be.

She closed it softly behind her.

'Good morning,' a voice came from behind her.

'Jesus!' Alice screamed once again, jumping this time in fright.

Vivienne stood at the kitchen counter, sipping on a mug of coffee, dressed in trainers, leggings and her bright yellow wind-cheater. Her blonde hair was pulled back into a very tight bun, making her face look even more pinched than normal. She looked like she was about to head off for a run. Her eyes were puffy and red as if she hadn't slept well. Alice wouldn't be surprised if that was the case, not after what they'd witnessed last night. She tried to not stare at Vivienne in alarm. Now that she knew they were up to something nefarious, she didn't want to spook them. If Vivienne was going for a run like she had yesterday, she'd be gone for a good long while. With Mac sleeping off last night, that gave them time to get away without drawing immediate attention to it. She just needed to act now like nothing had changed.

'Sorry to give you a fright,' said Vivienne, as ever not sounding in the least bit sorry.

'I didn't expect anyone to be up so early.'

'I couldn't sleep.'

Alice nodded then looked about the kitchen, unsure what to do next. Her eyes rested on the broken kitchen chair, placed close to the door, the splintered legs sitting on top of it. Vivienne followed her gaze.

'Mac had an accident with the chair last night. Happens a lot at his size.' Vivienne turned to the sink and emptied the last of her coffee down the drain. She rinsed the mug and set it down on the draining board. She looked back at Alice. 'We'll pay for the damage. Don't worry.'

'Okay, thanks,' said Alice, nodding again. She felt like one of those nodding dog ornaments for the back shelves of cars. She had to cut it out, it was too suspicious, too over-conscious 'acting normal'. She was desperate for a coffee herself, the aroma of Vivienne's just finished mug snaking its way towards her. But she needed to get upstairs, rouse Finn and be ready the moment Vivienne left and was out of sight. She edged towards the stairs.

'Emm, going for a run?'

Vivienne looked down at herself, at her running gear, and just stared at Alice in reply.

'Ha, yes, I suppose you're hardly off to dig the garden in that outfit.' Alice felt her cheeks redden. She had to get out of here before she gave the game away entirely. 'Enjoy!' She turned and flew up the stairs, not looking back, not waiting to see what reaction she'd induced in Vivienne.

Finn was still out for the count on the floor when Alice fell into the room, panting from the effort of running up the stairs, and from nerves. She'd no idea how he could be so fast asleep on such a hard surface. She dashed to the window and pulled back the curtain. She waited, her breath taking its time to return to normal, and a couple of minutes later, Vivienne emerged. Alice ducked back as Vivienne looked up, as if searching for her in the window. Watching from a remove, Alice followed her as she walked towards the drive and gradually began to jog as she reached the gates.

She spun around and went over to Finn. She crouched down and shook his shoulder. He opened bleary eyes.

'Finn. Finn. Come on now, wake up. We have to hurry!'

TWENTY-EIGHT

'C'mon, c'mon, no time to lose.'

She stood up.

'We gotta get going. Vivienne has gone for her run and Mac is fast asleep. We need to leave.'

Finn pulled himself up off the floor. He screwed up his eyes and rubbed the palms of his hands down his face.

'Do you honestly think they're up to no good? Do we have to do this?'

'Yes, I do think they're up to no good,' said Alice, annoyed. 'And yes, we do have to do this.'

'Okay, fine.' Finn looked tired, dark rings under his eyes, his curls dishevelled. Stubble was shadowing his chin. Alice thought he'd never looked more handsome. But she wished he'd hurry up.

'Come on. Time to go.'

He pulled a blue fleece hoodie over his head. Then ran his fingers through his hair, untangling some of the kinks. Alice dragged the two bags to the door.

'I'll drive,' she said. 'You look too exhausted. We'll be hitting Letterkenny in an hour and we'll be home by lunchtime.'

Finn looked at Alice. 'I'm sorry about all this, love. It really wasn't what we'd planned.'

Alice went over to him and placed a hand on his cheek. 'Shssh, don't apologise. This isn't your fault.'

She took his hand and they went to the door. They grabbed a bag each and went out onto the landing. Alice could feel her heart thumping a mile a minute.

Like mice, they wove their way down the stairs making barely a noise. Alice grabbed Finn's wetsuit from the bathroom and they slowed even more as they passed Vivienne and Mac's bedroom, though Mac's insistent snores reassured them he was in no danger of waking up. They finished their descent.

Once in the kitchen, they hurried out to the car. With exaggerated care, they put their bags down by the boot. Finn carefully popped it open.

They were confronted by the tangle of equipment Alice had dumped there the day before, in a hurry to hide it before Vivienne returned and was triggered.

Alice left Finn's wetsuit on top of the mess.

'You make some space here as quickly as possible,' Alice whispered. 'I'll go and grab our coats and the keys, okay?'

'Okay,' he said, pulling out gear from the tangle.

'Be quick, and don't be too picky,' said Alice. 'I don't want to hang about in case she takes a short run this morning.'

Alice dashed back into the cottage. Finn hadn't found the keys yesterday morning, but he said he hadn't looked too hard for them either. She went to the countertop where she thought she remembered him putting them. They weren't there. She checked their coats, hanging by the door, searching pockets and patting them down like security guards. Alice was sure she'd find them there. But no, nothing. Then she circled the room, looking around and behind everything there. No sign of them. Like her phone. Then the living room. Alice pulled out the sofa cushions. Got on her hands and knees and looked under the sofa. And then she repeated everything again. The keys were nowhere to be found.

This is so frustrating, thought Alice. They were losing so much time. Every second they delayed was a second Vivienne could be on her way back, or Mac might wake up. But they were going nowhere without the keys.

Alice pulled out all the cushions from the sofa and the armchair for a third time with no joy. She pulled open all the kitchen presses and drawers, just in case the keys had somehow gotten put away. But they were nowhere.

She straightened up and caught a glimpse of Finn outside, his brow furrowed. She abandoned her search, went over to the cottage door and opened it. She grabbed their coats, but she'd have to tell him she couldn't find the keys. He was going to have to help her if they were going to get out of here.

'Finn,' she whispered as loudly as she dared.

He had his back to her. He didn't react.

'Finn?' she repeated a little louder again. Still nothing. She walked right over to him and the car. Dumped the coats on top of their bags. He was standing there, looking down at the piece of equipment in his hand. A length of tubing which looked like it would join to the mouthpiece was in his hand. He was staring at it as if in a different world.

'Finn?' she tried for a third time. He looked up at her this time, dazed, as if he'd forgotten she was there at all. 'I can't find the keys anywhere.'

He said nothing.

'You okay?' Alice asked, getting worried at Finn's weird behaviour. She waved a hand in front of his eyes. 'Finn?'

His eyes focused and he finally looked at her properly. 'Sorry, yeah.'

'You look like you've seen a ghost.'

He shook his head.

'Finn, what's wrong?'

'Nothing.'

'It's clearly not nothing,' Alice hissed quietly. 'Don't lie to me.'

'It's nothing!' Finn snapped and threw the tubing into the boot of the car. Alice shot a darting look up at the first-floor window, willing the clatter of the equipment not to wake up Mac.

'Finn!' she hissed again, this time through gritted teeth and a clenched jaw. 'Be quiet!'

Alice looked from him to the jumble of gear in the boot. She leaned over, picked out the tubing and waved it at him, whispering, 'And don't throw your things around like a spoiled toddler!'

'Give me that,' Finn said.

Alice stepped away, holding it out of reach. 'No, not until you tell me what's wrong. Why've you gone all weird?'

'Please, Alice, give me the regulator hose, now.'

Alice looked down at the tubing – the regulator hose – in her hands. Finn seemed awfully keen to get it back. And then she spotted it. A tear.

'This is damaged,' she said, looking up at him.

'It was the rocks. I was thrown against them so much. You saw how knocked about I was.'

Alice thought of the cuts and bruises all over Finn. 'Why'd that make you look so freaked out? What's up, Finn?'

'Don't you think that's enough?'

Alice was about to say 'maybe' when she spotted Finn shooting a quick glance into the cottage, his eyes flashing an emotion she couldn't quite place. Panic? Fear? Anger? She felt the lightweight regulator hose in her hand. She ran her finger over the tear.

Then she gasped. Looked down at the equipment, eyes widening.

She looked up at Finn, her mouth agape. Finn looked

scared. Alice stepped closer to him and dropped her voice even more.

'Finn,' she said, her finger trembling as it touched the damage. 'This isn't a tear.'

'Alice...' said Finn, his face flushing. He took a deep breath, and he seemed to gulp in the air, like a throwback to the accident in the water yesterday.

'If it was a tear, it would be jagged and uneven,' she said. Alice felt the blood drain from her face. 'But this...' She held it up and slid her finger back and forth. 'This is a *cut*.'

TWENTY-NINE

'No, it isn't,' said Finn, shakily. He snatched the regulator hose out of Alice's hand and flung it back in with the other gear, shutting the boot with as much force as the quiet would allow. He grabbed their bags, coats and his wetsuit and tried to squeeze them into the small back seat of his sports car.

'Look at it, Finn! How else could it have been damaged like that? Christ.' Alice's voice vibrated with shock. 'A cut is deliberate.'

'Stop it. It was, as I said, a rock. Just a sharp one.' He looked back at her from the car door.

'Right... is that so? Why wasn't your wetsuit ripped then? Tell me that.'

They argued like parents threatening divorce with their children in the room, hushed but angry, words expelled through locked jaws.

'The hose juts out, I don't know. I don't have all the answers.'

'Right. Well, humour me. You told me yesterday that you spent most of your time snorkelling, not diving properly. But, if you'd been able to dive for longer what would have happened?

You're the expert – what would happen to your gear with a rip like that, however it was caused?'

Finn thought about it. Spoke slowly.

'A rip like that? It's small enough so there might only have been a small hissing leak initially. But, if I'd gone deeper, when it came under increasing water pressure... at some point the hose would have ruptured.'

'A rupture sounds pretty serious. Could it have killed you if the storm hadn't got there first?'

A shifty Finn nodded. 'Yeah, it would have been an emergency.'

'That sounds like the sort of terrible possibility that would leave you looking as freaked out as you have been for the last few minutes. I don't believe you think it happened afterwards, that it was the rocks. I think you agree with me that this is a deliberate cut.'

'Alice, come on...'

'Finn, I don't blame you for not wanting to agree with me! This... this... is unbelievable.' She pointed at the boot of the car. 'I thought that maybe those two were after you for money. Or, I dunno, perhaps they were hired by a competitor, or something like that. But this... this is a whole different level!'

Finn was deathly pale. 'Alice, they didn't. They couldn't... I can't believe...'

He came round to the end of the car, picked up a set of goggles nearly lost and forgotten on the ground. He opened the boot again, both their gazes immediately drawn to the regulator hose. Alice could see Finn's hands shaking. He threw the goggles in, then gently shut the boot again. Alice listened to the soft, dull click of the boot's latch. Her eyes narrowed. She stared at the car. At the boot and its lock.

'Finn,' she said. 'The car, it's been unlocked since we got here. They could have gotten in at the gear at any time, interfered with it. They'd have had ample opportunity.'

A seagull screeched overhead.

'But... Mac, he saved me,' said Finn, shaking his head. 'He risked his life to pull me out of the water... Why would he do that if... if...'

He dragged a hand down over his face.

'He did do that,' Alice agreed, thinking. She looked up, straight at Finn. 'But... that doesn't rule Vivienne out.'

Finn shook his head.

'Don't shake your head at me! Remember, I *saw* her, outside, the first night. The night before you went diving. Screaming her head off like a madwoman. She looked possessed! I thought it was weird at the time, but now... with all this? She's an angry, angry woman. What did she take the opportunity to do when she was out here?'

Alice reached out to Finn, his face pale but his cheeks red. Her pulse was slamming through her veins.

'I heard her come straight back in after the cliff screaming,' said Alice, her words tumbling quicker from her, eyes widening with each syllable. 'But I didn't hear her *leave* the lighthouse before. She would have had plenty of time to sabotage it.'

Alice started pacing, not sure if the roaring in her ears was the sea or the rapid pulse of blood coursing through her veins. Her fingers tingled and her breath felt shallow.

'The broken landline, that's looking more serious now, right? And my missing phone. This whole double-booking claim, I bet it's nonsense. They probably knew GetaGetaway wouldn't do anything for days. You're agreeing to leave just to make me happy... but can't you see it? Can't you see she's trying to kill you? We've got to get the hell out of here, now!'

Finn sighed, long and heavy. He nodded his head. 'Okay. Okay, alright. I think maybe you're right.'

'Finally!'

Alice felt a weight lift. Finn appreciating the seriousness of the situation was vital. As he'd said last night, they'd know where he lived and worked. Getting away from here was just the first step. He'd need to go to the Gardaí when they got back to Dublin. The police would have to be made aware. Conscious of her own – now abandoned – scheme, Alice knew she might have to let him do that on his own.

'Good. Right then, let's haul ass.' Alice turned around, looked at the lighthouse. Did they need anything else? Or could they just hop in the car and put the foot down?

Finn was at the opened driver's side door of the car.

'Throw me the keys,' he said, holding his hands up.

Oh. The keys.

'I can't do that.'

'Why not?'

'Because I couldn't find them. I looked everywhere.'

'But they have to be somewhere, they can't have disappeared—'

Finn stopped talking. They both looked in the direction Viv had run, and then back at the lighthouse.

'Alice,' he started, slowly, 'do you think that perhaps...'

Alice nodded her head, her heart trembling. It wasn't that big a house. There were few places for the keys to get lost.

'Maybe the keys aren't missing?' she finished for him. He nodded. 'Maybe someone was making sure we didn't leave.'

THIRTY

VIVIENNE

The road was rough and uneven under Vivienne's feet as she ran. Gravel slid as she pounded the ground one foot after the other. Running helped her think. She ran faster, urging her brain cells to keep up.

Alice had a big happy head on her this morning, hadn't she? That giant gormless grin spread across her face when she came back into the kitchen. No one is ever that happy before 8 a.m. unless they're up to something. Vivienne had enjoyed giving her the fright of her life by wishing her good morning. Waiting for her moment after realising Alice hadn't spotted her. She'd been too focused on closing that front door quietly and too distracted by whatever it was she was up to. That wiped the smile off her face goodo. And while Vivienne had no idea what had put her in such a good mood – especially since Alice had hated every moment they had been there – it did tell her one thing: she had no idea what Vivienne's plans were. If she did, there'd be no smiles at all.

Vivienne had hoped to have it all sorted by now, but not everything was going her way. Mac was right that they should worry about the girl. Vivienne couldn't believe that even after all this time and all the kicking life had given her, she still had some hubris left. She needed to listen to Mac more. Because he was right about Alice. That girl could be planning anything, and Vivienne didn't have a clue. She might be about to ruin it all.

Until the photo, Vivienne hadn't suspected a thing. She'd picked up her book last night, not long before Mac had kicked off and all that hassle. When she'd opened it, there the photo was, unfolded, in all its eviscerating glory. And though she'd never be parted from this photo – it was the only memory she had of her child – she never kept it like that. She always had the top part hidden. She didn't have the heart to mutilate it by ripping the top half off. But still, she couldn't stand to see what should have been her bleary-eyed joy. Instead, she'd already known it wasn't possible. Without David, without her family's support, without her degree, there was no way she could keep Hannah. And she couldn't stand to go back to that moment, to repeat it like some twisted version of a Hollywood movie where the instant repeats over and over until a lesson is learned and there is a happy ending. She learned a lesson alright –that life is cruel and unfair – but there was no happy ending.

So, the girl had been snooping. Her curious, careless hand had flattened it out. It had to be her – Finn had still been asleep, where they'd left him, when they'd come back with the food. And she was coming downstairs, as guilty-looking as a child caught with their hand in the proverbial cookie jar.

Her lungs were burning, but Vivienne welcomed the punishment. The sweat on her brow trapped any flyaway hairs. The breeze blowing lightly around her chilled her where the moisture sat. She thought it was going to be a nice day today, finally. The storm was reconsidering its weekend plans. There was only space for one unwelcome visitor at the lighthouse, and the storm knew it wouldn't win against her.

Vivienne slowed down then stopped. As she bent over to

catch her breath she listened to the sea loll gently into the shore. Her breath was laboured and she was panting like a dog. She was pushing it too much. And like a dog with a bone, her mind was fixated on Alice. She'd been cross, sure, but in the greater scheme of things Vivienne had only been mildly put out after she found the photo. Alice had gotten nosy; Vivienne might have done the same in her shoes. She didn't entirely blame her. Vivienne had folded the photo back and shut the book. After that she'd been distracted trying to calm Mac down. There had even been a chance she'd have forgotten about it.

Except then she'd found the phone.

Not the one she'd accused Vivienne of taking. No. The girl had a second phone. It wasn't the pink-cased, large iPhone Alice had described to her. This was a small Android phone. Vivienne had found it when Mac was melting down, storming about the place, fit to trash the room. Her poor friend, overtaken once more by his waxing and waning trauma. He'd knocked the girl's coat off the hook, and as he stumbled around, Vivienne heard a worrying crunch. She'd thought there were glasses in the coat pocket which had succumbed under Mac's boot. But when Vivienne had picked it up, felt around the fabric, she'd finally found a damaged phone tucked away in a pocket. She didn't know what to think. Well, no, she knew exactly what to think. No one had a secret phone for noble purposes. She didn't need to unlock the phone to confirm that. Not that she could have even begun to try with its crazy-paving cracked screen. But what it meant was the girl was more than nosy. She was up to something. And a secret phone suggested Finn was in the dark too. Poor Finn, caught between the devil and the deep blue stormy sea.

Vivienne had decided to run this morning as it helped her think. She wanted to come out here and put a few miles in. She'd work a few things out. How much of a threat was the girl? What was her game plan? What was Vivienne's next move? She was none the wiser, and she was beginning to think it was time she was as cautious as Mac. She woke up early this morning, unsettled by everything. She didn't sleep well. Which was lucky because the girl was up early too. Vivienne saw her from her window, off down the drive again, sneaking out as everyone slept. What was she up to? Off to make secret calls? She'd have gotten a bit of a surprise if that was the case.

Vivienne didn't like it.

Right now the girl didn't know what they were up to, and they didn't know what she was up to. But Vivienne had an advantage. The girl hadn't a clue that Vivienne was on to her. Vivienne looked back in the direction of the house. Maybe she shouldn't leave them alone for so long?

Vivienne took a deep breath, felt her lungs stretch, expand, fill with air. And she started to run again. Back the way she'd come. Back to the lighthouse.

She pounded the uneven roads, faster this time, pumping her arms. She got closer and closer, then slowed down. When she saw them she ducked behind a half-collapsed old cottage wall. She took off her beacon-like bright yellow windcheater, held it out of sight. Crouching, she watched them outside, by the car. That was not good. She couldn't believe she was right.

Thinking of doing a runner, Finn? I can't believe it, after what I told you I'd do.

No, no, no.

You don't get to leave.

THIRTY-ONE

ALICE

'We need those keys, we've got to get out of here. Are you sure they're not downstairs?'

'Completely certain. There's only one place I didn't look,' said Alice.

'Their room?' said Finn.

Alice nodded.

They both looked up at the first-floor window.

'What are we going to do?' said Alice. She didn't fancy the job of creeping around the bedroom searching as Mac slept. The only consolation seemed to be that Mac wasn't, entirely at least, in on what Vivienne was up to. So, if he woke up, they might not be in mortal danger. She still didn't like the idea though. And she couldn't say for absolute certain that Mac wasn't in on it. He could be biding his time, playing good cop.

'If we're going to get out of here, we're going to have to search the room.'

'With Mac in there, asleep?' asked Alice tentatively.

'I guess?' said Finn, just as unsure as Alice at the prospect. 'Perhaps we could wake him up and one of us could distract him while the other searches? Something like that?'

Alice thought about it. 'I don't know, Finn. We can't be sure he's completely harmless, just 'cause he saved you.'

'We need those keys.'

'I know,' said Alice, brow furrowed, thinking. What were they going to do? She looked up at Finn, a flash of inspiration. 'Okay, out-of-the-box thinking – let's get another car.'

'What?'

'Yep, forget this one, we need another.'

'Where do we get it exactly?' Finn sounded a little irritated. 'We're miles from anywhere. And by the time a taxi is out to us, Vivienne will definitely be back.'

'I realise all that,' replied Alice, irritated right back. 'I was thinking of those neighbours, the lovely people who dropped the eggs into us on Friday. I've met the son a few times, he's very nice. They have a car, I've seen him driving around in it. Maybe he wouldn't mind dropping us into Milford, or maybe even Letterkenny? You can send someone for your car when we're safely gone. What do you think?'

'What if they can't give us a lift?'

'What if they can! C'mon, Finn!'

'Look, what about this... you go and see if they can give us a lift, and I stay here and see if I can creep into the room and look for the keys.'

Alice shook her head furiously. 'Oh no. I don't like that idea at all.'

'It'll be fine.'

'Mac is a big guy, Finn. If he wakes up... I wouldn't rate your chances.'

'It'll be okay. I'll be very careful. If I don't think I can do it, I'll come straight out and follow you to the neighbours'.'

'Finn...'

'I'll be okay, don't fret.'

'I'm not sure—'

'I am. C'mon, we don't have a lot of time. Get to the neighbours'. Hurry. I'll give it five, ten minutes with the search, then I'll head to you. On foot if I've no luck, in the car if I do. Okay?'

Alice felt like stamping her foot, but she could see the determination in Finn's eyes. Instead she grabbed him and kissed him, Finn returning the intensity of her embrace.

'You've five minutes to check for the keys,' said Alice, gripping his hand. 'Then it's ten minutes to the neighbours, walking. If you're not outside in fifteen minutes, I'm calling the Guards.'

'I'll be there.'

Finn squeezed her hand back, then turned for the cottage. He stopped and turned back to her. He was handing her something.

His mobile.

'Take this. It'll work once you're out of here. I'll feel happier if you have it. It'll keep you safe. Like... if you have to call the Guards.'

'I meant I'd use the neighbours' phone... giving me this leaves you with nothing, Finn.'

'It doesn't even work here. It's useless to me. It's better for you to take it. Take it!'

'Okay,' Alice said with great reluctance. She made a note of the time: 7.05 a.m. At least with the phone she could keep track of time and know when he needed to get out of there.

'Be careful!'

He nodded and disappeared into the lighthouse. She then turned and hurried down the long driveway, watching out as she went, just in case Vivienne was returning. She didn't need to bump into her at this stage, not when they were so nearly out of here.

Alice ran through all the options in her head as she hurried down the drive. While sure the neighbours would be happy to drive them somewhere, if for some reason they couldn't, Alice felt they wouldn't mind letting her and Finn hang out in their house until a cab came for them. Either way, this was the last of the lighthouse for Alice. With that thought, she turned around and looked back at the looming building. She shook her head and kept going. It had all seemed so promising. At least, despite the worry of the moment, the future that awaited her in Dublin was a life without The Plan. A good life. She had to keep reminding herself of that.

A blur in the corner of her eye made her spin around. Was that something? The fear of Ted's photographer reared up in front of her. They'd have gotten a brilliant shot there, her kissing Finn so fiercely. Why did she do that? Stupid. She spun around, searching the surrounds. But she didn't see anything else. Hopefully it had been an animal in the fields. Or nothing. Just her stressed-out subconscious.

At the end of the drive she turned left, thankful Vivienne had gone the opposite direction of the neighbours'. She wasn't two steps along the road when a phone in her jacket pocket began to buzz. She took out the two phones. Her broken one, and Finn's. Much to her surprise, it was her phone that was vibrating in her hand.

Alice stopped, looked left and right, then stepped back, onto the side of the road, where a hedgerow of hardy, spiny bushes lined the roadside ditches. It wasn't much concealment, but it made her feel less obvious. Not that Finn could see or hear her here. But she felt guilty and wanted to hide all the same.

She didn't know who was calling. It was a gamble. Maybe it was Molly, overwrought and anxious, frantic and manic. The only way to get her off the phone would be to hang up. A solution that only ever made things worse. And there'd be the questions. Where was she? What was she doing? Who was she with? These could all wait. Had to wait.

But it could also be Ted. The only other person who had this number. It was worth the risk to try and answer. She pressed what was left of the home button. She pressed hard enough to feel a splinter cut her thumb. But, after several tries, it worked.

'Hello, Alice?' Ted's gruff tone rang out.

Oh thank God.

'Hi, Ted?' she said quietly. She looked up and down the road again.

'Alice. Sorry for the early call. But I just wanted to check in with you 'cause my guy has let me know he's in situ. Got up to Milford late last night.'

'What?'

'My photographer got up there—'

'I heard you, Ted. I just... has he started yet? Is he here somewhere?'

'He's a lazy bugger so I doubt it. But there's a chance he just hasn't gone to bed yet.'

Alice, frantic, rapidly scanned the horizon. She couldn't see anyone. Feck. This was all she needed.

'Ted, I'm sorry. This just can't happen. I was going to call you.'

'Don't worry, dear. All you need to do is get Finn down to Portsalon Beach—'

'No, I mean it can't happen at all. I'm calling it off. Things have changed.'

'Oh, I see. Well. No. That's not how this works. You came to me, remember? This is a great story, I'm not backing out now.'

'But you have to!'

'I don't have to do anything I don't want. Why have you suddenly got cold feet? Gotten used to his money, that it?'

'That has nothing to do with it!' Alice hissed into the phone. 'I'm not getting cold feet. Things have just changed.'

'I'm not sure I give a damn.'

'You need to drop it. He's not the bad guy.'

'You've changed your tune. You're letting your mam down, you know that?'

'Leave her out of this!'

'I have a lot of what you gave me already, I can use that.'

'Don't try to blackmail me!'

'I'm only saying,' he said, and then the line went dead. Alice looked at the phone. Its cracked and splintered screen black.

'Shit.'

Ted was going to be a problem. She gave the countryside another paranoid sweep. But, the truth was, he wasn't the worst problem she had right now. And everything would get better if they just got away. She started walking again, faster, anxiety speeding her journey. The euphoria of last night, the prospect of her and Finn together, was diluted. The stakes had suddenly gotten so much higher, the situation much more complicated. Her ambition for them right now was just to get out of Donegal alive.

THIRTY-TWO

VIVIENNE

Vivienne could hear quite clearly from where she was sitting. Alice might have thought it was a wise move to get closer to the hedgerow, getting out of sight. But she'd no idea that Vivienne was right there, on the other side of the thorny thicket, with a hotline to her secrets... Vivienne waited, like a priest on the other side of a confessional, only Alice was unaware she was confessing.

As Vivienne had got closer to the lighthouse, she'd seen Alice taking off up the road. Just her, no Finn. At the end of the drive, Alice had pulled to a stop and taken out the secret phone. Alice had looked surprised, and then anxious. Throwing a look back to where she'd come from, from Finn. This was followed by a few furtive glances before a dash towards a sheltered spot. Vivienne had reckoned she was close enough to quietly catch her up. If the phone was working well enough to take a call, Vivienne wanted to eavesdrop. That was too good a chance to pass up.

And it had been worth the mad dash. Alice had no idea Vivienne had dropped low and scampered across the fields unseen to this spot.

Vivienne's only regret was she couldn't hear both sides of the conversation. It seemed quite the chat. Her eyes widened with each passing moment. *Cold feet. Leave who out of this? Blackmail.* Although she wasn't privy to the whole conversation, one thing was clear: this was bigger than she could have guessed. She'd thought the girl could be your basic grubby money-grabber, but this sounded different.

Things have changed. She'd said that twice. What things? Who was this girl?

An obscene invective slipped through the branches to Vivienne's ear. The call was over. And Alice wasn't happy. Her footsteps on the slipshod rough boreen began again. She was off. She was such a mystery! Vivienne gave her a moment, letting those footsteps fade a bit before she popped her head up. Where was the girl going?

Vivienne peeked above the hedgerow. Alice was far enough away that she could risk it. Keeping to her side of the hedge, Vivienne followed Alice at a distance. The hedgerow was tall enough to give good cover, and Vivienne could duck down again if Alice looked back. Her trainers were getting wet, squelching as she trudged through the grass, soaking up the late-autumn bogginess. But she kept going, hardly noticing, curiosity consuming her. She needed to know more.

Alice was fast. It was hard to keep up and stay hidden in the fields. There were dips and hidden divots trying to trip Vivienne up, and the level of the land was rising. Soon Alice would be able to see her if she turned around. But the rising land also meant Vivienne could stop here and watch her, if she dared. She decided to take the risk.

If the girl wasn't a gold-digger, then what? Last night Vivienne had wondered if she could be her anonymous correspondent. Was that it? Perhaps Finn talked in his sleep, his secrets slipping unconscious from him, and Alice realised she had to tell someone, but didn't want to give herself away. But the half-heard conversation now didn't seem to fit that theory.

Alice had pulled a good distance away now. She hadn't slowed down or turned to look back. For some reason, she was turning into that drive, the one with the distressed pillars and the black gate. That's where she'd been going. What was of interest with the neighbours?

Vivienne looked back towards the lighthouse. She had about five minutes. That was her minimum head start. It would take her five minutes to get back to the lighthouse. If Alice were to turn around right now, leave the farmhouse, it would take her ten. Vivienne presumed whatever she was up to would take longer, but she had to work off of the worst-case scenario. So, five it was. It should be enough.

By the looks of things, this might be the last opportunity. This might be it.

Finn.

It was time.

THIRTY-THREE

ALICE

Alice hurried on, turning into Mary's long drive, passing stone gate pillars with animals atop them so eroded by the salty air she wasn't sure if they'd been lions or eagles once upon a time. She was relieved to see the red car was there, up nearer the house. That was something.

A black cat slunk around the side of the house as Alice reached the door. It eyed her suspiciously.

'Hello, kitty,' Alice said as she raised a hand and knocked on the door. The cat continued to stare at her. Wasn't it bad luck, thought Alice, for a black cat to cross your path? She didn't think she could cope with any more bad luck.

A moment later, the door opened.

'Ah, hello there.' Mary stood with the door in her hand, her white hair mussed, wearing an apron over a beige tweed skirt and thick woolly cream jumper. Daubs of flour, like war paint, dotted her cheeks. 'You're the lovely cailín from the lighthouse, how can I help you, dear?'

'Hi, Mary, isn't it?' Alice forced a smile onto her face.

'Yes, that's me.'

'I hope it's not too early to call by?' Alice checked Finn's phone. It was 7.15 a.m. now.

'Not at all! This is a farming house, sure we've half a day's work done already,' she chuckled.

'Ah, good. So, we have a bit of a problem and I was hoping you might be able to help us.'

'Of course, come in, come in.' She beckoned Alice into the cold dark hall of her farmhouse. A building built for the functions of another era, long before light and space became king. She directed Alice down to the kitchen at the back of the house.

'I'm not sure I ever got your name,' she said.

'Alice.'

'Lovely to meet you, again, Alice,' Mary said with a smile, as they entered the kitchen. Another dark room, dark wood presses and cupboards that hadn't had a makeover in decades. Two armchairs were positioned at the end of the room by a large open fire, already lit. A radio was on a shelf, among books, beside the fire. A hum of companionable chatter emanated from it. Mary pointed Alice towards a kitchen chair at a large oak table. She flicked on the kettle and took a tea towel out of a drawer, covering up the dough she'd been working on.

'Cup of tea?' she said, already taking out a teapot.

Alice sat on the edge of her seat. Her hands crossed on her lap. She just wished Mary would dispense with the rituals. Time was ticking.

'Oh no, but thank you. I don't think I've time.'

Mary put the teapot down on the counter, frowning. 'That's okay, dear. So, what's the little problem you have that we can help with?'

'Ah, yes. So, it's a bit of an ask, but our car is out of action. We need to get to somewhere where we can arrange a hire car or hop on a coach or train.'

'That would be Letterkenny then,' said Mary. 'I don't think anywhere closer would be any good to you.'

'Okay, I see.'

'That's nearly an hour's drive.' Mary's frown deepened. She looked out the window as she thought. 'I'm afraid I don't drive such long distances any more. But I can ask Michael, maybe he'd be free to drop ye. When do you need to go?'

Alice shifted in her seat. 'Emm, sort of as soon as possible. I know, I'm sorry, this is an imposition.'

'Don't apologise, dear. Is everything alright?' She looked at Alice more closely, eyes narrowing.

Alice nodded vigorously. She didn't need to make Mary suspicious.

'Yes, don't worry. Everything – other than the broken car – is fine. We just need to be back in Dublin for tomorrow. Finn is anxious not to be delayed returning to the office... he has some big meetings...' Alice babbled on, giving far too much detail and feeling like she had a neon sign lit up above her head, pointing to her saying, 'Liar!'

'Of course, I understand. I'll just pop out and have a chat with Michael, he's out in the shed. Just give me a moment.'

The old woman opened the back door. Alice watched her shuffle across the courtyard, the large corrugated metal shed on the other side. She knocked on the door, the echoing clang reaching Alice's ears in the kitchen. A moment later Alice saw Michael emerge, dressed in overalls, pulling a fist across a sweaty brow. He looked towards the kitchen, in the window at Alice, then back at Mary, nodding.

This looked promising. Alice stood up. She checked the time. It was nearly fifteen minutes since she'd left Finn. He should knock at any moment. She peered down the hall, looking to see if she could spot any hint of his fuzzy outline through the frosted glass. But there was nothing.

Mary and Michael came to the kitchen door.

'Letterkenny?' Michael asked.

'Only if it isn't any trouble,' Alice heard herself say. She should have been saying, *It's a matter of life and death, get us out of here now!*

'Let me finish up what I'm doing. It could be half an hour, but I don't think it'll be much longer than that. Then I'll take you in, sure. I've to go to Roche's to pick up some feed anyway. It's much the same direction.'

'Oh, that's brilliant, thank you,' said Alice.

Michael nodded, then turned back to the yard.

A half-hour delay wasn't ideal, but at least it was a route out of here. In thirty minutes she and Finn would be gone, getting away from those crazy people. And no photographer would know she was here. She could feel tension easing, just a little. And you never know, maybe Finn would find the keys.

'Will you have that cup of tea now?' asked Mary, flicking on the kettle again. 'I have some freshly baked scones here too. How does that sound?'

'That sounds great,' said Alice. She still didn't feel like it, but she could hardly refuse, considering they were going to help.

Mary bustled about the kitchen, mugs clinking, kettle boiling and jam and butter put on a tray, ready to be served. If Alice hadn't been having such a dreadful weekend, this would have been quite the treat. She checked Finn's phone, fifteen minutes on the nose. She peered around the kitchen door again, looking down the hall.

No sign of him. She felt her tummy tighten again. It was risky, what he was doing... What if Mac woke up?

'I hope you've been having a lovely time since you got here. A shame you are leaving a bit soon. You should come for longer next time.'

There'll so be no next time, thought Alice. She was never setting foot in the county of Donegal ever again.

'We've been having a great time,' she lied. 'Though the bad weather has put a bit of a crimp on it.'

'Ach, the weather up here. That's all it does, puts a crimp on everything.' The old lady brought the tea and scones over to the table.

'This looks lovely, thank you, Mary.'

'Not at all.' Mary sat across from Alice at the large oak table. She handed Alice her scone on a delicate china plate. 'It is a shame about the weather, there is so much to see and do up here, and so beautiful when the sun shines.'

'I got out for a nice walk,' said Alice. 'And I read that tourist info about the lighthouse and that World War I shipwreck which was very interesting. The missing gold was all very *Boy's Own* adventure.'

'Yes, I suppose it is,' she said.

Alice got the distinct feeling she'd said something wrong. 'I'm sorry if that was flippant...'

Mary looked up at her, a smile back on her face. 'No, no, dear. It does make a good story. There are so many of them up here, but you see, they're all tragic. I remember my grandfather – the last lighthouse keeper I told you about – telling me all the sad stories when I sat on his knee as a child. All the lives lost at sea. Each one of them heartbreaking. And they aren't all ancient history either. There was a particularly sad one only about twenty years ago, and it was linked with that gold too.'

'Oh really?' said Alice.

'Yes, a young man lost his life. Near that wreck. I heard from around the place that he'd been searching for the missing gold. There's some awful lesson in there about greed, don't you think? But, ah goodness, I'm speaking ill of the dead. Forget I said that. I shouldn't have...'

'Oh, don't worry, Mary, I understand what you meant.' Alice, who'd been doing her best to be a good guest despite her nervous energy and impatience for Finn to get here, felt her interest piqued. If Mary had said twenty-six years ago, not twenty, she'd have wondered if it could have been the accident where Vivienne's David had died.

'Might that have been longer than twenty years ago?' Alice couldn't keep her curiosity bottled. 'Twenty-five or twenty-six perhaps?'

Mary, scone midway to her mouth, paused. 'Hmm. Maybe? The old noggin isn't what it once was.' She put down her scone and stood. 'My late mother used to keep scrapbooks, with all the clippings about the lighthouse. Because of her father, of course. I still have them. Hard to throw that kind of local history away...'

'Oh, no, Mary, don't worry.' Alice beckoned her back. 'Sit down, enjoy your scone, it was just an idle question.'

'It's no bother, I know just where it is,' Mary muttered as she left the room. Alice heard footsteps on the stairs moments later. She hadn't meant to put the old woman to any trouble, but she did seem keen to share – and sure, at least it was a distraction as she waited for Finn. Alice did a time check. It was now over twenty minutes since she'd left him. Nearly twenty-five.

He should've been here by now.

Alice got up and left the kitchen. She walked down the hall and opened the front door. From there, standing on her tippy-toes, she looked as far down the road as she could see. Nothing. Not a sign of him.

Alice felt her pulse quicken. She looked back into the house then down the road again. Should she stay here, and keep waiting? Maybe he was just taking longer to search the room, so as not to disturb Mac... But what if Mac had woken up? Or Vivienne had come back? Alice took a step out of the house. Maybe she should go back?

'Here we are.' Mary was coming back down the stairs, wearing her reading glasses and with an open, tattered scrapbook in her hand. She reached the bottom step and smiled at

Alice. Alice came back in with a worried look over her shoulder towards the door.

'So, yes, you were right! It was about twenty-five years ago. Twenty-six to be exact,' Mary said as she walked down the hall. Alice followed reluctantly.

Back in the kitchen Mary gave Alice a curious look over the top of her glasses. 'Was it something you knew about?' She pushed the butter and jam out of the way and placed the open scrapbook down on the table.

'Not really,' said Alice. 'I heard someone mention something about an accident and I'm twenty-five, so the time stuck in my head.'

Mary nodded, satisfied with that. She pushed up her glasses and began to read. Alice was finding it hard to pay attention, despite her earlier curiosity. She kept glancing towards the hall, willing Finn to show up, waiting for his knock. He was taking too long.

She was going to go back. Alice turned in the direction of the kitchen door. Mary didn't notice, engrossed as she was with her scrapbook.

'"Two young men were pulled from the water. One is currently seriously ill in hospital following an unauthorised dive at the SS *Laurentic* location. It is reported they were searching for the reputed missing World War I gold..." I'm certain I heard that the seriously ill one didn't pull through... Silly boys, if proper divers couldn't find it, what were they thinking? Oh, and they look so young.'

They look so young.

That stopped Alice. There was a photo? She looked back at Mary and the scrapbook. What had the charismatic and much-missed David looked like?

The yellowing newspaper snippet was taped onto the page. The headline, 'Accident Near Lighthouse', and underneath:

'Young men get into difficulty, one in serious condition in hospital.' The black-and-white photo had stood up quite well, only slightly discoloured and brittle. She peered more closely at it.

And then her blood ran cold.

THIRTY-FOUR

VIVIENNE

Finn wasn't at the cottage door. He was lucky, because Vivienne was, and the eternal flame of her rage was turned up to maximum. She passed their car and saw the bags packed and ready to go in the back seats. She'd been right – they were planning on doing a runner. Light-headed with anger, she nearly ran into him as she pulled open the front door, meeting him as he barrelled out, a rat deserting his sinking ship.

'Oh!' he puffed, skidding to a halt in front of her.

It took Vivienne a moment to speak, her fury transcendent, robbing her of coherency. She jabbed a finger at his chest. Forcing him backwards, back into the cottage.

'You!' She made contact with his chest, jabbing again, 'how dare you try to leave?'

Finn backed off, keeping his distance from her. *As well he should*, thought Vivienne.

'We're just going on a walk. That's all. There's no need for that,' he said, pushing away her arm.

The part of Vivienne's brain that wasn't consumed with anger reminded her it was a two-way street – she should be as wary of Finn as he was of her. She needed to be careful. She knew what he was capable of.

'A walk with all your bags?' she replied, forcing herself to take deep breaths, to regain control. She couldn't let her emotions limit her, overtaking her to the degree that she didn't see danger coming. 'I'm not a fool, Finn. You were trying to disappear while I was out. I thought we talked about that. No going anywhere before we had our chat.'

'I've changed my mind. We can talk another time, Vivienne. Back in Dublin.' He put his hand in his jeans pocket and pulled out a wallet. Taking out a card – embossed on heavy cardstock, not cheap – he handed it to her. 'That's my personal number, not too many people have it. You can get me there.'

Despite the quiver in his voice, the notion that he could palm her off with a stupid business card made fury flare within Vivienne again. She crumpled up the card and stared him in the eye as she dropped it at his feet.

'We are going to talk *now*,' she hissed. 'You're not going anywhere.'

Finn shook his head. 'I'm sorry for what happened, so sorry you cannot imagine, but this is no solution.'

'I think it's a fine solution!' she growled. 'You're not CEO here, Finn Tobin. You don't get to decide what we do or don't do. And don't you think your little child bride will be sad if you head off without her?'

Finn threw his arms up in frustration, unfamiliar anger flashing across his face. 'I'm obviously not leaving her behind!' he snapped.

'You'll find it tricky bringing her with you though,' Vivienne said, a smirk telling him all he needed to know.

His face went pale. 'What have you done with her?' He only managed a whisper now, the fright stealing the air from his lungs.

'Nothing yet. But if you don't do as I say now, I'll go wake up Mac and send him to the neighbours' house, to wait for her. Do you want me to do that? He could take her for a nice little walk...' The fact she knew Alice was at the neighbours' gave her words weight. Finn realised she'd been watching them. And he didn't know that Mac wouldn't do anything to her. Mac was her rock, but he was also her weak link. He'd agreed to what they wanted to do this weekend, but he didn't hate like she did. He wasn't driven by it. It wasn't lit in his toes and didn't scorch its way up through him like it did in her, building and building until a volcano of molten rage exploded from her head. And unlike her, he wasn't willing to do anything to get what they wanted.

Finn picked up the crumpled business card and retreated to the kitchen table. He pulled out a chair and sat, his shoulders slumping, his head bowing. A ripple of triumph flowed through Vivienne. It could be intoxicating if she let it, having this power over someone else. Finn's brief rebellion was easily quashed. Unseeing, he picked up Mac's book, which had been sitting there all weekend. He gripped it white-knuckled, probably imagining it was her neck. Vivienne had learned the lesson long ago that love left you vulnerable, stripped you of your armour. Finn was counting the cost of love now. It had made him a prisoner.

'Okay,' he said. 'Let's talk then. Let's get this over with.'

'That's more like it.' Vivienne looked out a window, checking that they were still alone. They were – no approaching Alice to disturb them. She was still at the neighbours' doing whatever it was she was doing there. Again, Vivienne felt a hint of unease... She didn't like not knowing who the girl was and what she was up to. She couldn't feel one hundred per cent in control while it was a mystery. But she had to do this before they succeeded in bolting.

So, the time was now. Right now. And not in the lighthouse. Her instinct yesterday to go check out the hostel had been spot on. She'd also made the right decision to leave what she needed there, what she needed for their... chat.

'We're not doing it here.'

'What?' Finn looked at her, a new struggle between anger and powerlessness flaring across his face. She watched as he suppressed it. He knew what was best right now.

'A trip down memory lane is in order. I think we might head to the hostel.'

'Where— oh... right. Is it still there?'

'Oh yep, it is.'

Vivienne turned towards the door and opened it with a tug. Finn remained sitting.

'C'mon, then.'

He put down Mac's book and, with great heaviness, stood. Vivienne thought his blue eyes were so sad. Like a man walking to his own funeral.

THIRTY-FIVE

ALICE

It was as if the physics of time changed as Alice stared at the twenty-six-year-old newspaper clipping. Specifically at the photo. She understood it instantly. Her brain successfully processed the black, white and grey pixels, the building blocks of this shadowy photo taken back in 1998. But, simultaneously, another part of her brain stood sentry, denying entry to the terrifying implications of what she was looking at.

The photo was grainy. And the paper see-through thin. This was from a local newspaper, the incident not serious enough to prove worthy of national coverage, so the quality was cheaper. But it was good enough for her to clearly see three wet, huddled figures, blankets over their shoulders, spotlighted by multiple sets of headlights and pairs of flashing lights from emergency vehicles. So many lights in fact that the illuminations belied the 6 a.m. timestamp of the incident.

A huddle of paramedics, at the rear of one of the ambulances, the feet of its stricken passenger just visible, is the focus of everyone in the image, all eyes directed there. Including those of the drenched, blanketed figures. Arranged three abreast a little distance away from the ambulance. The middle one sitting back against the bonnet of a police car.

Alice didn't get to see the famous David's face, just his feet. But she found she wasn't interested in him any more. Instead she was far more interested in the faces she could see.

Alice's finger reached out, touched each of the faces. Tracing their contours.

The first, eyes wide and her delicate hand over her mouth, looking even more than twenty-six years younger. Even in the horror of the captured moment she looked less burdened than she did now, today.

Vivienne.

The second, his hand on the middle figure's shoulder. His face beard-free, his hair short, but still, unmistakably him. His oak-like limbs, his rootedness, his bulk and strength, clear even then.

Mac.

And lastly, in the middle of the trio, wet hair plastered to his forehead, face twisted in anguish, tortured. Familiar. And now, for Alice, utterly unfamiliar too.

Finn.

THIRTY-SIX

'Are you alright, dear? You've gone very pale.'

Alice looked at Mary, watched her lips move but her brain was too in shock to take in what she was saying. It was as if she was down the end of a very long tunnel. With effort, Alice looked back at the photo.

Vivienne, Mac and Finn.

The three of them. Together. Twenty-six years ago. She forced her freewheeling brain to slow down to look at the text. To search for some sort of explanation.

The words skipped and jumped. There were no names, they were just referred to as students from Dublin. But there was no doubt that it was them. What on earth was going on? How could this be? Alice felt weak, shaky. Like her heart had stopped in her chest, too shocked to continue beating. But it also felt like it was huge, had quadrupled in size, pushing against her lungs, her throat. She reached out, fingers fumbling for the edge of the table.

'Alice?' Mary was staring at her, concern writ large across her face. The old woman reached out and touched Alice on the upper arm. 'What's happened? What's wrong?'

Alice shook herself, tried to get hold of herself. 'Sorry. It's nothing.' She looked wildly around. 'I'm sorry.'

Alice spun around, her hip knocking against the table, the mugs of tea clanked, banging against each other. The sound of the crash and crack of something falling off the table followed her as she dashed out of the kitchen and down the hall. She pulled open the front door and ran, leaving it swinging behind her.

'Alice!' the old woman's voice called after her. But she ran and didn't stop. Ran till her lungs burned.

She got to the spot where she'd taken the call from Ted and shuddered to a halt. She bent over, sucking in gasping breaths of air. She forced herself to straighten up, her hands braced on her thighs. Still panting, she looked out over the fields, out across the grey sea.

What the hell was going on?

Finn was there the night Vivienne's David died. This thought kept repeating itself. Was there, watching David being loaded into the back of an ambulance, ready to be taken away. And everything about that picture screamed intimacy, people who knew each other well.

Finn knows Mac and Vivienne.

Finn knows Mac and Vivienne.

Finn knows Mac and Vivienne.

How was this possible? A wave of nausea swept over Alice. She bent double, feeling wave after wave of bile ripple through her.

This was madness. They'd all been acting for the last two days as if they were complete strangers. Not a hint from any of them that there was a shared history. And what a shared history. Not likely to slip your mind. And... Vivienne was trying to kill Finn!

Who were these people and what had happened between them?

Alice felt her breath quickening again. Her hands were shaking. She closed her eyes, tried to calm her breathing. Tried to hold off the panic before it overtook her once more. She let herself slide to the ground, to sit there at the edge of the road, in the damp rotting remains of nature.

Alice slipped a hand into her pocket and took out Finn's phone. Her hands were shaking so much it took her a few tries to unlock it. When she finally did, she opened a browser window. If she had more information, then maybe everything would make sense. She first tried searching for anything else about the accident, but there was nothing. The only reference at all was a short mention of it on a parish newsletter archive page. None of them were even named. The article in Mary's scrapbook wasn't online, no one had scanned and added the old newspaper to the bottomless pit of information on the internet. She was sorry now that she'd run away so quickly. Where exactly had she been heading? Back to the lighthouse, to Finn? Shaking her head, forcing her thoughts to calm down, she tried to recall what she'd read. It said they were students. And they'd been diving. Finn had said he'd been diving for over twenty-five years. So he must have started diving during his university years. Maybe that would help. Something that might help her find some more information, work out what was going on. If they were all students, then maybe they'd been part of the diving club at university? She typed 'scuba, university, club, 1998' into Google, and added their names.

Links came up and Alice scanned them. She clicked on the third link, it looked the most promising. It took her to the UCD sub-aqua club page. To a page deep in the club's archive. As part of a longer article, there was a photo of four people in a row, standing beside a swimming pool. All wetsuited-up, right down to the neoprene balaclavas, masks and breathing appara-tuses. Arms all around each other's shoulders, the divers on each end with their thumbs up. It was impossible to see their faces, tell who was who, but their names were listed underneath: Vivienne O'Brien, Finn Tobin, David Johnson and Macdara Ryan. On second glance Alice realised it was clear that the slim female at the end had to be Vivienne, and the tall, broad man on the other end was Mac. The other two, obscured by the scuba gear, were indistinguishable. According to the names below one was Finn and the other was the doomed David. She couldn't tell which was which, but one of them was definitely the same Finn Tobin she'd been dating for the last six months. So, they'd been friends at university. It wasn't as if he'd been some passing stranger who had come to the rescue on that day twenty-six years ago and accidentally ended up in the newspaper report, the only other possibility Alice's frantic brain had come up with.

Alice sat there, staring at the photo on her phone. Even though the gear obscured their faces, you could still feel how full of the joys of life they were, how their youthful exuberance flowed from them. It was like the opposite of the newspaper photo. Full of the horror of death. She looked more closely at the photo. She settled on the figure beside Mac. Those eyes. Behind the diving mask. Oh yes. Now that she looked more closely, that was definitely her Finn.

Alice put down the phone. Let the frigid wind wash over her.

Alice released a deep, confused, sigh. *My Finn?* That mightn't be the right choice of words. For a brief few hours, he had been her Finn. Last night it all seemed possible, a whole new world opened up to her. But that hadn't lasted long. Because it was built on lies. And lies that hid something bad. Because there was no other reason for the three of them to deny knowing each other. Old college friends are usually happy to see each other.

And old college friends don't tend to try and kill each other.

Alice felt dizzy with confusion. Joining her fear at what was happening came anger, bubbling up within her. She was furious at Finn for lying to her. Hiding all this from her. And furious at herself for letting herself have hope. For giving in to it. That mirage of a happy future, it had seemed so real. She'd been ready to abandon everything that had been driving her forward and giving her existence meaning – despite how unhealthy it had been – to be with him. She had to say she was impressed with this new, next-level ass-kicking life was giving her. Tempting her with the poison apple of a perfect future. Giving her just enough time to think it was going to happen... then snatching it away.

'God dammit!' she screamed, startling a group of birds who leapt into flight with disgruntled caws.

Alice stayed sitting on the damp, cold side of the road and looked out to sea. What was she going to do? All the time she thought she was hiding secrets from Finn, he'd been hiding secrets from her. Alice had always understood, even if she'd never admitted it to herself, that she'd used The Plan as a way to feel in control in a world where she had no agency. It made her feel safe, secure. But now she was spinning, like one of those parachutists you saw in videos online, where their chute only half-opened and they were falling and spinning, falling and spinning. With only the cold, hard ground waiting for them.

It looked like she had two choices. The first: give Finn a chance to explain. Hadn't she been lying to him herself? And not just for the weekend, but for months. She'd want a chance to explain herself, let him know she wasn't a bad person. But... Finn's secrets came with attempted murder. Maybe there was nothing he could say to make it alright. Perhaps she needed to just get out of here. Escape these strangers and the games they were playing. So, the second choice was to turn around and go back to Mary's. Take that lift herself and just go.

Alice stood and brushed herself off. Her secret phone buzzed yet again and she looked at it. From the buzz after buzz that obsessively came in, she knew the messages were from Molly. She couldn't read them, but she'd see her soon enough when she went home. If she went back to that life, she'd have nothing. She wouldn't turn up for work tomorrow, or, in fact, ever again at TobinTech. She would probably move back in with Molly so she couldn't be found. A new, rather bleak life stretched out in front of her. But at least she'd know what was happening. She could trust herself, rely on herself. This was what happened when you let yourself love someone. You lost control. And bad things happened.

Looking at the two phones, Alice sighed. Two choices.

Alice noticed the time. It had now been a full thirty minutes since she'd left Finn.

Finn should have been here, either on foot or in the car, after fifteen minutes. Even giving him some wiggle room, that was a big delay. Despite everything – despite the lies, despite the confusion, and despite the very tempting decision to go home and start afresh... she couldn't shake off the ball of fear for Finn in the pit of her belly. Because even though she had no idea what was going on, there was one fact among all this mess that she knew to be true.

Someone, Vivienne, was trying to kill Finn.

So, where was he?

THIRTY-SEVEN

Alice got up and began to run again, towards the lighthouse, not Mary's. She hadn't a clue what was going on. Or how she felt. She wasn't sure if she should be running in this direction. It went against every self-preservation instinct she had. But she also knew that she couldn't leave Finn to some awful fate. She couldn't shake the feeling that something had gone horribly wrong. Mac had woken up. Vivienne had come back. And a little voice whispered in her ear... *Save him, give him a chance to explain, it's worth the risk.*

'Be there, be there,' she yelled, panting as she ran. She visualised getting back to the lighthouse and they'd all be there, in the kitchen. She and Finn would share knowing looks – all that had happened was that Vivienne had appeared back unexpectedly and he couldn't blow their plan by leaving. They'd be sitting, having tea, the atmosphere as terrible as ever. That was all. That's what she would find.

She felt the uneven road under her feet, adrenaline fuelling her. She made it to the driveway and, from somewhere, found the reserves to speed up.

She passed the car, with the bags in the back, and wasn't

sure if that was a good sign or not. She didn't slow down to look through the windows. She came to a skidding halt at the cottage door. Her heart was pounding. And only pounded harder when she saw that the door was ajar. She stretched out a shaking hand. And pushed.

The door creaked open.

The kitchen was empty.

'Finn?' she called out. She stood stock-still, listening for a reply, anything to indicate he was still here. There was nothing. Just the echo of her words bouncing off the walls.

Alice looked about the kitchen. For a moment, doubt crept in. What if there was even more to Finn that she didn't know? She'd by sheer chance discovered that he and Vivienne and Mac knew each other. What else might she not know? In forever she'd never have thought what she'd discovered was a possibility. So, what was to say there weren't other, worse things to know?

Alice shook her head. She couldn't think like that. Not right now. In truth, she wanted to give him the benefit of the doubt. There could even be an explanation for why he'd been lying to her. Couldn't there?

She headed for the stairs. Running up them. Tugging at the rope banister as if climbing a mountain. Halfway up, she stopped. Realised Mac might still be here. The clang on the metal stairs could wake him if he was still asleep. She skipped lightly up the remaining steps to the first floor. Held her breath. The same loud snores reverberated. So, whatever had happened, he was still here and it hadn't disturbed him.

She kept on. Up to the next floor. There, the bathroom door was open. The room empty. She hurried up again, to their floor, their bedroom. She fell into it, lungs complaining, breathing heavily. But, again, empty. The room exactly as they'd left it. She returned to the landing. She looked up. Only the lantern room was left. She couldn't see why he would be up there now, but she had to search it.

She took the last set of narrowing stairs up and emerged into the lantern room. The bright daylight from the encircling glass windows left her blinking. As her eyes adjusted she confirmed what she knew already. There was no one here.

Other than the sleeping Mac, the lighthouse was entirely empty.

Alice grabbed the binoculars which hung from a hook by the small hatch door that led out to the gallery deck. She unlocked the small opening and clambered outside. The wind immediately whipped around her, shaking her. The hatch door slammed shut behind her. She spun around. Spooked. But it was just the wind that had caught it. Fighting the wind-induced blinding tangle of her hair, Alice reached out and grabbed the top rung of the chest-height red railings that ran around the gallery deck. It felt like the wind would lift her off and take her out to sea.

Frantic, barely able to hold the binoculars, Alice raised them. All the while the wind grabbed at her and shook her, whipped the sound from her ears. She scanned the roads to the horizon of the lighthouse. Maybe she would catch sight of Finn, or Vivienne, out there somewhere.

Alice shivered violently. The icy chill was worse up here and whirled around her unimpeded. Her teeth began to chatter as she searched. She moved, slowly, carefully, circling the lighthouse balcony. She was now on the opposite side to where she'd started, but she'd seen nothing.

Alice stopped.

And brought the binoculars down. Had she heard something out there, outside the cottage? The wind was so wild up here, robbing her ears of anything but the whoosh and wails of the violent gusts, she couldn't be sure. Maybe it had been Finn or Vivienne coming back. Maybe the worst hadn't happened?

Quickly, Alice shimmied back around the narrow balcony. She saw nothing in the immediate surroundings. Directly below her, under the gallery deck, was hard to see clearly. Down the seventy feet to the ground. If the wind wasn't so horrendous, she'd have risked stepping up on the rungs and leaning over to look down. But right now, that would mean certain death. She had to leave it, she couldn't be sure she'd heard anything.

Alice gave up. Finn wasn't here. It was time to go to the Gardaí. It was that simple. The police were needed.

She circled back to the hatch and grabbed its handle. She was beginning to lose feeling in the tips of her fingers, it was so cold. They tingled painfully as she tried to pull the hatch open. She gave it a tug. But it didn't move. She tugged again. It had slammed shut in the wind, so perhaps it was more firmly shut than usual. She used both her hands and pulled. It didn't budge an inch. A different sort of chill crackled down Alice's spine. With growing dread she circled the gallery and looked in at the hatch from the other side.

The bolt was shut. That couldn't have happened by accident.

What little warmth was left in Alice drained out. She was stuck. Out here in the freezing wind.

She banged on the door, hammering it with her fists.

'Help!' she yelled as tears froze in the corners of her eyes. 'Help!'

Not even the seagulls heard her.

THIRTY-EIGHT

She was stuck out here. Deliberately locked out. Who had done this? Mac? Or had Alice been right when she'd thought she'd heard someone come back to the lighthouse?

With her two near frozen fists she hammered on the glass.

'Let me in!' she roared. 'Let me in!'

She knew it was futile. A violent shiver shook her whole body. She tried ramming against the hatch. It remained stubbornly shut.

Alice began to wonder how long she'd survive out here. In these icy, wind-chilled sub-zero temperatures. How soon would hypothermia set in? The two phones she had were useless; she couldn't summon help. Would Mary come after her? Or Michael? But they'd probably be here by now if they were coming.

Alice turned to the railings.

'Help!' Her frozen hands gripped the rail. 'Help!'

But her screams barely left the gallery deck: fledglings, scared of the drop, unwilling to fly. Hot tears streamed down her face. She wanted Finn. She wanted to be right that he wasn't with Vivienne, in mortal danger. She wanted to be right that he had no more secrets to share. She imagined his strong arms around her, keeping her warm, taking her away from all of this. This was punishment. Karma for her horrible plan to hurt him. She deserved this. She didn't care that he'd lied to her too. Not now. Alice cried harder, self-pity fuelling her anguish.

Her head dropped, her hands were shaking. She was shivering non-stop, her breathing felt like it was being stolen by the wind with each gust. Alice tried to stem the rising panic. How the hell was she going to get out of this? She looked up to hammer once more.

Alice screamed.

A dark shadow. A distorted face through the curved glass. It disappeared again. Noise at the hatch.

Then Mac's voice, and his face appearing through the now opened door.

'Christ! Alice! Get in here!'

She dashed towards the opening, fell through, sprawling into the lantern room.

'Alice! What happened, who did that to you?' Mac, dishevelled, bleary-eyed and stinking of last night's alcohol, knelt down beside her, helped right her. 'Who locked the door?'

Alice scrambled backwards in the confined space. Away from Mac. Her back up against the tight, close walls of the lantern room. Away from his touch. As if it had burned her. Mac looked confused, his head to the side like a puppy.

'Stay away from me,' Alice gasped.

'Alice, what the—'

'What is wrong with you people!' she said, roiling further. She was scared of big, strong Mac. Scared like she hadn't been before. Brave Mac, always there to save the day. Finn yesterday, her today. In the right place, at the right time, two days in a row? And yesterday she hadn't known he was part of this perfidious charade. She'd just been grateful he'd been there to save Finn.

What messed-up game were he and Vivienne playing at?

'What... Alice... What's going on? You don't need to be afraid of me...'

'I-I know... I know that you've been lying.'

'What?' Mac frowned but backed off a bit.

'I know your secrets.'

'Secrets? Alice, what do you know?' The frown was still there, but Alice could tell Mac was forcing it. His eyes had changed entirely. Fear.

'You!' Alice rasped. 'And her. *And Finn.*'

Mac went pale.

'You all know each other.'

'Alice... I can explain.'

'And you're trying to kill us.'

'Kill you?' Mac blanched. 'Alice, that's crazy talk. You've got to calm down.'

'What, so you can attack me? Finn's and my life expectancies have plummeted since you two got here. The hatch just locked itself shut there, yeah?'

'I've no idea how that happened—'

'Of course you don't!'

Alice gradually shimmied to her left. Inching carefully around, getting closer to the stairs out of here. Out of this tiny space.

Before Mac realised what she was doing, she made a dash for it. Throwing herself into the narrow stairwell, grabbing the thin metal banister. Then half-jumping, half-falling down two, then three stairs at a time. She slammed the door to the lantern room stairs behind her. Ran for the next flight of stairs. Behind her the loud lumber of Mac followed. She felt like Jack from the fairy tale, pursued by the giant down the beanstalk.

'Alice! Come back!' Mac's voice calling after her.

She was down, past her bedroom, then past the bathroom. She sped up, finally passing Mac and Vivienne's room. She rounded the steps, the rope banister burning under her hands, and Mac in pursuit. The last few steps into the kitchen. Her foot slipped. Alice tumbled.

'Ow!' she cried, her ankle twisted, her knees slamming against the tiles as she sprawled into the kitchen.

Mere moments later, as she scrambled to get up, Mac was looming above her. She looked over her shoulder. The door was so close. She yelped in pain again when she tried to put weight on her foot.

'Would you ever stop!' Mac bellowed. 'We are not trying to kill you, Alice. Just calm the hell down!'

Alice crawled crab-like away from him. Mac threw his hands up.

'I woke up and heard you on the lantern balcony – I rushed up there and saved you! Are those the actions of someone trying to harm you?'

Alice looked up at him. 'Just like you saved Finn yesterday?'

This made Mac pause. He frowned, confused. 'Well. Yes, like Finn yesterday,' he said slowly, looking for the trap he couldn't see.

'Quite the coincidence, no? Both of us needing saving two days in a row.'

'Unlucky, I'd say,' Mac replied, but the conviction in his tone was unsteady.

'Really? Unlucky is the best you have? I don't believe you. I don't know what is going on with the three of you. But I know Finn and he's a good guy and whatever happened between you all, you need to get over it and leave him alone. Trying to kill him? Really? Where is he now, Mac? Where is Vivienne?'

Mac let out a disturbing laugh. Closed his eyes, laughed again and shook his head. 'That's a good one.'

Alice stopped. Stared at Mac, scrutinising his face. Stunned into silence by his unsettling reaction.

She pulled herself up into standing using a kitchen chair. Never taking her eyes off Mac, she tested the twisted ankle. It was okay, she'd be able to move. It would be sore, but she could do it. She scanned the room, desperately searching for something to help her escape. A weapon would be good. The kitchen was the most likely source of such, but Mac was standing between her and it.

'I don't think this is a laughing matter,' she said, standing up as straight as she could, looking him in the eye.

'Damn right it isn't.' Mac slammed his fist on the kitchen table, his bitter mirth replaced with a fierce, terrifying glare. Like a fire and brimstone preacher. Hair swinging and spittle flying. 'You're quite right, you have no clue what is going on! Do you know who actually needs to be afraid for their life? If Finn and Vivienne are together? Vivienne, that's who!'

'That's ridiculous!'

'Do you want to know his secrets, Alice? Do you want to know them all?'

Alice stood there. Said nothing. Afraid, not just of Mac but what he might say.

'Vivienne would be right to be afraid. Because she knows who he is. I know who he is. Do you want to know too, Alice?'

Mac took a step closer to her. His stench of body odour and stale alcohol filled her nostrils.

'He's a murderer.'

THIRTY-NINE

Of all the things she thought Mac might say, that would never have been one of them. Her body didn't even react with shock, it didn't go cold, it didn't shake, just nothing. At most, like Mac a moment ago, she wanted to laugh. Such an accusation was absurd.

'Finn wouldn't hurt a fly,' she finally managed, shaking her head.

Mac stood there glaring at her, the fire of his anger still burning. But then, suddenly, like the air released from a balloon, he collapsed into himself, shrinking, looking more like the man Alice felt she'd spent the last couple of days around. He sank down heavily into one of the kitchen chairs. It creaked under him. He sighed, looking at his clasped hands on the table, quiet.

'I know. I find it hard to believe too. But—'

'But nothing! Finn, a murderer? No. And why would you expect me to believe something so ridiculous after you've been lying to me the last two days?'

'It's complicated.'

'I'd be very disappointed if it wasn't,' she snapped. 'That is some accusation. Who is he supposed to have killed, then?'

'David.'

'What? The guy who drowned?'

'He didn't drown.'

'Okay, right, whatever it was, scuba accident then.'

Mac shook his head. 'No, I mean he didn't drown, he didn't have an accident with his gear. Finn killed him.'

Alice's incredulity wobbled at the look in Mac's eye. A tortured mix of pain, loss and anger. Whatever the truth, it looked like Mac genuinely believed this about Finn. And what was also definitely true was Finn had been hiding things from her. He'd kept his former friendship with these guys secret. And a pretty good reason to do that would be if they knew a terrible truth about him. But... kind, gentle Finn? A killer? Surely not.

'If Finn did that... then why?' She didn't know what to say. 'I just can't believe...'

'I'll tell you the whole sorry story. You can decide then what you believe.'

Alice shot a glance at the clock. 'Time is passing, Mac, and Finn is missing. Whatever about the past and the truth of it, I know he's in danger now. There's no time to explain, we have to find him!'

Mac looked up at her, his previous anger flashing across his face. 'I think we have plenty of time.'

He was still between her and the kitchen, she wasn't getting a weapon. And she wouldn't get far if she made a dash towards the front door, not with her sore ankle. Alice wasn't seeing many options other than letting Mac say what he wanted to say. And praying he was quick.

'Okay. Tell me all. Convince me. And do it quick.'

'I'll take whatever time I need,' snapped back Mac.

Alice fought back an urge to scream. But she kept it in. For Finn.

'It all stems from that day David died.' Mac shook his head. Rubbed his eyes. 'I told you a little about him yesterday. But I didn't tell you about how it was the four of us – me, Vivienne, David *and Finn* who were the friends. It was the four of us together, real halcyon days. Most weekends, we'd travel with all the guys in the club, all around the country. Go to hostels by the coast and spend our time diving. David keeping us entertained. Funny, loud – his dad was American and he'd spent half his childhood in the US. We told him that's where he got his brashness from.' Mac smiled sadly at the memory. 'He was smart but wasn't the best student. I'm not sure he was on target to graduate, I think he spent too much time having fun. But we were all young and stupid.

'We were here, in this part of the world. We'd been diving, having a fantastic time. Then David heard about the wreck from one of the locals. The World War I ship, with the gold. Nobody was allowed to dive there – the salvage owner had gotten so frustrated with all the treasure hunters it was off-limits. But David wasn't one to listen to rules. And he and Finn were thick as thieves. What David wanted, Finn delivered. And vice versa. The bond those two had. And risk-takers, both of them.'

'Finn, a risk-taker?' That didn't sound like the man she knew. 'I find that hard to believe.'

'He was different then, Alice. We all were. That day changed us.'

Mac sat up straighter.

'We went to the site of the wreck at dawn the next day. When no one at the hostel would know what we were up to. I dived with them, but the conditions weren't great. But those two. They were just determined. Vivienne didn't go down, she wasn't feeling well so she didn't dive. It was morning sickness, but none of us, not even her, knew at the time. And thank God she didn't, what might have happened...'

'What did happen?'

'Well, I left them. I came up, just in time to see a garda car coming over the crest of the hill. Their blue lights flashing. I assumed there was an emergency nearby. But they slowed down and stopped by the wall where we'd clambered over to the shore. I suppose stolen gold is a serious matter. Someone had called them, seen us go in.

'It took Finn and David a while to surface. Afterwards, Finn told me that through the water they'd seen the Gardaí's flashing lights, refracted but bright against the dawn sky. And stayed down there, hoping the Gardaí would leave. But then David had gotten spooked, freaked out that his oxygen was getting too low and he'd panicked. He came up quickly. Too quickly. You can't do that with diving. You get decompression sickness. The bends. Finn dragged David from the water. It was awful. He died a few days later.'

Mac sighed a deep, heartbroken sigh.

'Afterwards... our lives, they were ruined. College kicked us out. Gross violation of the code of conduct... breaking the law by diving there, causing an accident where a student perished. I can see their point now. But I was angry then. That was when my problem drinking began. And Vivienne, she discovered she was pregnant a few weeks later. But with no David, and no degree... she had to give up her baby, Hannah. It was like a second bereavement. She was never the same again. You've seen her this weekend, she's tough and bitter and utterly without joy. That wasn't her back then. She was so smart, and funny. She was wonderful to be around. We used to joke that her name should have been Vivacious, not Vivienne... but we lost that Vivienne just as surely as we lost David and she lost Hannah. Our lives were ruined.'

'I'm really sorry that happened to you,' said Alice, 'but it sounds like it was an accident. A tragic one, sure. But not murder.'

'I would've agreed with you until recently. But we learned some new information, Vivienne and I. We came up here this weekend to talk to Finn about it.'

'What new info? What's so compelling?'

'We learned it wasn't an accident. Against all the odds, Finn and David had actually spotted a few of the missing bars of gold. Can you believe it? But what should have been something wonderful... well, Finn had other ideas. He didn't like the idea of having to share the gold. So he messed with David's air, restrained him, keeping him down there until David was forced to make his panicked ascent. Finn knew exactly what that would do to him, and knew it would look like an accident. Later, a few weeks after David was dead and the fuss had died down, Finn went back for the gold. It was all about greed. Finn is a murderer and we want a confession. And that's why we're here.'

'But where did you get this new information? Where does new information come from, twenty-six years later?'

'Where we got the information isn't any of your business. We know it is legit and that's enough. On the other hand, you can't deny Finn is a rich man now, can you?'

'Of course he is. But that's TobinTech. A few bars of gold would be a drop in the ocean compared to his overall wealth...'

'Now, sure, but the seed capital to start, to kick it all off twenty-five years ago? Where'd that come from?'

'He said investors...'

'Of course he did.'

Alice didn't like where this was going. Mac was making everything sound so credible. But something Mac hadn't addressed, and something she would really like to have some answers to, was that the only killing she had witnessed was Vivienne's attempt to drown Finn.

'Well,' she said, 'all you've said may be true – though I find it hard to believe. But I know for certain you are lying about something.'

'I'm not! What?'

'You didn't come here to get a confession from Finn. Just to talk to him. I understand it now... you're here to exact revenge on him in the same way you think he killed David!'

'Oh my God, this again! Where have you gotten this idea? We just want a confession.'

'What about the sabotaged regulator hose then? Huh? Explain that to me.'

'Sabotaged? What?' Mac looked very confused.

Alice marched as best she could, her ankle smarting, to the car outside. Mac jumped up but she was back in the cottage with the equipment before he had a chance to get outside. She held it up.

'Look, do you see?'

She handed it to him.

Mac held it up, stared at it. Turning it around, he spotted the cut. He frowned as he examined it. And, just as Alice had done, he ran his finger over the cut. With some satisfaction, Alice watched as his already pale face washed out a further level. He understood.

'Oh, Jesus.' He turned to Alice. 'This wasn't me. I swear.'

'I have nothing but your word for that,' said Alice, 'but what about Vivienne? Can you say the same for her? Are you still so sure she just wants to talk?'

Mac stood there, staring at her. Like she'd been minutes ago, shocked, unbelieving.

'Oh God. Oh no, no, no. I knew she was angry, I knew it was hardest on her most of all...'

'Do you believe me now? That damaged hose was meant to kill Finn.'

Mac nodded. 'Where are they?' he asked.

'That's what I've been trying to get you to think about!'

'We have to find them,' Mac babbled, eyes wide. 'We have to find them before it's too late.'

FORTY

VIVIENNE

Finn twitched, looking over his shoulder at Vivienne from where he walked a few steps ahead. She knew he was wary of her, being careful not to get too close. His eyes darted left and right, his body tight and tensed, ready to run. But he wouldn't, Vivienne knew that. Invoking the threat to Alice was all it took to keep him in line. Vivienne didn't have to physically force him out of the lighthouse, down the drive and onward. She propelled him with her words, using his love for Alice as a cattle prod, urging him forward.

A gull screeched, and Vivienne looked up at the blue sky, no clouds in sight. It reminded her of their youth before that morning, no clouds until that storm arrived – a storm that never left.

'Why are we going to the hostel, Viv?'

'We just are,' Vivienne replied, deliberately obtuse. She wanted to irritate him.

'Okay,' he said, compliant, not rising to it. Acting as if they were just going for a stroll. As if the narrow roads with the musty, mulching notes of winter and death in the autumn-scented air were just part of the weekend away. And she'd been right to let Mac think all she wanted was a confession from Finn. Maybe she'd even believed it herself when they hatched this plan. But not now. Now it was time to rebalance the universe. An eye for an eye. A life for a life.

Vivienne slipped her hand into her trouser pocket, running her thumb over the smooth wooden handle of the flick knife she'd brought from Dublin. The knife she hadn't told Mac about. He'd have been appalled. But Mac was still, after all this time, too gentle. Forgiving. Trusting. Not Vivienne. She had learned her lesson. It had been a long time ago, but they'd underestimated Finn once before. They had fallen for his nice-guy act. Not again.

They'd fallen for it because he'd been so convincing. He'd seemed like such a nice guy. Or, rather, a nice kid. She remembered how she'd felt about him back then. Wanting to look after him. Mother him. He'd looked too young to be in university. Once they'd got to know each other, she'd had to ask him if he was some sort of child prodigy. He'd laughed, telling her all about how he'd started university early to escape foster care. That had only deepened her maternal yearning. He was two or three years younger than the rest of them, but only a year behind academically. That's how they'd ended up meeting during freshers' week. David and Vivienne had been manning the scuba club desk, signing up new members. Finn had come over, quiet, reserved, asking about joining. Gradually, they'd got to know him during diving weekends away, time spent on smelly buses to coastal towns, in run-down hostels, in the thick of noisy pubs. They'd discovered his shyness was a survival tool. He didn't let people in easily. But slowly, he'd told Mac all about his awful childhood. His mother dying, soul-crushing foster care, and the father who could have saved him from all of it but rejected him. Mac had been like a confessor even then, inspiring confidences and doling out absolution. Between him and David, they'd drawn Finn out. No one could resist David.

With his smile that charmed whoever it fell on. And he'd bestowed it on Finn.

But it wasn't a one-way street. By Finn's second year, Vivienne had watched amazed as David was in turn besotted back. He took modules in computers, got himself into classes with Finn. This quiet, super-smart kid and the gregarious, not quite as bright charmer became best friends. The left and right chambers, the beating heart of their group.

The emails had forced Vivienne to reconsider these memories. Look back on that time. Re-examine it. How had they all been so wrong about Finn? Had there been something off that they'd missed? The emails claimed money was the motive. The truth was that down in the silt-speckled deep, unbelievably, David and Finn had actually found a few bars of gold from that wreck. And Finn had made a decision as it gleamed and called to them from its sandy grave. And that was the why. It made sense, looking at Finn now, making Croesus look like a pauper. But that seemed so grubby. He did it just for the money?

Perhaps Vivienne wanted it to be more than that. Would jealousy somehow make it better? Finn could have liked David too much, envied his easy charm, his easy life. Not to sound conceited, but he could have envied that David had her. For all his smarts and his undeniable good looks, life was harder for Finn back then. All while David just sailed through. But she was kidding herself. None of that would make it better.

They walked in silence. Finn began to follow the path unguided. Like she had, he was recognising the way now. His pace slowed. He took in a deep breath, opened his mouth, then closed it again. He snatched quick glances at Vivienne. He was clearly thinking of saying something.

'What is it?' Vivienne snapped.

'I just wonder...' Finn said, 'how you found out. After all these years?'

Vivienne looked at him. She thought he might ask this

when the shock wore off. She thought about that first email when it had landed in her inbox. Out of the blue. Subject line: 'Information about David Johnson's death. Murder.'

Murder.

That word had grabbed her by the throat. Nothing could have prepared her for the contents of the mail. That the accident had been no accident. That David hadn't foolishly waited too long, avoiding the Gardaí. That he hadn't panicked about his oxygen, and come up too quickly. Instead, Finn had wrestled the breathing apparatus from him, and kept him down there, long enough that David hadn't stood a chance. The real culprit wasn't the nitrogen in his bloodstream – the bends, decompression sickness – but Finn.

Vivienne thought part of her hadn't fully believed it. Not until Finn opened that front door to them on Friday night. The only look on his face after the surprise had slipped away had been guilt and fear. There'd been no denials, not even an attempt. If she'd needed any confirmation, that had said it all.

'Someone told me. I started receiving emails. Someone had all the details from that awful day.'

'Emails from who?' Finn looked perplexed. 'Who told you?'

Vivienne shrugged. 'They were anonymous. But they knew enough to convince me they knew what they were talking about. Don't worry.'

'I see,' he said, and then he was quiet. After a while, he looked at her. 'Maybe it was the doctor.'

'Which doctor?' Vivienne didn't want to engage too much with him, but she was curious.

'You never met her. She was in Belfast. At the second hospital, where they took David after Letterkenny couldn't help him. The one who certified his death.'

'Why her?'

Finn sighed. 'Because I told her everything. Without her help, to cover it up, I wouldn't have gotten away with it.'

'Ah.'

'I heard she lost her job afterwards. They realised she'd altered records or notes or something. I imagine she was struck off the medical register too. She sounds a good bet if I were to guess who was looking for revenge.'

'I agree with you. Why on earth did she agree to help you? That was a lot for her to risk.'

'She needed money, student loans, other debts. She was a single mother. I'd overheard her talking to one of her colleagues about her money troubles. I reckoned she might take my money to help me.'

'You took advantage of her.'

'I did.'

'Another life ruined because of you.'

Finn nodded, mournful.

'Pathetic.'

The wind, still strong, filled the spaces around them, keeping them cold.

'I never... I never meant for all this to happen... particularly...'

'Particularly what, Finn? What was the worst bit of all of this for you? Feel free to share that with me.'

He had the decency to look deeply ashamed. 'Hannah. Has she... has Hannah ever come back into your life?'

This stopped Vivienne in her tracks. The same discordant screeching bird in the distance cried out again, giving voice to her pain. She was unable. Winded by his words, silenced. She glowered – how dare he say her name? Finally she managed a guttural no. There wasn't going to be any ambiguity he could use to lie to himself.

'No,' she repeated, her voice stronger though shaken. 'She turned eighteen eight years ago, so she's been free to look me up ever since. But she hasn't.'

'I'm so sorry,' he said. 'And... this time of year, it must be extra hard.'

Vivienne thought of the scrawl on the back of the battered, folded photo, *October 23ʳᵈ*. Hannah's birthday, not long passed. A date she tried really hard not to think about. It was too hard. She barked a bitter, rasping laugh.

'Sorry? *Sorry?* I haven't fallen and scraped my knee. Sorry isn't even on the same planet as us any more. You can't talk your way out of this, Finn. There are only consequences now.'

She looked at him. He returned her stare with a cautious side glance.

She hated him.

She could see the turn in the road, those ash trees, their bare branches like a crone's bony fingers, beckoning them.

They were nearly at the hostel.

Her hand, in her pocket, closed over the knife.

FORTY-ONE
ALICE

'Where are they then? Where would she have taken him?'

Mac spun around. His hands in his hair.

'I don't know. The plan was to talk to him here. But then we turned up and you were with him. We didn't know about you, so we had to rethink everything. Vivienne said she was going to find somewhere else we could go, but she hadn't decided.'

Mac began pacing up and down. Alice watched him, every nerve and sinew tight and tense in her body.

'No hints?'

He shook his head. And then emitted a plaintive keen. 'How did I miss this? God, I'm a fool...'

'Mac, beating yourself up about this isn't going to do anyone any good. I want to save Finn and I am sure you want to save Vivienne from doing something she will regret. Just take a deep breath.'

Alice looked around the room. They needed a clue. Some indication of where Vivienne and Finn had gone.

'Nothing is out of place. There's no sign of a struggle.' She looked at Mac. 'Did he just go with her willingly, without a fight? Is she armed, Mac?'

A vigorous shake of his head. 'No! No!'

'You can't be sure.' Alice felt her pulse quicken with further reams of panic, depths of panic she didn't think existed. 'You didn't know what she was really up to. And a knife cut that regulator hose.'

'She didn't need a weapon to make him go. He'd have gone willingly.'

Alice's brows furrowed. 'Why?'

'Why do you think? You.'

'Me?'

'Yeah. He didn't want you to know about his past and Vivienne was using telling you as leverage. He'd have walked right out of here to make sure you didn't know. He loves you very much.'

Alice hung her head. Tears stung. He'd let himself go with a potential killer because of her. And she was a liar. Who'd been lying to him from the very moment they'd met. Even beforehand as she'd sought out a job at TobinTech, pretending to be just an ordinary career girl. If Vivienne killed him, sought her ultimate revenge on him, it would be her fault. He'd walked into the lion's den for a love that wasn't worthy. Oh God, they had to find them. She had to save him.

'Mac, think, think harder... where could they have gone?'

Mac looked at Alice, eyes full of pain. He held her gaze and shook his head.

'I don't know,' he repeated.

He lashed out, pushing his kitchen chair against the table, knocking and shaking it and the other chairs. There was a slapping noise as something fell off one of the chairs and hit the tiled floor. Alice followed the sound. She saw what it was. Mac's poetry book. It must have been on one of the seats, and Mac's shove had dislodged it.

She dashed to the table, dropped to her knees and reached out and grabbed it.

She stood back up.

'What are you doing?' asked Mac, who'd stopped pacing to watch her. Alice held the book up.

'This. It wasn't on the chair when I left. It was on the table. Neither of us has touched it. So how did it get on the chair?'

Mac screwed up his eyes. 'What are you talking about? What's my book got to do with anything? How can you be sure where it was even?'

'Because I searched this place entirely a few times over, looking for our missing car keys. It was on the table, right there.' She pointed to the end of the table where it met the wall. 'It was right there when I left. And I don't think Finn decided to sit down for a little poetry reading break. And there are no signs of any struggle. But even if there were, the book couldn't have gotten onto the seat. It must mean something. Doesn't it? Finn must have moved it for a reason.'

Mac took the book from her, all his body language screaming doubt.

'I don't see how...' His voice trailed off as he flicked through the book. And, for a second time that weekend, Alice saw a bookmark that made her stop.

'There. Go back.'

'What?'

'There was something in the pages. Midway. And there were no bookmarks when I was looking at this yesterday morning.'

Mac flicked through the book a second time, slower. He stopped at a page where a small rectangle of card had been secreted. He looked first at it.

'Finn's business card?' He handed it to Alice. She took it and smoothed it between her fingers. It was all creased, as if it had been crumpled up. This was one of his private number cards. He didn't give them out lightly. What did this mean?

Mirroring Mac's confused face, she looked from the card to Mac to the book. He was letting the pages loose.

'Stop!' she yelled. 'Keep the place!'

Startled, Mac did as she asked, snapping his hand on the original page, holding it tight.

'What poems are those there? On those pages? Maybe Finn was trying to tell us something... he has the book at home, he knows these poems, Mac.'

Mac scanned the pages. Alice came around and looked too. On the left-hand page was a poem called 'Summer'. She read through the lines, but nothing suggested itself. She looked at Mac and he shook his head. On the right-hand page was a poem called 'The Last Night Before'.

> Before and after.
> We sit with laughter here and now.
> Better before than after.
> Now he lies there, chequered tatters,
> Tiled red embers.
> I will remember
> Sitting. Laughing.
> Here.
> Before.
> After.

'The hostel!' Mac cried out. 'The hostel... this *is* a message!' His words tumbled out of him.

'The hostel where you stayed? Back then?'

'Yes, yes, exactly. I wrote this about the night before it all happened. We had a great night, laughing and singing and just being all together. We were so happy. And then, after the accident... Before and after. The chequered tatters were the seats, someone in the hostel had done a dreadful job on the chairs with this awful material. We laughed about them every time we went down to the kitchen, it became a running joke. But I felt afterwards that the imagery was right, everything ended in tatters, black and white. Before and after.'

'Is it somewhere she might have gone?'

He shrugged. Nervous energy pulsing through him. He couldn't stand still, he moved from foot to foot.

'Maybe? I don't know. I haven't been there since that night. I suppose so. But is it even still a hostel? Is it still there after all this time? And it's a bit odd to go there...'

'But that's definitely what that poem is about, yeah? And would Finn have understood it?'

'Definitely. The chequered tattered seats, and then also the red tiles in the fireplace. They were very striking. We talked about them too. He'd know. And the fact that he's marked it. You were right, he's telling us where he is, I'm sure of it.'

'Well, that's it then. Come on! Let's go.'

'Alice, I don't know where it is. It's close to here, it has to be, but I haven't a clue. It's been twenty-six years since I was there last.'

Alice grabbed Mac's hand. Started dragging him towards the door of the cottage.

'Well, Mac, they have this amazing thing called the internet now... we just get to the end of the road and signal and then we'll locate it. C'mon!'

Mac came easily under her tugging and they both raced to the door. She opened it and stepped out, her hand patting her pocket, making sure Finn's phone was still there.

The wind whipped her hair. And a hand grabbed her.

A rag stuffed in her mouth. An arm across her, restraining her, pulling her away. Alice let out a suppressed muffled scream.

'No!' yelled Mac, exiting the cottage two steps behind her. He launched himself after her, reaching out.

But her attacker's arm lashed out, slamming a length of wood across Mac's head. A jet of red, and the big man crumbled. Alice struggled. Screaming a scream no one could hear.

FORTY-TWO
VIVIENNE

Finn kicked around the debris on the floor: broken glass, bits of ceiling, all manner of derelict detritus. It made a scratching, sloppy noise as he moved it. He looked up at the ceiling, regarding the raindrops as they fell on him. It wasn't even raining outside.

'It sort of hasn't changed,' he said. Vivienne knew what he meant. It was unrecognisable in its dark dankness, but somehow it had remained utterly the same.

He'd stopped outside, just like Vivienne had, when he'd come to the red peeling gate. He'd looked at the hostel as if it were a haunted house. Which, Vivienne guessed, it was. Full of ghosts. He'd looked back at her, his eyes asking not to go in, his mouth smart enough not to translate. She'd urged him on. They were going in. Her heart had sped up as they'd walked down the path. The moment was nearly here. Vivienne may only have found out this year what he'd done, but she'd longed for retribution, revenge, redress for over twenty years.

Vivienne positioned herself by the window as Finn circled the room. She eyed up the old tea caddy, undisturbed where she'd left it yesterday. As he stared into the cracked and blackened fireplace, the only feature that had remained the same since they'd last been there, she ducked down and grabbed the caddy, popping it on the windowsill behind her. Ready.

Finn crouched down and rubbed away some soot marks from the tiles. The drinking teens had been lighting fires too, keeping warm while they boozed. The red was still there. Fiery. Red is always a warning in nature. Hot. Poisonous. Keep away. They should have paid more attention. They should have listened.

Vivienne kicked the chair across the room. It practically aquaplaned into place. Finn turned, looking at it and then at her.

'What's that for?'

'You. Sit.'

'That looks sodden. I don't think I need to sit. We can talk while standing.'

'SIT!' Vivienne screamed, the sound crashing about the room like one of those ghosts. But he didn't sit, stayed standing, looking at her defiantly. She put her hand into her pocket, felt the warm wooden handle of her flick knife, and brought it out. Finn's eyes were glued to her hand. What was she doing? With a practised movement – she'd spent time at home getting it right, taking no chances – she swung out the blade, no longer sheathed. Finn blanched.

'Do you want to reconsider the chair?'

'Christ, Viv... there's no need for that!'

'Then sit the hell down!' She raised the blade and stepped closer. He sat, quick and heavy. Vivienne grabbed the caddy from the sill behind her, opened it, and took out some cable ties. She threw one at him.

'Tie your right arm to the armrest with that.'

'Viv...'

Vivienne ignored his plea, just waiting and watching until he began to bind himself.

'Tighter. I can see the slack.'

He did as she said, pulling the end of the plastic until there was no air between his limb and the rusting, mottled metal. The next bit was tricky. Securing his free hand... without giving him a chance to fight back.

She approached him from behind, brushing the dull side of the blade across the back of his neck. A warning. She felt him shudder. And it made her think – would she be able to do it? When the moment came? She'd think of Hannah, of David, of Mac. Would that give her the strength? She supposed she would only know in the moment. When it was time for Finn to atone.

Behind him, she put the knife between her teeth and, in two swift movements, secured the cable tie around his other wrist before he understood what she was doing. He yanked and twisted the arm, growling like a captured wild animal.

Vivienne circled him, stopping once they were face to face. She stood there, watching him as he pulled at his restraints. As he tried to stand, denied by the chair's vice-like embrace. He gave up, and the metal chair clanked to the ground again. Finn was red in the face. Trapped. Angry. He glared at her.

'What is going on, Viv? This is hardly the way to talk.'

'I don't think you get to dictate terms.'

'You know how sorry I have to be, Vivienne. I could never have wanted it all to end this way. But,' he shook his hands, 'you can't want it to end this way either.'

'Don't tell me what I want and don't want! I'll be the one telling you that. I want David! I want Hannah! I want the life I was promised, which you snatched away from me because of your greed.'

Confusion spread across his face. Vivienne didn't expect that. Fear, guilt, more anger. But not confusion.

'What's the problem? Huh? Why the stupid look on your face?'

'Greed?' he said, looking up at her with scrunched-up eyes. 'Greed? Why do you think greed had anything to do with it?'

'You did it for the gold,' Vivienne snapped. 'This isn't complicated.'

'The gold? What gold?'

Vivienne released a long, exhausted sigh. Why was he doing this? Acting the fool wasn't going to make a difference. She supposed she had him tied to a chair and had been waving a knife in his face. She might have played the fool if their positions were reversed. But he was forgetting that he had already admitted his guilt. All weekend, they'd been able to manipulate him, get him to do what they wanted – the only weapon they had was the threat of exposure. He couldn't backtrack now. No matter how much he wished he could.

'The gold. From the wreck. Ringing any bells? The gold that you and David found during the dive, but which you decided you didn't want to share. Coming back to you now?'

'I have no idea what you're talking about,' he said. 'David and I, we never found any gold.'

Vivienne had to admit she was a little unsettled. He sounded like he meant it. He was a very good liar.

'It's been a long time, twenty-six long years. So I suppose your memory could have gotten hazy.' Vivienne let the sarcasm bite.

'I don't remember because it didn't happen,' he growled. 'I don't know where you got that idea.'

'Right. Maybe there was something a little more memorable about that day, something that you might recall better? For example, what about when you murdered your best friend? Kept David in the water, deprived him of his oxygen? Hmmm, anything?'

Finn's jaw actually dropped, just like in the cartoons.

'You'd think,' Vivienne said, 'that that's the kind of memory that would stick around.'

'Murder?' he finally uttered, the word barely formed. 'David?'

'There we go, it's coming back to you now.'

Vivienne took out her phone. She hadn't lied to Mac about wanting a confession. She just wanted justice as well. She looked down at the phone. Five missed calls. From Mac himself. God, she hoped he hadn't worked out what she was up to. But, even if he had, he didn't know where she was. She swiped them clear. Then she unlocked the phone, opened the recording app and held it out towards the shell-shocked Finn.

'Shall we try this all again, then? Now that it's coming back to you. Once I press record, you can tell us all about it, how you murdered David Johnson, and that you did it for the gold. If you do as I say, I might just cut those ties with this knife, and I won't cut anywhere else.' This was a lie. But she wanted him to think there was a chance she would let him go.

She pressed the large red button on her phone and cleared her throat.

'The next voice you will hear is that of Finn Tobin, CEO of TobinTech. He wants to share his personal recollection of what happened near Fanad Head, on 4 April 1998, between him and his friend, David Johnson.'

Vivienne got as close as she dared to Finn and held out the phone.

'Go on,' she said when he didn't utter a word.

'But... but... I didn't kill him.'

Vivienne rolled her eyes. She was tired of this now. 'Finn, I don't know why you're denying this now. You've already confessed!'

Finn looked at her as if she was the crazy one. 'What? No, I didn't!' He actually had the temerity to look annoyed.

Vivienne's phone buzzed in her hand. It was Mac again. She hit decline, made sure it was still recording, and tried again with Finn.

'So you just went along with whatever we wanted all weekend, just for fun? 'Cause you were happy to see us?' She laughed. It was so preposterous.

'No, I went along with your threats and blackmail because I thought you'd found out what I'd done.'

'Exactly. And what you did was kill David,' she snapped.

'Well, you're right in a way,' he said, then sighed as the temporary fight that had flared burned out. He looked down at his lap, head hanging. All she could see was his messy mix of curls. 'I did kill David, yes. But just not how you think.'

He looked up at her. His blue eyes were pale and anguished.

'How can it not be how I think? This isn't that complicated, so please stop speaking in riddles.'

'When you appeared on the doorstep on Friday... When I saw you standing there, I didn't think you'd found out that I'd murdered David. I thought the opposite, Viv.'

'The opposite?'

'Yeah, I thought you'd uncovered the biggest regret of my life... my awful, unforgivable lie... that David was never dead.'

FORTY-THREE

'What?'

It wasn't the smartest response, but it was all Vivienne had.

'I don't know how else to put it. David is alive,' Finn said.

Vivienne stared at him. 'Or at least he was twenty-six years ago. After the accident. I don't know what has happened to him in the intervening years. He could actually be dead now, for all I know. We didn't keep in touch. But he didn't die then.'

This was bizarre. Unbelievable.

'David is dead, Finn. Seriously.'

Finn said nothing. He looked away, peering out the cracked glass of the hostel window. He spoke, still staring out at the world outside.

'I understand that you don't believe me. I worked hard so you wouldn't.'

Vivienne looked down at her phone and stopped the recording. She felt the weight of the knife in her other hand, letting her thumb touch the blade. It wasn't very sharp, but it had a very narrow point. And she was strong. It wouldn't take much.

'You're right, I don't believe you. I saw his death certificate... and, rather like most dead people, he isn't here any more.

I have a portion of his ashes at my home, sent to me by his mother. And a beautiful note from her about how much he'd loved me. What more do I need?'

'All those little details... I did a good job convincing you all.'

'Right. I think what's really happening here is you're trying to get yourself out of this.'

'That's not it, but I'm not sure how to prove it to you. I can't, not here, not right now.'

'Ha! What's that? Is this some gambit to get out of here? Do you really think I'm so foolish that a promise of David being alive is enough to save you? That I'll let you go so you can falsify some proof? Nice try.'

Vivienne shook her head and picked up her phone to delete the previous recording, this nonsense of David not being dead.

'Right, let's try that again, shall we? I promised Mac a confession, and he's going to get one.' She pressed record and held it out again.

'You weren't looking for a confession yesterday when you could have killed me, so why worry about it now?' Finn snapped.

'What? Who tried to kill you yesterday?'

'You did! The sliced-open regulator hose? Ringing any bells?' He used her own words against her. 'Looks like we're both getting a bit forgetful about who we've been trying to kill.'

'I don't know what you're talking about.'

'No? Sure you don't... If the storm hadn't kicked up and nearly killed me, your sabotage to my regulator hose would have done the trick just a well. '

'I didn't try to kill you!' she yelled, frustrated.

'And I didn't kill David!' Finn yelled back.

Silence fell as they stared at each other.

'I'm not just saying that to get out of here. Though, that would be nice,' he said, shaking his wrists, straining against the cable ties. 'The truth is what I told you at the time – that David panicked in the water and came up too quickly. I tried to stop him and could have killed myself too in the process. But that's where the truth stopped. He didn't die. But, I can understand why you find that hard to believe. You saw a legitimate death certificate. And other things, like ashes and letters. Everything was engineered to make sure you thought he was dead. Things I made happen. I did what I could to make you, and everyone, believe he was dead. And, to my great surprise, it was easier than I thought.'

'You can't have.'

'You'd be surprised. When they stopped you going to the hospital because you weren't next-of-kin, it gave me a chance to create the lie. Didn't you ever wonder about the lack of return address on the letter from his mother? The death cert was real though. Just not the death. The doctor I told you about, on the way here. The one I suggested might be sending you those emails. She issued that cert. I paid her to. I gave her some money, and she changed some records. She got caught in the end, career ruined. I don't know why she'd wait so long for revenge, but I wouldn't blame her.'

'Surely I'd have heard if a doctor did such a thing. It would've made the news!'

'Why would it? It would have been important to us, but not to anyone else. Doctors get struck off all the time. And it wasn't for a few years after that it got found out. We were scattered to the wind by then. It was in Belfast too, in the UK, so anything official was in a different jurisdiction. I'd be more surprised if you had heard about it.'

Finn shrugged his shackled shoulders.

'You might be able to find some reference to her being kicked off the medical register online... but it's been such a long time I doubt it.'

Vivienne looked at her phone, considering it. Then she shook herself. He was getting into her head. He was succeeding.

'Stop it!' she shouted at him. 'This doesn't make sense. None of it. Why would you have done such a thing? Why would David have let you? This doesn't add up. The simplest explanation is the correct explanation. David died. That's it.'

Finn closed his eyes. His tense body went loose as if the fight had left him. He slumped in the chair, shaking his head slowly. He opened his mouth to speak but stopped himself. He did this again. And again. Then stopped.

He finally looked up at her, straight in the eye. 'Vivienne, I can tell you why. I can connect it all up so that it makes sense. But I don't want to. You've been through so much already.'

'Don't do me any favours.'

'I'm telling the truth.'

'I saw how quickly you came up with the lie of the double-booking on Friday night. I've seen you think creatively and quickly. So you can hardly blame me for not believing a word that comes out of your mouth.'

Finn shook his head. His eyes were sad.

'He was leaving you, Viv.'

The words hung in the air.

'Oh God. Vivienne, it's time. I've got to do what I should have done then. Tell you the truth, no matter how awful it is... He was leaving you.'

'No, he wasn't.'

Finn sighed.

'He was. He was pretty sure you were pregnant. You were only getting suspicious at that point, but he was fairly certain. And he didn't want that, the whole family thing. He knew you would. He was flunking out of college. I know you know that. We were both helping him, doing our best to drag him over the line. All he could see was no degree and a new baby. It filled him with horror.'

'David wouldn't have done that to me. He loved me. He'd have loved Hannah. We would have been together forever.

How dare you tell such lies! You expect me to believe he got you to help him fake his death to get away from me? Come on!'

'He didn't ask me to help. In fact, he was a bit annoyed when he found out.'

'Huh, what?'

'I decided to do it, on my own. *I* faked David's death.'

Vivienne stared at Finn, blinking. 'What?' she said again.

'Yeah... it all happened in Belfast, after we were transferred to the hospital there. They knew in Letterkenny that I probably wasn't serious enough to need the bigger hospital, but they sent me with him, just to be sure.' Finn kept going. 'And then, when we got there, David rallied. He wasn't quite as bad either as his doctors first feared. He improved hugely within twelve hours. But they weren't telling me much because I wasn't family. That's why my messages to you weren't accurate when I told you there was no change. I wasn't trying to deliberately mislead you. Not then, anyway.

'I went to see him the next morning. Finally got someone to tell me what room he was in. But when I got there, his bed was empty. I still remember the shock. I thought he was in the morgue.'

Finn shook his head, going paler at the ghost memory.

'But that wasn't it. A nurse told me I'd just missed him. He'd discharged himself. She wasn't happy about that, but he was well enough to make his way out. I ran after him and caught up. I was delighted, embraced him. But he didn't return it. He was pissed that I'd found him. Furious. It took me a while to realise what was happening. He was doing a runner on his life with us. Leaving.'

Finn took in a shaky gulp of air. Vivienne felt transfixed, Finn's words flooding over her, but she couldn't move, couldn't think.

'He told me you were pregnant, and he wanted nothing to do with that. He was going to head to his father's place in

Arizona, and he was never coming back. I was all, "But what about us? What about Vivienne? You can't do that to her." He just laughed. He said, "Watch me." Like a loser, I asked, "What will I tell them?" He just laughed again and said, "I don't care. Tell them whatever you like. You can tell them I'm dead for all I care."'

Finn's eyes bored into hers with each word.

'He wasn't going to stay and do the right thing. My dad left me like that before I was born. He didn't give a damn, and it nearly destroyed me. I loved you, Vivienne. Not just as a friend, but in a stupid puppy-dog way. You looked after me, cared for me. You were the first person since my mother died who'd done that for me. I was appalled that this was happening and that I'd be the one who had to tell you. And that's when I had the thought. What if I made David's flippant remark come true? Because if he was "dead", that would be easier for you. He'd never break your heart. He'd always remain your great love, and that would be enough to sustain you and see you through. I thought I was being brilliant. I think because I'd dealt with death and loss so much I'd become a little inured to it. I'd survived it, and so would you. And you'd have a new baby, something joyful to keep you going.

'I didn't realise that college would kick us out. It hadn't even entered my head as a possibility. And I'd assumed your family were as kind and lovely as you – I'd never imagined they would be horrified that you were pregnant and alone.'

'Yeah, surprised us both.' Vivienne scowled.

'By the time I realised how much I'd messed up, it was a runaway train.'

'Why didn't you pull the brakes, then?'

'I tried, believe me. I contacted Professor Clarke, I thought he might be able to help. I wanted him to see if there was a chance to get you, at the very least, back into the college. I gave him this whole "hypothetical" scenario, *what if maybe I'd done this, what if perhaps this was the truth about what happened*. He used some back channels at the college, talked to the provost. He maintained the hypothetical and kept my name out of it. But regardless, the provost didn't want to know. Unsurprisingly, lying about a student being dead is just as bad as being part of a rule-breaking incident where a student dies. And the provost didn't care that the dive hadn't been your idea and you hadn't even gotten in the water. The university had washed their hands of us. Prof Clarke told me he wouldn't alert the authorities to what I had done. I'd been his favourite student, so he saw my expulsion as punishment enough, my bright academic future in tatters, but that was all he could do.

'After that I tracked down the doctor who'd helped me pretend David was dead. I asked her to help me undo it all but she freaked out. She said she'd be struck off for sure, there was no way to resurrect David without landing us all in a whole heap of trouble. I'd have taken the chance but she'd a family, she begged me not to. It just felt like the more I tried to make it better, the worse it got.

'You gave up Hannah and disappeared into yourself, Mac just crumbled... and that doctor, she ended up being struck off anyway. When it was too late to fix things, a year or two later, she contacted me, looking for a payoff – she'd covered for me when they'd discovered that she'd falsified the records. But she needed money, she was desperate. I gave her what I could. And then I added her to the growing list of lives I'd ruined.'

Vivienne watched Finn begin to cry, his handsome face crumpling as tears traced a path to his jaw. His chin dipped. His bound wrists stopped him from wiping them away.

'By the time I'd tried everything, the only thing the truth would have done was add more pain to your life, to Mac's, to that doctor's.'

There was a tiny shake of his head.

'It's crushed me every day of my life since. It's why we

drifted apart. I couldn't bear the guilt, watching the toll it took on you. That's what I thought you'd found out when you turned up on Friday. That's what I thought you knew. And I didn't want Alice to know.' Finn shook his head. 'I'd just let my heart open up to her. I'd punished myself by not allowing myself a relationship. Not letting myself have the comforts I'd caused you to lose. But something about Alice... Somehow she broke through. She wouldn't take no for an answer.

'I wanted to atone. You'd found me. I was willing to talk, explain, to finally tell you the truth and, for what it's worth, say I was sorry. And believe me, Vivienne, I am so very, very sorry.'

Vivienne had no words. She didn't know what to think, to believe. Was this true? Could David have wanted to walk away from her? Did that really happen? She felt a ghost of the pain that that would have caused grip her heart. The pain that Finn's lies were meant to prevent.

Bang!

Bang!

Her head shot up. So did Finn's. Someone was hammering on the back door.

'Alice,' he murmured, and she saw hope ignite in his eyes.

She rushed to the door and tugged it open.

It wasn't Alice to the rescue.

Instead, it was Mac.

Bloodied.

Hair matted red, he collapsed through the door. She caught hold of him as he stumbled.

'Christ!' cried Finn, still restrained in his chair. 'Mac!'

Vivienne steadied him, her eyes darting frantically around, trying to see where he was hurt.

'What's happened? What's happened? Are you alright?'

He was clearly not alright. He grabbed her windcheater, bloody hands staining it.

'Someone... someone's taken Alice!'

'What?' Her head snapped from Mac to Finn.

'We were leaving the cottage. He grabbed her, and hit me, to stop me stopping him.'

'Get me out of these!' roared Finn, trying to stand, shaking and pulling at the chair arms.

Mac looked over to him, confused.

'Who is "he"? Who grabbed her?' Vivienne asked, dragging Mac's attention back from Finn.

'I don't know, Viv. I don't know... but I think I'm going mad because he looked just like David.'

FORTY-FOUR

'David? *Our David?*'

'Yes!' Mac said, bewildered. 'I'm losing my mind, seeing a dead man. His ghost has been haunting me... but this, this was so real.'

'What happened? What did you see? Why do you think it was him?'

'I just caught a flash. He tried to hide his face. But, Viv, his face is burned into my memory. I could never forget him. And... he even looked older, like us. Ghosts don't age.'

Vivienne turned to Finn, shaking.

'Finn, could he really be here?'

'How the hell would I know!' Finn came alive again, battling against the cable ties. 'The last I had to do with him was twenty-six years ago!'

Finn said he couldn't prove that David wasn't dead. Now, tumbling through the door was this bloody envoy, a timely Hermes messenger from the gods. With news of a very mortal man.

'If that was him,' Finn said, 'and he's actually here? Christ! And he's got Alice? Get me out of these!'

'What's going on?' Mac asked. He looked from Vivienne to Finn. Then looked more closely at Finn and saw the cable ties for the first time, realising Finn was not sitting by choice.

'Oh no, Viv... no. This was never the plan.' He ran to Finn.

'Mac, wait. You're bleeding. You need help.' Vivienne went to him, but he put up his hand.

'It's stopped. I can manage.'

Vivienne hung back as Mac tried to use his bare hands to rip the ties apart, but they were too strong. She offered him her knife.

'I don't think it'll be sharp enough,' she said.

Mac snatched it, and the look he shot her made her die a little inside.

'Alice said this was what you were planning to do. She showed me the regulator hose. Oh Viv, I love you dearly, but no.' He forced the knife underneath the tie and dug it into the plastic. The ties didn't give an inch. He sawed and pulled while Finn, using superhuman strength, sat still to let his friend help him. He was bursting to get out of there.

'I didn't try to kill you, Finn. I didn't damage the hose. Look at that knife, it's useless. I swear I didn't.'

Teeth gritted, he glared at her. 'It isn't the only knife in the world.'

'And these.' Finn pulled at the wrist that Mac wasn't working on. 'This was just a game, huh?'

'I thought you killed David.'

'And that would have made it okay? Jesus Christ!'

'No. No, it wouldn't.'

With a grunt, Mac broke through. Half of Finn was free. Adrenaline reviving him, Mac didn't bother trying to cut the second tie. He tore the arm from the chair, rust and screws scattering, and Finn was released.

Finn grabbed Mac's shoulders, hugging him. Then, still holding him, he leaned back and looked him in the eyes.

'Old friend, there's a lot going on and there's a lot to explain. But you are not going mad... David is alive. I didn't kill him.'

'David alive? What?' Mac was stunned.

Vivienne nodded. 'I think it's true.'

'Someone has been manipulating you guys,' Finn said. 'Maybe it was him? Mac, I will tell you all that I've explained to Vivienne about David. And I will spend the rest of my life apologising for what I did. But right now I need to know what happened. Where has this person taken Alice?'

'I'm sorry,' he said. 'I wish I could tell you more. It all happened so quickly. We stepped outside the cottage and he grabbed her. Hit me across the head. So hard, the world was spinning. I think I heard a car, so I guess they could be anywhere now.'

'I gave her my phone! Quick, give me yours, Viv. I have an app work made me install, so I can find my phone if it's ever lost. I can track her.'

Vivienne dashed to Finn, phone outstretched.

'Stop,' Mac cried. He drew something out of his pocket and handed it to Finn.

'Is this it?'

Finn took the phone from Mac and nodded wordlessly.

'It must have fallen out of her pocket when he grabbed her. I found it on the ground by the door when I came to.'

Finn steadied himself.

'Well, I'm going to go search anyway. I have to find her.' He rushed to the door, looking back at Mac. 'Stay here with Vivienne. Let her call you an ambulance; your head looks bad. I have to go. I have got to save Alice.'

'I'm calling them now,' Vivienne said, but her fingers were shaking. There was so much happening. Her life seemed to have become a kaleidoscope, each twist taking all its parts and rearranging them, making new patterns with every turn. It was overwhelming, confusing. She was sick to her stomach.

'There is no way I am letting you do that on your own,' Mac said to Finn, following him to the door. 'I can manage. It must look worse than it is.'

Mac turned and looked at Vivienne, pale and bloody but his eyes alive. 'Vivienne, I'll be okay. I must help Finn. Alice needs us.'

He caught Finn's eye, and they nodded and ran towards the door.

'Wait!' Vivienne called out.

They did as commanded, stopping and turning to look at her like eager children, obeying but unhappy.

'Mac, tell me again what happened?'

'Viv, sorry, but we have to go!' Finn said. 'We can't waste another second.' He grabbed hold of Mac's arm, starting to drag him.

'No. Give me a moment... trust me, this is important.'

'But...'

'If you mean it that you're sorry for everything, then you owe me this!'

It was a low blow, unfair. But they had to wait.

Desperate frustration had a hold of Finn. Vivienne saw how it shook his body, fight or flight coursing through him. But he stopped and did what she asked.

'Mac, it's important. Tell me again what happened. Tell me everything.'

'Okay.' Mac closed his eyes, taking a deep breath. 'We were in the kitchen. She was calling you a killer, Viv. I told her no, it was Finn who was the dangerous one.' Mac opened his eyes again, looking at Finn, who shook his head.

'Lies, Mac, I swear,' Finn said. Vivienne nodded, reassuring Mac. Backing up Finn's assertion lifted a weight from Mac. He continued to talk but stole glances at Finn, excited to be allowed to care for him again.

'Alice told me then about the sabotage, Finn's damaged

scuba gear. And I got afraid. Afraid that you were too angry, Viv. That you were going to do something that you regretted. You've been on edge, teetering since we got here. Alice found my book, Finn. And I worked out from it that you must be here.'

'It worked, thank God.'

'It was smart. And she's a smart girl. We ran then, from the house. But he... the guy...' Mac's eyes widened once more at the possibility that it could have been David, still too unreal to be possible. 'It was only moments, but he was outside, waiting for us. We stepped outside and he grabbed Alice and he swung a branch or a plank. I don't know what it was. But it knocked me down. When I could stand again, when I came to my senses, they were gone. As I said, I think I heard a car. And that's it. I raced here after.'

'I need you to think, Mac, close your eyes and remember it. When he grabbed her. Was it a grab? Or was it a pull?'

'What do you mean?'

Vivienne glanced at Finn but had to go on.

'Was he forcing her to go... or helping her to go?'

'Helping her?' Finn's voice was as sharp as her knife was dull.

'I'm sorry, Finn, but I think I'm just getting a taste of how you must have felt after the accident. How you must have felt to have such an awful secret. I don't want to have to say this... but...'

'Spit it out!'

'Alice isn't being straight with you. She's hiding something. That person could have been collecting her, not taking her. You're right, someone has been manipulating us. Bringing us here this weekend. I didn't damage your equipment, I swear. Maybe it was David. But it could also have been Alice.'

FORTY-FIVE

Vivienne started with the photograph, recounting how she had found it. Unfolded, mocking her.

'She was just snooping,' Finn interjected. 'She told me about that. You can't blame her, you guys showed up, acting the way you did.'

'Finn, that isn't all of it, okay?' Vivienne pressed on.

Finn stared at her, eyes challenging her.

'She has a secret phone. You're a grown-up, you don't need me to explain how that's no good.'

Finn opened his mouth to refute this, but Vivienne held up her hand to stop him. She then told them both about the conversation she had overheard.

Blackmail, cold feet, you need to drop it, he's not the bad guy.

'Who was she talking to?' Mac asked.

Vivienne shrugged. 'Not a clue. But she wasn't catching up with an old friend.'

She watched Finn wither before her.

'I just can't... no. There must be an explanation. Something.'

'I agree,' said Mac. 'I like her.'

'Oh, for heaven's sake, Mac, you like her?' Vivienne snapped.

Mac scowled. 'I obviously mean she seems genuine. I'm shocked at all this.' He put his hand on Finn's shoulder, giving it a reassuring squeeze.

'If David is here, and Alice is shady, maybe they're working together?' Vivienne suggested.

'No!' Finn snapped.

'I know you don't want to hear any of this, but you can't deny it's suspicious timing. When did you meet her, Finn?'

'She joined the company in February.'

'Meaning she applied for the job in January sometime?'

'That would be about right.'

'So, she applied for a job at TobinTech in January, just weeks after your *Times* profile came out.'

Vivienne shared a look with Mac, unseen by Finn. Mac shook his head, his eyes sad.

'And around when we began receiving our emails,' Vivienne added.

The three exchanged glances, the possibility of this new truth, the play within a play, revealing itself. David was alive. She believed Finn. And as impossible as it seemed, this very alive ghost might just be here. She was breathless at the speed at which everything was changing.

'Vivienne... I can't, I can't write her off without giving her a chance to explain. And all you have is a theory. She could really be in harm's way.'

'But what if I'm right? And running after her is running into a trap? Should we not take a moment... just to try and work out what's going on? Whoever is behind this all, they're months ahead of us.'

'She's right, Finn,' Mac said.

'I thought you said you liked Alice?' Finn retorted.

'I liked David. I loved David. And he did this to me.' Mac touched his bloody head.

Vivienne eyed Finn, watching him process and agonise.

'Can we at least get out of here? Go and look for her while we try to work out what is going on?'

'Of course. Let's go.'

Vivienne hung up the phone and tucked it back in her pocket, battling against the wind with the others.

'I think they thought it was a prank call.'

'I don't blame them,' Finn said. 'It is pretty unbelievable.'

Vivienne could see the lighthouse. They were hurrying back there to start their hunt for the truth. The wind was picking up, and the blue-sky promise of the morning had gone. Dark, bulging clouds gathered in the distance. Finn scoured the roads and fields for any signs of Alice or David.

'The sergeant said they'd send a squad car to the lighthouse, but they couldn't say exactly when it would get there, we're so far out.'

'That doesn't suggest they took you seriously, no,' Mac remarked.

'"A dead guy might be trying to kill us." I wouldn't take me seriously either,' Vivienne grumbled.

They hurried on. Finn took out his phone.

'I'm going to try ringing her.'

'Wasn't her phone missing?'

'Yes, but...'

'Maybe she was lying about that?'

Finn shrugged.

'I just want to try every possibility.'

'Are you sure that is even wise? We don't know what's happening.'

'Exactly, we don't know what's happening, so let's just ask!'

Finn dialled the number as Vivienne watched. It rang and rang. Hope leached from his eyes with every unanswered trill. Eventually he hung up.

'Finn, she has two phones. You're probably not even ringing the right one.' Vivienne couldn't spare him. It felt kinder to speak the truth.

'Oh,' he said, 'alright.' He put his phone away. His shoulders slumped.

'Let's talk about what we know,' Vivienne said, moving things along. Distracting Finn.

'Okay, tell me about the emails,' Finn said. 'Tell me everything. It's a good place to start.'

Vivienne took a deep breath, thinking back. 'They started not long after you appeared on that magazine cover. When they did the profile on you.'

'That's how we discovered what you were doing now, after all this time,' Mac joined in. 'Maybe it was the same for David. That's what brought him back.'

'If it's David, wouldn't he have to have been back in Ireland to see it?' Vivienne asked.

Finn's head bobbed from side to side. 'Depends, it would've been online too. But he'd have needed to be looking for it, at the very least searching for my name.'

'Maybe he did that. Was feeling nostalgic.' Vivienne's words were corrosive. She was only getting used to this new reality. Sainted martyr David was dead. A demon springing up, alive, in his place.

'The timing of the emails right after is too coincidental. I think we can say for sure that the profile was the catalyst for whatever is going on,' Finn said.

'And it wasn't hard to notice from it how rich you are,' Mac added. 'That is quite the lure, for some.'

'Yeah, maybe. But I don't see how he, or anyone else, is getting a penny out of me if I'm dead.'

Mac frowned. 'True.'

'Tell me more about the emails. Weren't you suspicious of them? Emails out of the blue, telling you such a shocking thing. Why didn't you think, just like the police right now, that it was a prank?'

'Whoever it was knew stuff that only we would have known. And I'm not talking about some cold reading trick. Real stuff. Not lucky guesses.'

'Did you ever try to follow their digital trail to find out who it was?'

'I told her we should,' Mac said.

Vivienne hung her head. 'You did, Mac. I should have listened.' She took his hand and squeezed it. She looked over at Finn as they walked three abreast down the narrow road. 'I think I didn't want to know.'

'What exactly did they tell you?'

'After the initial info that gained my confidence, they explained how you and David had spotted the gold on your dive. And it wasn't the hurry to avoid the Gardaí that caused his injuries. You deliberately inflicted them, there and then. That you dragged him out as if you were helping once you knew it was too late for him to be saved. They pointed out how you'd distanced yourself from us afterwards, and how you were now so rich. They were very convincing. And it was subtle. It went from wanting to just let me know to planting ideas. Pushed me towards punishing you. I can see that now. I was a very receptive audience. They made me think it was all my own idea.'

'Using you to get at me.'

'Yes. Keep their hands clean.'

'But why would he want all of us out of the picture? Because that's what it looks like to me. If you'd gone through with it, I'm sure the Gardaí would've been tipped off. No "we'll send a squad car if we can be bothered". You'd have been caught, blood on your hands.'

Vivienne groaned at the mention.

Finn squeezed her hand now.

'It's okay. You wouldn't have done it, I know you wouldn't have. And that's why there was help – moving things along by sabotaging my scuba gear. All that was needed was you in place, acting suspiciously, and me dead.'

His faith in her was built on shaky ground. The rage was true and all-consuming.

'I agree with Finn,' Mac said as he put his arm around Vivienne's shoulders. Pulling her close. 'In the end, you wouldn't have done it, I know you. You can let this go,' he whispered in her ear.

Finn carried on. 'If this is David, we need to ask ourselves – what does he get, killing me and blaming you? Any ideas? Any grudges, anything he gets to gain? I know he was cross at me at first, after I killed him off. He discovered he was dead when the college emailed his parents. An official 'please don't sue us' commiseration. But he was right there, so they knew he wasn't dead. They wrote it off as an administrative error and, being much like David themselves, they ignored it, unconcerned. He got in touch with me, furious I'd done that. But he soon saw the advantages. Realised he'd never get stuck for child support, wouldn't be followed up for his debts. He never intended coming back to Ireland, so he hung up the phone, thanking me. That was the last communication we ever had. And he seemed to think I'd done him a favour. What about you guys?'

Mac and Vivienne shook their heads simultaneously.

'I don't know,' Vivienne said. 'I'm that twenty-year-old, frozen in time when it comes to David. I can think of nothing. He can't begrudge that Hannah was adopted. He left me no choice by leaving. And other than her, there is no other legacy of our time together.'

'Unless he didn't like the poems I wrote about him, I've got nothing either,' Mac laughed with gallows humour.

'So if he has nothing to gain, shouldn't we ask the same about Alice? Could she have?'

'No,' Finn said, shutting it down completely.

They walked on, all deep in thought, probing memories for any possible link. They kept searching the landscape too for Alice and for David. They slowed down as they approached the faded black pillars of the house near the lighthouse. Vivienne looked down the long drive.

'This is where I saw Alice go after the phone call. Do you know why she was coming here?'

'Yes. We needed a car, we were trying to get away but our keys were missing. I take it that wasn't you guys?'

'No,' Vivienne said. 'It was. I'm sorry, I took them.'

'Ah,' said Finn.

'Sorry,' Vivienne repeated.

'Forget about it.'

Mac was looking around, scanning the horizon. 'About what time did she come up here? Roughly?'

Finn leaned on the pillar, thinking. 'It would have been seven-ish.'

Mac turned and looked down the drive.

'She came back to the lighthouse not long after that. And something had changed. She knew we all knew each other then. She was raging. Something happened here and she found out.'

'What on earth could it have been?' Finn wondered.

All three of them turned and stared down the long drive. They looked at the grey, simple, two-storey farmhouse. A black cat watched them from halfway down the drive. A few drops of rain began to fall.

Vivienne heard footsteps behind her, quickly getting louder. She swung around.

Finn heard them too and turned on a dime.

'Alice?'

FORTY-SIX

It wasn't Alice.

Instead Vivienne found herself looking at a little old lady, white-haired and startled. Her eyes flicked to Mac and stayed there. Vivienne looked at him too, seeing him, seeing them all, through the old woman's eyes. Strangers at her gate, one of those strangers big and broad like Mac. And bloody. It was understandable if she was wary. It would be understandable if she was terrified.

'What... what are you doing at my gate?' she stuttered.

'Ah!' Finn's eyes lit up. 'You must be our neighbour.'

She eyed him suspiciously and said nothing.

'You've met my partner, Alice. Young woman, auburn hair, we're staying in the lighthouse. You gave her eggs. And she came looking for a lift this morning?'

Vivienne saw that Finn had found a crack. The woman's face relaxed a fraction.

'Ah, I see. And is she okay? She rushed off, she seemed upset all of a sudden. It was a bit odd.'

'Well, it's complicated,' Finn said, shooting Vivienne a side glance. 'She hasn't been back, I take it?'

'No.'

The woman looked pointedly at Mac, who Vivienne had to admit looked a state. And she was regretting now not insisting they call an ambulance. He was mess. The old woman's guarded expression threatened to return.

'We're friends of Finn and Alice,' Vivienne said. 'I'm Vivienne, and this is Macdara. He had a small accident – it looks a little alarming, I know.'

'We're having a bit of a day, I'm afraid,' Mac added. His deep baritone vibrated like a cat's purr, and he smiled his gentle, disarming smile, tricks learned over a lifetime to defuse the trepidation inspired by his size.

'Are you Macdara Ryan, by any chance, the poet?'

Mac laughed, surprised. 'I am, that's me. I don't get recognised often.'

The old woman nodded, this recognition changing things.

'You write beautiful words about this part of the world. I know your work. I wondered was it you underneath that nasty bash.'

'It is, indeed.'

'I was a nurse before I retired,' the woman said. 'Would you like me to take a look at your head?'

'Mac, that is a good idea,' Vivienne urged him. He looked at Finn, seeking permission to look after himself. Vivienne pushed down a burst of anger. He was not going to ignore his injuries because Finn wouldn't believe his girlfriend was a danger.

'Mac, do, please,' said Finn.

Mac nodded, then looked at the old woman. 'Okay. Thank you, I would be most grateful.'

'Good. Come with me, let's get you sorted out.'

She started down her long driveway, and they turned to follow.

'I'm Mary,' she said, looking over her shoulder at them.

Finn fell into step beside her. 'Do you mind me asking,

Alice didn't tell me, but what upset her? When she dropped in to you?'

Walking just behind them, Vivienne listened closely.

'Oh, I don't know at all. One moment we were talking about an accident that happened here a long time ago, and then the next she was off out the door, a face on her like she'd seen a ghost.'

Finn shot a look back at Mac and Vivienne.

They reached the door, and Mary guided them in. A dark corridor led to a kitchen that smelled of home baking. She sat Mac in a seat by the fire and came back to him with warm water and a cloth. Standing over him, she squeezed out the excess water and began to dab. Vivienne saw Mac wince, but he didn't say a thing. Mary washed all the blood away, carefully clearing the dark red stains from his hair.

'Is Mac okay?' Vivienne asked.

'You're lucky,' she replied to him, not Vivienne. 'The skull is designed to take a knock or two. And head wounds gush, it can look worse than it is.'

'That's good news...'

She looked up at Finn and Vivienne. 'There are scones in the cupboard, and you can boil a kettle for tea if you fancy. I wouldn't normally be so rude, but your friend here needs attention.'

Vivienne looked at Finn; scones and tea were not quite what she was in the mood for.

'We're fine. But thank you, Mary,' Finn said, using a voice, a tone Vivienne didn't recognise. One full of confidence and ease. That lost little boy she'd first met in university was a faint memory.

'In that case, sit, sit,' Mary said, as Finn and Vivienne stood like strangers at a party. She pointed to her kitchen table. They did as they were told, but Vivienne could see it was hard for Finn. He wanted to be searching, for Alice and for the truth.

'What accident was Alice interested in?' Vivienne asked, mimicking Finn's calm, assured tone. Nothing to see here. She wasn't up to anything.

'It was one that happened a little further up the coast. Twenty-six years ago. She's a young pup,' a glance of disapproval at Finn, 'so it would have happened before she was born. Some young people. One of them died.'

Mary looked up from her work, the cloth now stained red. She squeezed it, and ruddy water splashed into the bowl.

'Perhaps she lost someone in a similar way. Maybe that's why she was upset. Would I be right?'

'I'm not sure,' replied Finn. 'I'll have to ask her.'

Mary looked back down at Mac and dabbed his temple again.

'You don't even need stitches, I don't think. But you will have a nasty bruise and black eye. Let me go fetch some antiseptic and bandages. I'll be back.' She left the room, and they turned to each other, quiet, giving her a moment, then they talked.

'Our accident,' Finn said.

'Clearly,' Vivienne agreed.

'We're missing something though. How did she add it up?' Mac said from his chair by the fire. Then Vivienne's eye fell on a scrapbook pushed to the end of the table. She grabbed it and flicked through powdery pages of disintegrating clippings. She stopped when she found it.

She laid the page open on the table. Their stricken younger selves stared back at them.

'Ah,' Finn said. 'That mustn't have been a fun moment for her.'

'No.'

His shoulders slumped, but then he brightened, sitting up straighter. Vivienne heard steps in the hall. She shut the scrapbook and pushed it back to the end of the table. Mary didn't need to see their younger selves and connect them with the people in her kitchen right now. She came back into the room laden with supplies. With practised hands she anointed Mac with cream, carefully applying a bandage to the wound. Mary was nearly finished with him. It was time to get out of here. They caught Mac's eye. A tiny, near imperceptible nod from him, and he looked up at his nurse, his smile turned on.

'Thank you, Mary,' he said. 'That feels so much better.'

'It might well feel worse again tonight, I warn you. And if you're dizzy, sick or seeing double, don't wait – get to a hospital because that will mean you probably have a concussion.'

'Thank you for looking after our friend.' Vivienne smiled as well at the old woman. 'And don't worry, we'll keep a close eye on our Mac.'

'Good,' she said. 'Keep watching him for twenty-four hours.'

Vivienne nodded. Mac stood and they headed for the kitchen door. Mary followed them as they walked down the hallway.

'Oh,' she said behind them.

'Yes?' Finn turned, eyebrows raised in question.

'The car. Alice, when she came, she said you were having trouble with yours. Is that still a problem?'

'No, that's okay now. Thanks for checking.'

'That's alright. Wanted to be sure. Michael has headed off now to Roche's for some animal feed, so the car is gone again. He'll be back later if anything changes. I'm sure he'd still be happy to drop you anywhere if you need it.'

'You're very kind, Mary, thank you. Hopefully we won't need to ask your son for that favour.'

Mary laughed. They all stopped. There was nothing funny in what Finn had said. Was there?

Finn looked at her, then at Vivienne, an eyebrow raised.

'Oh, I'm sorry,' she said, the chuckle dissipating. 'Michael isn't my son. I'm not married. Though I suppose these days those two things don't go together like they once did.'

'Alice said he was your son.'

Mary bobbed her head like a chicken a few times.

'She just assumed, I imagine. Easy mistake. But no worries, I won't hold it against her.'

'Who is he?' Vivienne asked, feeling dread pull at her edges.

'My lodger!' she replied cheerfully.

'How long?' asked Finn, his voice quivering.

Mary scanned the trio, not oblivious to the change. She looked now like she had when she'd stumbled upon them earlier – wary, suspicious.

'How long has he lodged with me?'

'Yes.'

'Since just after Christmas.'

'Of course,' Vivienne said.

Another confused but curious look from Mary.

'Mary, I know this is an odd question,' Finn said, rolling out his most suave, CEO, trustworthy and persuasive voice. 'But would you have a picture of Michael anywhere? On your phone, perhaps?'

'Oh no, not at all. He's like one of those religious types who thinks cameras will steal your soul! Very camera-shy.'

They all shared a look.

'It's probably nothing,' Finn started, 'but... he might be someone who you... who you might need to be careful of. It's a very long story. But we'd need to see a picture to be sure he's who we think he is.'

'This is all very odd. He's been absolutely fine from day one. He's worked for his board and kept to himself. No problems.'

'We could be wrong,' Mac said. 'But we'd like to be sure. For your sake. I couldn't leave here thinking you might be at risk. Is there anywhere his photo might be? Online? Local Facebook area page? Mart day? Anything?'

'Well, I suppose he might have been in the background of the village mart photo that appeared in the parish newsletter. He brought some sheep down there for me. Let me see.'

She pottered back to the kitchen, and they followed her like ducklings. She rooted among papers, letters, bits and pieces. Finally, with a smile, she picked something up.

'Here it is.' She flicked through it, stopping to study a black-and-white photo on a photocopied page. A smile formed on her face. 'Aha!'

She turned the page round, and they crowded in, eager to see. She raised a finger to point him out, but she didn't need to. They all saw him. In profile, at the back, going somewhere. Caught unawares. Caught.

David was alive. And he was here.

FORTY-SEVEN
ALICE

'I don't think he really saw me? I don't think so!' Michael slammed the steering wheel with the ball of his hand. The car swerved. Alice cringed, forcing herself closer still to the car door. As far away as she could get from this man. He glanced over at her, eyes blazing. His foot pushed down on the accelerator, tearing round narrow roads. They were going to crash if he wasn't careful.

'You, you silly little bitch! This is all your fault. Months of careful planning. Years! A brilliant plan! And you, mystery girl, show up like a one-woman demolition crew! Who the hell are you?' With a quick, darting look at her, he returned his eyes front and centre, back at the road, but his driving didn't improve. They were still careering around sharp bends, Alice thrown around, unable to stop herself, her hands tied together behind her. He wasn't looking for an answer from her either. The rag he'd stuffed in her mouth when he'd grabbed her was still there. Terrified, Alice didn't think she'd have been able to talk even if it wasn't in her mouth.

They'd been driving for what felt like forever. From the

passenger seat Alice had stolen a glance at the clock. It had probably been half an hour, maybe a bit more, since he'd snatched her. They'd been driving all that time, but she wasn't sure he knew where he was going, that he had a plan. He was taking out his rage on the roads. Alice wasn't even sure they were going away from the peninsula. Landmarks in the distance moved away but then came back. Wherever they were, Alice didn't think they were far from where they'd started. It was the only bit of hope she had.

This was Michael. Mary's son. But he looked different with this wild look in his eyes. And he was talking differently too. He had a slight American accent now, which was really very strange. This didn't bode well. Nothing right now was boding well.

'I can't believe you made me break cover. That was the one thing I had going for me! The world thinks I'm long dead thanks to Finn. It's quite the alibi. A dead man can get away with quite a lot. But not if he has to show his face!' Michael slammed the steering wheel again. He hit the horn by accident and the car cried out, startling a couple of horses in the field next to them. They galloped away.

'Macdara would have only had a moment, and I had my hood up, and the scarf too... It was just my eyes and I gave him quite the wallop. Dammit.' Alice listened as he talked rapidly to himself, speaking a mile a minute. 'Should I have killed him? Made it look like part of it? Vivienne on a rampage... dammit, I should have thought about that back there. I suppose it won't matter, if I stopped you in time. It will come out eventually...'

Suddenly, he skidded the car into a layby and hit the brakes. The car tyres sent gravel spitting. The smell of rubber invaded the car interior. Alice was thrown forward and narrowly avoided bashing her head against the dash when Michael grabbed the scruff of her neck, her top choking her in the effort.

He deposited her roughly back down into the passenger seat. With angry hands, he pulled the rag from her mouth. Alice glared, an alliance between fear and anger in her eyes.

'Who are you?' he spat at her. This time he wanted an answer.

'I'm... I'm nobody.'

'That's not true. You're dating the wonderful boss man Mr Tobin. In secret.'

Alice nodded, too afraid to say anything more. She couldn't believe that her worst fear, when she got here on Friday, was that the board would find out about them before she could break the story herself. Now she was in a car with a guy who'd been pretending to be someone else, had assaulted Mac, was driving erratically and didn't seem to care if they crashed and died. And if they didn't die in a blazing car fireball? It didn't feel like it was going to end with a handshake and a 'no hard feelings'.

'You've been quite the spanner in the works. We'd have been done and dusted Friday night if you hadn't been here.' He shook his head and looked away from her. Stared out the windscreen, out to sea. 'And then, getting back in time to get Finn out of the sea? Aw, c'mon! I thought that was definitely going to work.' He turned his head and looked at her, his eyes full of hate. 'But despite this, I tried to be nice about it! I locked the lantern room hatch to keep you out of things. If you'd just stayed put, I wouldn't have had to grab you.'

'If I'd stayed put, I'd have died of hypothermia.'

'You'd have been fine. Don't be dramatic.'

Alice opened her mouth to object, she wasn't being in the least bit dramatic. She was telling the truth. But this guy, he wasn't interested in that.

'So, like everything right now, girlfriend, it's your own fault I had to grab you. Whatever happens next, it's on you. Despite your best efforts, Vivienne was *finally* doing what she was supposed to do and no way was I letting you and the giant teddy-bear-man stop it happening. Fuck's sake.'

'Who are *you*?' Alice couldn't help herself. Throwing his question back at him. She knew who Mac and Vivienne were. She knew they knew Finn. She thought she'd stumbled across all the secrets this weekend had to reveal. But she'd been wrong. Michael had seemed to be the kindly neighbour's son, local farmer and nice guy. Clearly he wasn't. Was anyone who they said they were? Even she wasn't.

'Me? Don't worry about that. You don't need to know.'

He leaned forward and looked at the clock on the dashboard.

'Yeah, yeah, okay, okay... it's been a while, we might have blast-off. It's been nearly fifty minutes, that should be enough. Ring him. Let's see if he's still alive.'

'W-what?'

'I'll dial for you, don't worry. I'm not going to untie you. That'd be a stupid move.'

'I-I don't have a working phone.'

'I know.' He leaned forward and opened the glove compartment in front of her. There, her missing phone. He pulled it out with a grimace.

'I couldn't crack this. Waste of my time stealing it. I just really wanted to know who you were, where you'd come from...'

He rotated the phone in his hand, getting the feel for it. He pressed the home button and it flashed on, looking for a thumbprint. He pushed her forward, Alice grunted in pain, and he twisted her thumb around.

'Owww!' Alice yelped, feeling the joints in her thumb twisted beyond their natural range. Tears of pain and fear and humiliation began to fall. She heard the tell-tale click of the phone unlocking. Michael sat back in his seat, an amused little grin on his face as he looked at it. He tapped and scrolled through the phone.

'I'm feeling less disappointed now. It's completely vanilla.'

Alice sat there in miserable silence. He turned the phone for Alice to see the wallpaper – a picture of her and Finn.

'You're the perfect girlfriend, aren't you?'

Alice flinched, the happy image a gut punch.

'And you sounded so happy together in the lighthouse. Soppy in fact.'

'What do you mean?' Alice was shocked from her silence. 'How do you know how we sounded in the lighthouse?'

'How? I have some of the lighthouse bugged. I heard a lot. How do you think I knew I had to swoop in now and stop you?'

'Have you heard anything else?' Alice asked cautiously, replaying the last few days in her head. Had she said anything inside the lighthouse that suggested she was anyone other than who this guy thought she was? She hoped not, and he wasn't acting as if she had. Knowledge was power right now, and she needed as much of it as she could get.

He looked at her more closely. An eyebrow raised.

'What are you worried I heard? You misbehaving? Have I got it all wrong? Oh, poor Finn! Unlucky in love again. Though, I guess Vivienne is available now... not quite the attractive prospect she was once, granted... but I'll tell you one thing I did learn, listening back over the grumpy whining out of all of you lot. Finn will do anything for you. Even the merest hint of threat to his beloved Alice, and bam! He'll do whatever he's told to do. Do you know how many times Vivienne was able to manipulate him, make him do what she wanted, just by threatening to tell you all his secrets? So. Many. Times! Imagine what he might do if I threatened to harm you! Oh boy! Hot-frickin'-dog!'

'Oh, Finn, I'm sorry,' Alice couldn't help but mutter with tears streaming down her cheeks.

'I'll be keeping that little idea in my back pocket,' Michael said. 'Let's just hope he's dead already and we won't have to pull it out, hmm?'

Alice couldn't suppress a sob. *Oh, Finn. Finn. Finn. Please let him not be dead, oh God.* She wouldn't be able to go on if Vivienne had succeeded.

He turned the phone again for the crying Alice to see. He was looking at her camera roll.

'I like this one, it's cute.' It was one of Alice and Finn, just about to leave his apartment on Friday morning, looking like love's young dream. She was snuggling into him, fitting that space, his arm around her. It looked not just a million years ago to Alice but like a complete alternative universe.

'I'm going to dial him now, and see what's what.'

'And when he answers?' She had to have hope.

'*If* he answers,' he sighed with unhappiness at the prospect, 'well... you'll tell him you got away from the big bad man and... let me see... you're heading back to the lighthouse. You'll see him there. Then at least I'll know where he's at.'

'He knows my phone was missing, he'll know something's up.'

'You can just tell him you finally found it. Simple.'

'What makes you think I'll help you set him up?' Alice spat.

'Good point,' he said.

He reached out, and with a crack, he slapped Alice hard across the face with her phone.

Alice cried out. Her ears rang and her cheek stung. Tears and snot streamed down her face.

Michael pointed the phone at her and took a photograph. He examined the shot.

'Well then, plan B it will have to be. Where I won't need your help. I told you he'll do anything for you. If he's still alive, I'll use this little gem to do what we can to rectify the situation.' He turned the phone for her to see. Her pathetic, red-faced terror and misery on full display. 'But hopefully it won't come to that.'

Alice felt tears of despair mix in with those of pain.

'Right,' he said. 'Let's make this call. Let's see if you're single again!'

FORTY-EIGHT

VIVIENNE

They all stared at the photo. Mac had caught a glimpse of David earlier, enough to trigger a quarter-century-old familiarity. But this photo showed him clearly, not covered up as Mac had described. David was there, in all his shocking glory.

'He's here,' Finn whispered, as if David were in the next room. 'He's really here.'

Vivienne understood Finn's caution. This ghost – no, this demon – must have been summoned by some incantation.

'What's wrong with Michael?' Mary asked, disturbing their shock.

'Who's Michael?' Vivienne asked.

Mary touched the photograph as if Vivienne were an imbecile. 'Michael, my lodger, this guy. Who you're so interested in.'

'David,' Vivienne corrected her. 'His name is actually David. David Johnson.'

'But, Mary, if you see him, don't call him that,' Finn said, shooting Vivienne an annoyed glance. She realised that maybe she shouldn't have told Mary his real name. It might put her at risk if David realised they were on to him. And it would definitely let him know they were on to him. Finn was right.

The old lady looked properly worried now. No one liked someone with a fake name.

'Am I in danger? Should we call the Guards?' She looked down the hall to her landline.

'We called them already,' Vivienne said, leaving out the part where they hadn't believed her.

'And?' Mary was too sharp for Vivienne.

'They're coming, but they mightn't have us as a priority.'

'Oh, I don't like this at all. What's wrong with him? What did he do?'

'Does he have a laptop? Or a computer of any sort?' Vivienne asked. 'It would really help us if we could take a look at it.'

Mary shrugged. She might know the answer, but panic was taking over. All she could think about was her own safety.

'Do you have anyone who can come get you?' Vivienne suggested. 'You're not in danger, but if you wanted to get out of here, you might feel better.'

'My sister...'

'That sounds good,' Mac piped up. 'Come on, let's go call her.'

Finn looked at Vivienne and then at the stairs.

'Is his room upstairs?' Vivienne asked.

Mary hesitated, Vivienne watching her weigh everything up. Who were the bad guys? Were they a threat, or were they saving her? She was in danger either way – from them or from David. Vivienne saw the moment the decision was made. Mary was getting out of there, leaving them to sort it out.

'Top of the stairs. At the end of the corridor.'

'Thank you!' Finn called out, already hurrying up the staircase. Mac took Mary to the phone, and Vivienne raced after Finn, taking the stairs two at a time.

'Down here,' Finn said, his cheeks flushed, his eyes wide. Vivienne ran down the corridor after him, reaching him as he pushed open a white-painted wooden door.

They both stood in the doorway. The room was sparsely furnished and untidy, clothes lying on the unmade bed and on the back of the single chair in the room. A small wood-veneered wardrobe listed in the corner, its doors not fully shut. On a small pine desk, littered with empty beer bottles and dirty mugs, was a laptop. Finn sat and opened it.

It lit up.

'Okay, let's see if he's been sending some emails. And let's see if Alice has anything to do with him.'

A screen opened, asking for a password.

'Damn,' Vivienne said.

Finn looked up at her, a cheeky grin on his face. 'Don't worry, that is baby stuff.' His fingers began to fly. The screen changed from a familiar blue to strange black pages, streaming reams of white code. 'I'm not a tech CEO for nothing. There is always a back door.'

More familiar applications and programs flickered to life as well as a window for something she didn't recognise. He opened what looked like an email application and others. His hands flurried some more, the click of keys a frantic clattering.

'Well...' Finn turned the laptop around. He clicked on a folder with a strange lock-like symbol embedded in it. 'Do these look familiar?'

Vivienne leaned in and started to read. She knew all these emails by heart. 'Dear Ms O'Brien, it troubles me to have to send you this email, but I felt it was something you needed to hear... your college friend Finn Tobin... held David down, long enough to incapacitate him... I learned that his actions were all due to their discovery of some of the missing gold...' And then she saw her shocked but excited replies. She had been shaken from her habitual misery. Thinking David had been murdered, that it hadn't been an accident, had energised her. Woken her from her torpor. Given her someone to blame and exact revenge on. It had made her feel in control again. She had drunk from these emails like a woman parched.

And now she was ashamed. Ashamed that Finn got to read these. See how happy she'd been to believe he'd done this awful thing. How enthusiastically she had replied and let David manipulate her. Twisted her to his will.

'I'm sorry...' She could feel her face burn. This humiliation. Her old friend.

'No apologies,' Finn said quietly.

They heard the door slam shut downstairs. Then heavy steps on the stairs.

'Where are you?' Mac's voice called.

Vivienne stuck her head out the door. 'Here! She's gone already?'

Mac trotted down the corridor to her. 'Sister only lives down the road. They're going to head to her niece in Letterkenny, get right out of Dodge. I'm glad she's gone. It was a good move.' He spotted Finn at the desk. 'Find out anything?'

'The emails, that was definitely him,' Finn said, pointing at the screen, but maybe for her sake he moved on quickly. He was soon searching again.

'And what's at the heart of it?' Mac asked. 'Why is he doing this? Can you tell?'

'Yeah,' Vivienne said, 'why is he out to get us?'

'I don't know yet... but... let me look. He's encrypted everything. It would keep most people out, but – not to brag – for me it's a bit flimsy. He should have worked harder with me in college. Not skipped out on all those programming classes with Prof Clarke. He had potential but he never... Okay, I'm in. Let me see what he's so keen to keep hidden here.'

Mac and Vivienne stood behind him, watching the windows open and close. Old emails, documents, one after the other.

'Right... this is interesting. He was in contact with some

legal people, and some programmers... What's that all about? Okay... okay... oh.' Finn jabbed a key, minimising a window. He jerked his head around involuntarily, checking to see if Vivienne had seen it. She'd noticed one word.

Adoption.

'What was that? Show me!'

'It's nothing, Vivienne—'

'Open it!'

He hesitated but then clicked some keys, and the screen came alive with the hidden file.

'It's nothing really. But he did search for Hannah. That's what this is. He doesn't seem to have gotten very far.'

Vivienne's eyes scanned the file, and she saw that Finn was right. It looked like idle curiosity, nothing serious on his part. Like looking up an ex on social media, scratching a curious itch on a tipsy Friday night. A few notes from adoptee websites. The scant details he had. Nothing more. It would have been the final insult if he'd gotten further in finding Hannah than she had. The parent who had wanted her. Who had loved her.

'How dare he,' she spat.

Mac put his arm around her, pulling her close with his warmth and his safe, strong arms.

Finn looked up. 'I'm looking at his finances too. He's penniless. It looks like he had a property repossessed over in the States. He's bankrupt. I can see a bit of a trail here, going back around fifteen years in his emails – financial troubles, getting worse. It looks like he got a small inheritance when his parents passed away around seven years ago, but he squandered that too.'

'He's broke and desperate?' Mac asked.

'Looks like it.'

More searching from Finn.

'Oh!' He laughed a shocked little laugh. 'Look at this. Look, see how popular we've been...' Finn pointed to the browser search history he had just restored. Vivienne O'Brien. Vivi O'Brien. Hannah O'Brien. Hannah Johnson. Macdara Ryan. Mac Ryan. MCD Poet. Macdara Ryan POET. And then there was Finn's name. And pages and pages of searches. Finn Tobin. TobinTech. Finn Tobin applications. Finn Tobin net worth. Everything about TobinTech. Everything David could think of to scrape the internet for every last morsel of Finn's life, professional and personal.

'Wow.' Mac whistled.

'Nice he hadn't forgotten us,' Vivienne said.

Finn minimised the browser and kept looking through the remaining folders. He stopped and opened a document named *Fanad / Calendar*.

'Hmm. Bloody Paula.'

'Who's Paula?' asked Vivienne.

Finn shook his head. 'My assistant. She's been using her birthday again for a password.' He pointed at the screen. 'David has half my calendar hacked here. That's how he knew I was coming up here all the time, specifically to the lighthouse. Christ.'

'And any closer to working out what this was all for? What he was up to?'

'Not really... but I'm pretty sure of one thing.'

'What?'

'Alice isn't involved in whatever it is. There is no sign of her anywhere on this device. No emails, no Google searches, no IP trails back to my apartment or office. No hint of any connection at all.'

'Yay, Alice is innocent.' Vivienne couldn't keep the sarcasm out of her voice. 'She's just up to nice fluffy blackmail, you know.'

'We needed to rule her out, Viv! That she isn't working with him, that she didn't get into that car willingly. We needed to know how urgent this is!'

Finn jumped up, terrified, adrenaline sparking from him, ready for the fight. 'We have to go save her!'

'She is in danger, for sure,' Mac said.

'Thank you, Mac, for focusing on what's important.' Finn looked at Vivienne. 'I'm not saying she doesn't have her own agenda. But we need to find her.'

'Hang on,' Mac said, touching Finn's arm. 'I know we have to find her and find her quick, but are we finished here? Whatever he's been doing, it's been worth trying to kill you and incite us to do the same. He's not messing about.'

'I know, but—'

'Why is he doing this, Finn? What's his plan? We need to give it a few more minutes here to see if we can work that out. This is too serious to risk running in blind. And, like, where are they? We haven't a clue. I really doubt they're at the lighthouse. They could be halfway to Dublin by now. If you take another minute, have a look, maybe it'll give us a clue where to find them.'

Struggling, Finn nodded a tight, frustrated nod. He sat down again, looking back at the screen, his face burning.

Vivienne looked closely at the screen too. She squinted her eyes. The browser search history was still open. She read a few search terms and the websites they brought up.

'What are those ones about?' She pointed at intellectual property, code protection, heuristic algorithms, ownership.

Finn read the one she'd shown him, his lips moving silently with each word.

The colour drained from his face.

'What is it?' she asked, but he ignored her. He went back to what looked like emails. And there were even more documents, pages and pages of dense, unrelenting text.

'Well,' Finn slumped back into the chair, his hands on his lap, not the keys, 'this explains it all.'

FORTY-NINE

Finn kept them waiting. Searching more documents. His face darkening as he did so.

'What have you found? What was he doing?' Mac asked.

Finn took a deep breath, and when he spoke his voice wavered. 'He's after my life's work.'

'What?' Vivienne leaned closer.

'TobinTech. He's going to claim I stole the idea for the core code from him. And that he's owed all the money the company has earned in the last twenty years.'

'But that's preposterous!' Mac exclaimed. 'That was all you!'

Finn touched the screen. 'This is legal advice from some top lawyers in New York. They tell him he has a strong case. They're offering to represent him pro bono because he has nothing. But they're eager. And,' Finn flipped between tabs, 'these are his college transcripts. A full breakdown of all his marks and modules, including his top marks for Professor Clarke's project. And somehow – could he have had it all this time? – a copy of that project from twenty-six years ago.'

'I thought that was you,' Mac said, searching Finn's face.

'It was me. Completely, one hundred per cent me. Inside and out. But remember how we were all trying to help him pass his exams? Viv, you were cramming with him every spare hour you had after your own study, and Mac, you kept him fed and watered, making his every meal so he didn't have to do anything but study? Well, I went a step further. A stupid step further. I put his name on the project.'

'You did what? Finn!' Mac cried.

Finn held his hands up. 'Well, it's more accurate to say I didn't take his name off it. Prof Clarke had set it as a group project. David and I decided to work together, but he did nothing. He contributed absolutely zero. I could have gone to Prof Clarke and explained it all. He knew me well enough – and more importantly, he knew David well enough – to know I was telling the truth and it was all my work. But I didn't do it. I thought I could help him pass his exams, get him through. I knew the project was going to get a great mark. I thought it might even be enough to drag up his average overall. I thought I was going to save him. Christ.'

'But he can't do this!' Mac cried.

'But he can! As far as the college is concerned, this was a joint project. The work is just as much his as mine in their eyes. After he "died", I didn't see the need to correct the mistake. In fact, I wanted as far away as possible from all things David.'

'What about this professor guy?' Mac asked.

Finn chuckled sadly. 'He died ten years ago. I gave the eulogy at his funeral! He was the only person who could have verified that it was my work and my work alone. Without Prof Clarke, it would be my word against David's.'

'But he's legally dead, no? How can he do all this?'

'Sure, all he needs to do is turn up in the courtroom and it'll be pretty clear he's not.'

'It couldn't be that simple?' said Vivienne.

'Of course not, but, it's certainly just a technicality. His lawyers could get it straightened out I imagine. And then off he goes to make his claim.'

'Jesus,' Vivienne whispered. 'How much is TobinTech worth?'

'Fifty million euros.'

Mac whistled. 'He gets half that?'

'If he takes a legal case and wins, which he has legal advice telling him he has a very strong chance of doing...'

'I don't get it,' Vivienne said. 'If he could walk away with twenty-five million, if his lawyers – and you, it seems – think he'd have a strong chance of doing so, then what the hell is he doing here, trying to get us to kill you? For the full fifty million with you dead. Greed? That seems stupid, but for all his flunking out of college, he was never stupid.'

'I think...' Finn closed his eyes, running his own code through his head, running it to all its logical conclusions. 'I think he knows he'd face a few problems. Because, unlike his lawyers, he knows he's lying. If we faced off in court, I'd only need five minutes face to face, and I could demonstrate he doesn't have a clue. It would be thrown out of court in minutes. If I'm dead, though, and not able to show what a charlatan he is, then he has enough evidence to stand a strong chance of walking away with, if not all of it, then enough to keep him in the lap of luxury for a lifetime.'

'And us?' Mac asked.

'You guys were the only ones who might have been able to cast any doubt on his claim. What would you have said if he popped up after I died, claiming it was all him?'

'We'd have kicked up a stink,' Mac said.

'Thanks, Mac,' Finn smiled. 'I think you would have, alright. You guys were my best friends. You are good people.' His voice caught, emotion overwhelming him.

Mac squeezed his shoulder. Vivienne reached out, placing her hand beside Mac's.

Finn took a deep breath. And then another one.

'I think,' he continued slowly, 'I think he'd have framed you for my death, using the fact that I lied to you about his death as your motivation. It's quite convincing, wouldn't you agree? David dying ruined your lives... why wouldn't you take revenge on the person who did that? It's so very, very neat. I would have been gone, paving the way for him to claim his rightful share, and more. And you guys would have been locked up for murder with an ironclad case, all your credibility destroyed.'

A stunned silence descended on the room as they absorbed the weight of Finn's words.

Finn stood up. 'We need to find him. We need to find Alice. If he's seeing his fifty million slipping out of sight, he might get desperate. Showing himself to Mac tells us he's already taking risks. Bad things happen when people get desperate. We have to find her before it's too late.'

A vibration shook the desk into life. They turned as one to its source – Finn's phone. It was ringing.

FIFTY

ALICE

'This is a good sign,' Michael said with a smile, the phone flat on his hand in between the pair of them as it rang and rang. No one answering. Alice prayed it was just the confusion of seeing her number on Finn's screen that was causing the delay. Was he debating whether it was her or the crazy guy? Was he frantically trying to come up with a plan?

Michael, finger hovering over the red hang-up button, was grinning.

'Er, hello?'

Finn's voice! Tentative and unsure, but alive, it rang like celebratory clocktower bells through the speaker. Michael punched the side of the door.

'Oh thank God!' Alice blurted out.

Michael jabbed the mute button and held up a fist to her face. 'You say nothing that I don't tell you to say! Alright? Dammit. Can't believe she didn't do it. Again. Fuck. What am I going to do?'

'Alice. Is that you, Alice?' Finn's voice, swapping its tentative tone for increased anxiety, filled the car.

'Answer him. Tell him you're okay. Try to find out what

went wrong, where the others are. I want to know everything that's going on. Do it or I'll send him that picture of you and lure him to the lighthouse and kill him myself, okay?'

Michael unmuted the phone and pointed to Alice.

'Finn?' Her voice was weak and wobbly.

'Alice! It is you! Where are you? Are you okay? Are you with... eh, are you with Mary's son Michael?'

Michael shook his head.

'Eh, no. No, I got away. I'm okay. Are you okay?'

'I am, don't worry. Where are you? We can come and get you. Vivienne had the car keys all along.'

Michael shook his head vigorously.

'No, it's okay, I'm on my way back, I can meet you there. But Finn, what happened? I was afraid Vivienne was going to hurt you.' Alice's head dipped. She was struggling to keep from breaking down into racking sobs. She felt like whatever she did now, she was going to put Finn in danger. Whether she was forced to get Finn to reveal his location or Michael used her picture to lure Finn to the lighthouse, she couldn't find a way out. If only Finn could tell something was wrong from her voice. Was there anything she could say to warn him? Anything he'd understand, but Michael wouldn't?

'I'm okay, she didn't hurt me. And everything is all okay now. Vivienne is with me. So is Mac.' Alice watched Michael stiffen. He didn't like that. Alice cowered inside. How much more dangerous might he get if driven to it?

'We're at Mary's,' Finn continued, 'and Mac is okay.'

'Oh thank God, I was so worried,' she said.

'There's so much I need to tell you, Alice. Honestly, where are you? Let us at least meet you part-way?'

Improvise, mouthed Michael.

'No, it's okay, I'm, I'm nearly back at the lighthouse...' The misery tears were threatening again.

'Alright, we'll head back there now too. But you have to promise me one thing.'

'What?'

'Keep a very close eye out for Mary's son. Make sure he doesn't find you again. He's not who he claims to be.'

Alice looked up at Michael, her eyes widening further in fear. Like the slap of a minute ago, Finn's words seemed to whip and sting Michael. His cheeks burned and his eyes bulged. He looked like he was tipping on a precipice.

He jabbed the mute button and near foaming at the mouth hissed, 'Make him tell you more.'

Alice hiccupped and sobbed. 'Please. Pl-please—'

'Now!' He raised his fist to her face, then unmuted the phone.

Alice gulped in some raggy breaths, desperate to keep them quiet as possible. 'Wh-what do you mean? Who is he?'

'Are you sure you're alright, Al?'

'Uh-huh.' All she could manage was a sound; words would lead to tears.

'Look, I know you found out that I know Vivienne and Mac. I'm sorry for lying to you, and I will explain. But right now the most important thing is for me to warn you to keep on your guard. Michael, Mary's son, is really David. Vivienne's ex who everyone thought was dead. He's been trying to kill me and set up Viv and Mac.'

'NO!' Michael – really David – roared. With the force of an atomic cloud the bellow shook the car. He dropped the phone and with his fist beat the sides of the door and his seat, the steering wheel and the dash. Alice ducked away from him, making herself as small as possible in the passenger seat.

'Alice! What was that? What's going on?' From the footwell, Finn's voice echoed, fear quivering in his voice.

'Not what! But who!' David screamed at the phone on the car floor.

There was silence from Finn. Alice could hear he was still there, the line hadn't dropped. She began to sob.

David was panting, his furious energy electrifying his whole body. It was as if his rage had, hulk-like, made him bigger, stronger, more dangerous. Finally wrestling himself under control, he spoke again to the waiting Finn.

'Hello, old friend,' he spat. 'It's been a while!'

FIFTY-ONE

'David, you need to let Alice go.'

'Do I? I think perhaps it's the opposite. I need to hold onto her.'

David leaned down, found the phone on the floor and picked it up. Without hanging up, he sent the photo he'd taken of Alice, bound and crying.

'Take a look at that.'

Alice heard the gasp Finn tried to mask. She thought she heard a few other voices with him. What calibre of cavalry were Finn, Mac and Vivienne?

'I'm calling the Guards, David. You're adding kidnapping and assault to attempted murder.'

'You call them and you'll never see her again. Don't forget, I'm dead, I can slip away and no one will find me.'

There was another long pause at the other end of the line as Finn weighed up his options.

With a dart, David hung up the phone. He put it down by the gearstick.

'What?' Alice couldn't help blurting out. 'Why'd you do

that?' It had only been a phone connection, but just Finn's voice had made her feel less desperate.

David looked at her, sneering.

'I need to think. To re-evaluate. I spent a long bloody time putting that plan in place. It was foolproof. It was going to work.'

She heard her phone ring but David ignored it.

'Why are you doing this?' Alice whimpered. 'What did Finn ever do to you?'

'What did Finn do to me? Ha!' David looked genuinely amused. Then the smile fell away from his eyes. 'He killed me. That's what he did.'

Alice looked at David, who was now staring out the window at the sea. The wind was picking up and the waves were getting stronger, angrier, crashing against the shore. From the horizon, storm clouds were moving, heading for land.

Killed him? What on earth did that mean? David appeared to be very much alive right now.

Alice's phone kept ringing.

'I saw that business profile – quite by accident,' he said, ignoring Alice's question. 'I felt it was the universe reaching out to help me. Seeing his face after all these years. Little Finn Tobin, computer nerd. He's done pretty well for himself. Unlike me.'

He looked at Alice, eyes a little unfocused. He wasn't really seeing her, his vision somewhere far away, in the past.

'When he decided to tell the others that I was dead – and not just skipping out on them – I thought that it could be my big opportunity to be free and start again. No baby. No college failure. But it ended up just swapping problems. The college credits I'd managed to accumulate here? Couldn't use them there 'cause I was "dead". Funnily enough, dead men don't matriculate. I'd have to have started again, but college is too expensive at home. That was why I'd come to Ireland in the first place! Mom was born here so I could go to school cheap. My parents weren't impressed and kicked me out. I couldn't explain to them why I had to start at the beginning again, and they'd have to pay for it. They thought I was being a lazy asshole.

'And, after a few years, the idea of being a father didn't seem quite so scary, you know? I'd loved Vivi, I really had. I wouldn't be the first man to panic when he realised he had a child on the way. I decided to come back, restart where I'd left off. But I couldn't. I contacted the hospital and tried to correct the records but all that happened was the doctor Finn had paid to help "kill" me was fired. They started making noises of prosecuting me too. I did some googling and realised I'd need a court order to sort it all out. But by then I discovered Vivienne had given up the baby. I realised there was nothing left here to restart. So I've lived a shitty life that's gone nowhere. I've never settled down, and the older I get, the more I think about the child. My child. I never had any more. Hannah was it. And Finn Tobin took away any chance I had to know her. To be a *father*. Finn took everything from me.'

The last words, Finn's name especially, carried such venom it could have poisoned them both. Alice's phone, which hadn't stopped ringing since David had hung up, started a fresh attempt to get through to them. David picked it up. Stared at it for a moment, then clicked answer.

'Oh thank God! Alice, Alice, are you okay? Are you there?'

'She's fine, don't get your panties in a bunch.'

'David—'

'Shut up.' David cut him off. Finn did as he was told and went quiet. 'Here's what we're going to do. Revised plan. I'm going to let you live. I'm tired. I want to be done with this. But you're gonna pay me off. Five million dollars. Which is a bargain. If I find you and finish what I started, getting my share of TobinTech? That'd be ten times more.'

'But—'

'Don't talk. You find a nice, neat way to transfer that to me, untraceable. And, in return, I won't kill your girlfriend.'

'David, you've got the wrong idea about my wealth...'

'Don't lie to me! You have that money!'

Finn sighed down the line. 'Being worth that amount and having access to that amount of money are two different things! If you give me a few weeks I could realise five million, sure. Transfer it to a Cayman's account. But right now? I can't do that. You're a smart man, David, you have to know I don't have my wealth in gold coins in bags, all locked up in a room waiting for a ransom demand!'

David hung up and threw the phone across the dashboard of the car. It skittered to a halt not far from Alice. But with her hands tied behind her back it was of little use to her. Hands that were tingling painfully from restraint. Wrists that were aching and sore.

David spotted how close it was to her and leaned over, snatching it back. He wasn't taking any chances.

'He's not lying,' Alice said, her voice more full of fear than she would have liked. She wished she could sound tough and brave, not terrified as she was. 'He's... he's wealthy on paper but he wouldn't have lots of cash. And if he tried, people would notice. It would draw attention to him. To you.'

'Christ!' David growled. He looked at her, eyes narrowed, a snarl on his lips. 'So, how much then? How much do you think he could rustle up quickly and not draw attention? What can he pay for you?'

'I don't know, I'm an analyst, not his accountant... but maybe five hundred thousand?'

'Five hundred? One per cent of what I could get? You're making me think going back to killing him and framing the others is the best plan.'

'No!'

'No? I don't think you get a vote.'

Like before, the phone started ringing and didn't stop.

David turned the key in the ignition and pulled out. He turned the car and tore down the road, throwing Alice back and forth. She slammed into the side of the door, twisting herself, putting her shoulder facing the dash in the hope that she could avoid being thrown head first against it if he stopped suddenly. Twisted, she was facing him now. Watching his face, a symphony of grim determination. She had to stop him.

'Please. David. Please. Think about it... it's not nearly as much, but won't it be much easier to move on? Rebuild? You kill Finn, you're risking going to prison, for the rest of your life. And it'll be much harder to get away with now we all know what's going on. You'll have to kill us all. But five hundred thousand, Finn could square it away as a gift to an old friend. You can slip away and put this all behind you. You wouldn't have to look over your shoulder. It would be over.'

David said nothing. Letting Alice's words sink in.

He spun the steering wheel, careering around a sharp bend. Alice was thrown and walloped against the dash, her side taking the impact. She muffled her cry of pain, winded.

'Nope! I want more. I want it all.'

Alice tried to get her breath back. To talk to this man. To convince him. She had to stop him from hurting Finn.

'Th-think about it. I bet he can bring you back to life as part of it? Finn's a powerful guy, I'm sure he could call in some favours, make it right? He owes you that.'

Alice sat there. Bracing herself as best she could as he drove like a man possessed. Using her battered shoulders and feet to steady herself in her space. If he kept on like this, she wouldn't be alive to be used as a bargaining chip if she could convince him to go back to that idea. The phone kept ringing. Ringing and ringing. Left unanswered.

'My lawyers were going to sort that out for me.'

'Sure, but that still comes with the risk of being found out as a murderer. If you let Finn do it, then you get 500k and your life back, and, as I said, no risk of it all backfiring on you.'

'Get my life back, do I? It's far too late for that.'

'I don't think that's completely true.'

'No?'

'No. What about your daughter?'

FIFTY-TWO

David slammed on the brakes.

Alice crashed against the dashboard, the pain blinding.

'What about my girl?' He grabbed Alice by the arm and hauled her back onto the seat. The sky had darkened. The black, laden clouds were here. Fat, lazy raindrops began to land on the windscreen, exploding like water bombs.

Alice breathed through the pain. More tears she couldn't control.

'If you weren't dead, she could find you. Right now if she does a search, you died before she was born. That's probably the info the adoption agency has too.' She looked at him. 'But if the records were corrected here... isn't that something to live for?'

He said nothing. The only sounds were the waves and rain outside and the phone ringing incessantly inside.

'If you weren't dead, *you* could find *her*... you could do a lot to track her down with half a million.'

'I could.' He stared out to sea. Stilled.

'I bet she'd love to know you.'

He looked at Alice. A sly, sad sneer crossed his face.

'Don't try and butter me up, girl,' he hissed.

Alice shrank back.

But they stayed there. Staring out to sea.

'It's why I hate him most,' he said. His voice a low monotone. 'It's the pain that's grown while all the others have dulled. Does she look like me? Does she love the water as much as I always did? Does she love a practical joke? My parents are gone now. I've no brothers or sisters. It's just me... on my own. The last stop.'

'Then this is your chance. Maybe your last chance? But choose Finn's way. Because your way means you probably have to kill her birth mother. Sure, maybe she'd never find out... but maybe she would. Do a deal with Finn and you get money, no police looking for you, and a real possibility to know Hannah someday.'

'How old are you?'

'Twenty-five.'

'She'd be about your age. What was your dad like, was he good to you?'

'Ha, no. I never knew him. It messed me up.'

David looked back out to sea.

'Maybe she's messed up too. I tried to find her online. But I couldn't. I don't think I knew where to start.'

'Doesn't my plan sound like the best bet then? I know you're angry at Finn. Him paying that doctor to kill you off. But I know Finn. He'd want to make this right. He'll agree to this deal, I know he will. You'll walk away with half a million and a future. Maybe even a family. Isn't that worth it? Revenge just eats you up. It cuts you open and rips out all your love and hope, and then it stitches you back up with bitterness and hate. It's no life. You're right.'

David stared at her. As if really seeing her for the first time. The car shook as a gust of wind raced by. A seagull screamed and swooped out to sea. The phone kept ringing. Alice worried it might run out of charge before David could be convinced not to kill them all. Because that was certainly what was at stake, not just Finn's life. But Mac's and Vivienne's too. And hers. They all knew too much.

He picked up the phone. Answered it.

'Okay,' he said before Finn had a chance to say a word, 'here's the deal.'

He outlined Alice's plan to a listening Finn. Five hundred thousand, as a gift, no threat of legal repercussions. And bringing him back to life.

'If you hadn't done what you did, paying off that doctor, I could have come back. You closed that off for me. Vivienne might have been able to keep Hannah. Everyone's lives mightn't have gotten so messed up. I think you're getting a fair deal. But it has to happen today. I want the money transferred by this evening.'

'David, that's a big sum... I could do it for tomorrow or the next day. But today, that'll be hard. I'll do my—'

'You have till eight tonight. I'll be at the lighthouse, with your girlfriend, then. You'll have made the arrangement with the money. You will come alone. You will have proof of the legal, above-board payment, and you can have her back. You will have also instructed a solicitor to investigate invalidating the death certificate with no negative blowback on me. You will *not* ring the cops. Anything less and I kill her. And I mean that about the Gardaí... you involve the cops, I'll kill her just to punish you.'

'Understood. Okay. I'll make it work. Just don't hurt her.'

'Lighthouse. Eight o'clock.'

David hung up the phone.

FIFTY-THREE

VIVIENNE

'Call the Gardaí, call them now!' Vivienne said the second David hung up for the third time.

'No,' Finn replied.

'Sorry, what?' Vivienne blinked back disbelief.

'You called them earlier and they didn't believe us!'

'That was different, Finn! It sounded like we were talking a load of nonsense then. Now we have an actual person who is missing, kidnapped. We can just show them that picture he sent you! We have evidence.'

Finn shook his head.

'Viv, no.'

'Come on, Finn. Listen to her,' Mac chimed in, his face a riot of anxiety.

Finn shook his head again. 'I'm going to do what he asks.'

'What?' Vivienne exploded. She wanted to grab Finn and shake him. What insanity was this? 'Why would you do that?'

'Because it's fair!' he shouted back. He stood up from David's computer, shoving the chair aside.

He looked at the pair of them. 'I ruined all your lives by killing him off. His included. He never asked me to do that. He certainly never asked me to bribe a doctor to make it happen. I panicked. If I'd told you the truth, you could have reached out to him. He might have changed his mind. It might have all been okay.'

'Finn, he's been trying to *kill* you. You owe him nothing.'

'I drove him to it.'

'Oh man, you didn't,' Mac said, reaching out to take hold of Finn's hand. 'I forgive you, Finn. You don't need it, but I give it to you anyway. You don't have to do things this way. David is dangerous. You can't trust him. You can't trust him to give you back Alice safely.'

'I'm going to have to believe he will. And I think he will. I heard it in his voice.'

'Oh well, that's okay then, you heard it in his voice!' Vivienne laughed, a bitter laugh at the naivety, the stupidity of her old friend. Was he so crushed by guilt that he was willing to do this?

'Viv, you're not helping.' Mac glared at her.

She rolled her eyes. 'I'm surrounded by fools.'

'I understand that you disagree. That makes sense. But I'm going to do this. You don't have to help. I won't blame you. But I've got,' he looked at the time on his phone, 'about seven hours to raise half a million euro. I'm going to need every second to do that. You can go, that's okay, if you want no more part of this. You've been through enough for a lifetime as it is.'

'Finn, you can't risk this for her.'

'Why not?' He looked at Vivienne with innocent eyes, ignoring the truth they all knew.

'Don't act the innocent. She's been lying to you. She's been up to something and we have no clue what that is. Sure, she's not in league with David. But you have no guarantee that what she is up to isn't worse than what he had planned! And now you're going to risk dealing with David – giving him money! – on your own, with no Gardaí, and he's been planning for months to kill you. And already nearly succeeded once this weekend. And you'd do it all for her? This stranger?'

'David isn't the risk.' Finn looked at his feet. His breathing was unsteady, his voice cracked and broken. 'David isn't the risk. Happiness is.'

He looked up, meeting Vivienne's eye. 'And it's a risk I'm willing to take. I love her, Viv. Even if she's a tenth of who I think she is, I need to do this to save her.'

'Idiot,' Vivienne said, but the venom was gone. She, who had pined away years of her life for a love that never was, couldn't judge him.

She looked at Mac. He nodded.

'We're with you.'

Finn's face softened. 'Thank you,' he whispered.

And Vivienne felt a chill. Alice had better be worth it.

FIFTY-FOUR

ALICE

The rain stopped falling after an hour. It felt like the air was being used up in the car. The windscreen foggy like a car parked at a lovers' lane. Only here the two of them sat in silence. Waiting. She could barely feel her hands any more, but her pleas for him to loosen her bindings fell on heedless ears. She leaned against the side of the car, all her quiet attempts to release herself without him seeing came to nothing. She could feel her eye, the left one which had taken the weight of the slap, swell and partly close.

The other phone had rung. Alice had nearly gotten another slap as he'd manhandled her, looking for the source of the buzzing. Tiny fragments of Molly's name had flashed up on the broken screen. And Alice had felt a flash of hope. Maybe David would answer it. Somehow give the game away and Molly would call the police. Alice had then laugh-cried to herself. Molly could barely manage to cook for herself. She wouldn't be foiling any kidnappings today.

'What's this phone – who's ringing you?' David had demanded, holding it up.

'Just my crazy mam,' she'd replied without hope. 'It's just a phone for her.'

David pressed the off button, shutting down the phone. Something Alice had done on many occasions over the years when it had gotten too much for her. Molly wouldn't even register this as anything unusual. She'd just store up some added vitriol for Alice when she did eventually take her call. This time would be no different. This wouldn't be the clue that pushed Molly to finally wake from her torpor and call the Guards.

Slowly, the close, warm atmosphere, the stress, the late night and early morning, the sheer mental exhaustion, the waiting, dragged Alice off to sleep. An uncomfortable, uneasy unconsciousness devoid of rest.

She was woken by the movement of the car. Her head knocking against the window. The one eye that could, opened. It was dark. The sun set early in Donegal in late autumn, at only four or five in the afternoon. But it felt later than that still. There were no stars out, storm clouds hiding the heaven's jewels. Hiding their beauty. The sea was roaring and the wind was wild. They were speeding down the tiny country roads.

She could see the lighthouse beam ahead. It was time, it seemed.

She turned her head slightly, looking at David. He was gripping the steering wheel, knuckles white.

'We're nearly there,' he said.

'I saw the lighthouse,' Alice croaked, her throat achingly dry. She coughed. Her head hurt.

He said nothing more until they hit the familiar lighthouse drive. There were no lights on in the building. It was only the pulsing light from above and the car's headlights that illuminated the peninsula. The tyres crunched along the drive. He was going slowly, carefully in this almost total darkness.

'Whatever you do, don't think of getting clever.' He stopped the car a moment, leaned across and opened the glove compartment in front of Alice. She flinched out of his way. He snatched something from within. In the darkness, which invaded the car as much as the outside world, she couldn't make out what he'd taken.

She heard a metallic snap. And then a cold object stroked across her cheek. A knife. Alice froze.

'I will use this if I have to,' he said. 'It's sharp. Very sharp. And it's nearly killed before. I used it to damage your boyfriend's diving equipment. It slid through the plastic like butter. It could do the same to your throat.'

'I w-won't do a thing. I promise,' Alice whimpered, willing this all to be over. It was so close. She wanted them all to get out of this alive. She'd done everything she could to help make sure that happened.

He started the car again and rolled quietly towards the front door of the cottage.

'Can you see them? Are they here?' He peered out into the black. The lantern beam lighting up the headland, then plunging it back into darkness. There was no sign of life in the lighthouse and no sign outside it.

He got out of the car, battling the wind to come around to her side. He dragged her out. Alice nearly fell to the ground, legs cramping after hours trapped inside a car. Her only time outside it when he'd let her attend to her comfort. Short-lived and humiliating moments.

'Stand! Use your legs!'

'I'm trying to.'

His hand vice-gripped to her arm, he went to the door. Tried the handle. It was locked. He looked around him, uneasy. Alice felt the nervous energy in him. It fed her own.

Dragging her, he came away from the building, walking towards the cliff.

'Finn Tobin! Show yourself!'

David's voice echoed out to sea. Nearly swallowed by the competing cacophony of waves and wind. He looked around frantically. Behind them. Around the other side of the lighthouse.

'Where is he?' David's voice was sharp, worried. 'Why is the cottage locked? We need to get in there. Out of this bloody storm.'

Alice said nothing. She was scared too. Where was Finn? Had he left her to her fate?

Like a slow strobe, the next flare of the lighthouse lit up the space.

And they were there.

Finn. Mac. Vivienne. In front of them, between David and Alice and the sea.

Had they been here all along, watching them? Creeping around in the darkness?

David was unmoving beside Alice. Staring at them. All four old friends stood, just watching as the light flicked on then off then on again. Buffeted by the storm – the one around them and the one inside them.

Alice heard Vivienne gasp. In the next flash, Mac was beside Vivienne, holding her.

'Vivi...' The name slipped quietly, sad, from David's lips.

'Hello, old friend.' Finn's voice carried across the divide. Through her undamaged eye she looked at him, seeing his face register, then hide, shocked, when he looked at her.

'Is it done?' David called out.

The lantern flashed and Alice saw him nod.

'It's only four hundred and eighty thousand, that's all I could get, but it's close enough,' Finn yelled to be heard. 'It's already lodged to your account – we had access to your laptop at Mary's, so we had your details. There is a lawyer's letter, held with my people, witnessing that this is a gift. For an old friend.'

'And am I alive again?'

'You will be.'

The two men stared at each other.

'Finn...' David began. And then stopped himself. Alice felt his hold on her arm strengthen. 'How do I know this is true?' he called out.

'Take your phone out. And go to the end of the drive where there is signal. We had the details of your own lawyer, from your emails which I have seen. He's been given details of this legitimate transaction and he's going to call you. But you need to hurry, he'll be calling any second now.'

David, never letting go of Alice, started to run. Dragging her to the end of the drive and the low stone wall where she'd sat herself to make illicit calls. Where she and David had rescued that sheep. It felt like different people. A different life.

David's phone rang. He answered and Alice listened to one side of a conversation. David's tone one of surprise. Then delight.

He turned to her.

'He kept his word.'

With less hurry, he led Alice back down to the lighthouse. Her hair was blown across her face and with no free hand to tuck it away she stumbled blind next to him, nearly falling, righted by a rough jerk from her captor.

David slowed down, and the wind changed direction, whipping her hair from her face. Finn, Mac and Vivienne stood where they'd been. The wildness of the weather whirling around them.

'Confirmed?' yelled Finn, his voice carrying above the gales.

'Done,' replied David.

They stood there, rocked by the storm, staring at each other.

'Let Ali—' began Finn. But David looked away. Looked

bchind him. He'd seen a sudden change from Mac and Vivienne, the attempts to hide their frantic stare into the distance, beyond David and Alice. At the lights of a car. A squad car.

In one swift moment, Alice felt cold metal against her neck, David grabbed her, pulled her right up against him.

'I told you no cops! I can't believe you've done this, Finn! I thought we had a deal.'

Finn looked at Mac and Viv. Alice heard words from Vivienne on the wind: 'from earlier... they actually came.'

'I was on the level, David.'

'He was!' cried out Mac. 'These guys, we called them earlier, before you called. We didn't know they were coming.'

The headlights of the squad car, the illuminated blue light on top, snaked closer.

'I don't believe you!' David cried back. 'I told you I'd kill her! I told you I would!' He squeezed Alice closer to him. Pressed the blade to her neck. She felt a sharp pain and the wet trickle of beads of blood. She screamed.

Finn moved closer. Eyes wide in alarm. Viv cried out, 'No! Wait for the police!'

'I'm going to do it,' David growled. 'And then I'm going to slip away into the darkness. They'll never find me. You'll never find me. You'll regret this to the end of your days, Finn Tobin.'

Finn's face relaxed. Alice watched confused, then horrified, as it broke into a smile.

'Go ahead,' he said. 'Kill her. She's a liar and a charlatan. I don't care what happens to her. You'll practically be doing me a favour.'

FIFTY-FIVE

'Wh-what? Finn?'

Alice felt an icy-cold fist grip her heart. Even David's grasp loosened in shock.

'Lies since day one. I presume it was the profile piece that lured you in too?'

He turned to David.

'Kill her. Don't kill her. I don't care what you do. She means nothing to me.'

'What?' David looked from Alice to Finn. 'But... what? You did everything for Vivienne when she threatened you with her! You're bluffing. I'll really do it, don't think I won't.'

'Well, that was before. When I thought I knew who she was.' Finn looked directly at Alice, eyes blank. 'Vivienne heard you, talking on that burner phone of yours. Liar.'

David looked at Alice. 'Is this true?'

'I can explain!' Alice cried, looking at Finn, not David.

The squad car was getting closer. David looked to Finn. To Alice. To the car.

'Finn, I'm so sorry!' Alice pleaded.

'I've spent all day terrified for you. I've risked everything for you from the very day we met. And now, standing here, looking at you... I don't even know who you really are.'

Finn looked at David.

'Do what you want,' he said, then turned away. His back to Alice, he returned to Vivienne and Mac, their faces stunned.

'What... Come back!' roared David. 'Don't think I won't kill her!'

He pulled her tighter and Alice whimpered as the sharp edge of the knife pressed harder. Finn kept walking.

'This doesn't work if you don't care!' David roared to Finn's back.

To the sound of the Gardaí car tyres on the drive, the familiar crunch, Alice felt the pain at her neck sting. She twisted and fought, desperate.

Then she was tumbling. No hands to save herself, she fell to the ground, head smacking the hard earth. A bright light of pain flashing behind her eyes. Then there was movement around her. Mac's voice close and yelling as it passed her. Jumping over her. Screams and muffled thumps. She rolled into a ball, tucking in her head and knees, waiting for it to end.

FIFTY-SIX

'Are you sure we can't take you to A&E? That eye looks pretty nasty,' the young female garda asked her. Her colleague held a torch above them, lighting up the area. Lighting up Alice's battered face.

Alice shook her head. She'd get looked at tomorrow. Right now... she had things she had to do that couldn't wait. She had to stay here. She gingerly rubbed her red-raw wrists for what felt like the millionth time since the officer had cut her loose.

'Have you somebody to look after you now?'

Alice looked around for Finn. This was a good question. Did she?

'Yes, don't worry,' she said. She wasn't going to explain what was happening to the officer.

'Well, if you're sure. Take this.' The officer handed Alice a card. 'It has my number. You'll have to come in to talk to us again. From what your friends told us, I suspect the serious crimes team will be arriving from Letterkenny this evening. They'll want to talk to you.'

Alice nodded along. 'I'm not going anywhere.'

'Good.'

Alice looked at the back of David's head, through the squad car window. She looked at Mac, walking away, holding a sore arm. An injury acquired when restraining the fleeing David. He too was rejecting medical attention. The Gardaí had landed upon a confusing scene, and even after taking statements, Alice didn't feel they fully understood what they'd come across. As she'd listened, from a distance, she'd noticed the gaps in what the others had told them. Glossing over Vivienne's behaviour. The more complicated parts of their joint past. Probably why the officers were left a little confused. But thankfully they understood enough to know who to take away.

The Garda car pulled away. David was swallowed quickly into the dark night. Alice turned around. She needed to talk to Finn. She had to talk to him. Had he been serious in what he'd said to David? That she meant nothing to him now? Had it been a very risky bluff... or the truth? With her heart barely holding itself together, she thought she'd have preferred to have taken her chances with David than live with a rejection from Finn.

The lights were on in the cottage now, but their glow didn't stretch far. As she passed the windows, Alice saw no one inside. There was movement beyond, near the cliffs, where she and David had originally found the trio. They were in a huddle. Gathered away from the Gardaí. And her. The storm's rage had lessened but it blustered on regardless. Alice wished they'd gone inside. But she suspected the knowledge they now had of David's bugs kept them out here, where whispers couldn't be overheard.

Alice headed towards them. She made as much noise as she could. With the pulsing beam of the lighthouse only lighting her up half the time, she risked appearing to sneak up on them. They'd all had enough scares for a lifetime. She wouldn't be responsible for more. And she needed Finn to listen to her. To let her explain.

'Finn,' she said.

Despite her efforts not to surprise them, at her voice they all took a step back. Alice stopped. They were already a bit close to the edge, she didn't want her approach to push them closer. Following Alice's line of vision, Vivienne looked behind her and saw their proximity to the cliff edge. The dark disguising how near to the abyss they'd gotten. Finn in particular.

'Finn, come in, we've wandered a bit far,' she said. She and Mac nudged forward, Alice's proximity slowing them from a full retreat. Finn didn't budge.

'Finn,' Alice repeated. 'I need to talk to you. To explain. But please come in closer, it's still too wild to be so close to the edge. I promise I won't come any nearer if you come back in.'

He said nothing and still didn't move. With each sequence of dark and light, Alice hoped he'd move forward, but with each burst of brightness, he was in the same spot. He seemed transfixed by her. Rooted there.

She opened her mouth to plead with him, when he finally spoke.

'Who... who *are* you?'

Finn, face ashen, so pale its white glow was visible even in the dark, stared at her with hollowed-out eyes. The wind wailed around him, shaking him, unsteadying him, toying with him as he stood far too close to the cliff's edge, the waves beneath crying out for a sacrifice.

Alice looked at the other faces staring at her in the dark, the lighthouse beacon illuminating them in flashes, like secrets briefly whispered then concealed again.

'Finn, what are you talking about?' Alice stuttered, holding her hands out to him. 'You know exactly who I am. I'm your girlfriend, I love you.' She took a step towards him, her face crumpling in anguish. This was agony.

Finn recoiled, taking another step backwards, now so close to the edge that small loose rocks slipped under his foot and tumbled, falling, falling, falling into the deep, black ocean. Alice gasped. Her breath caught in her throat.

'Oh no you don't!' He held a hand up. 'Don't come near me.'

Alice could see the distress soaked deep in his eyes. Her own tears spilled down her face. Mac and Vivienne moved closer to Finn, like bodyguards, keeping him safe from her.

'Finn, please... please let me explain...'

'I said what I said to David to make him let you go. All I wanted to do was save you. But... but... now. Actually seeing you. Knowing you've been lying to me all this time.'

The beam of light continued its game of peek-a-boo. Darkness, then reveal. Darkness, then reveal – scaring Alice with what each new frame would show her.

This time Finn had turned and was looking at Vivienne. 'Viv, maybe you were right, I don't know her, I can't just trust that it was real. Maybe there is nothing for me here.'

'Finn,' said Vivienne, 'come in from the edge, seriously. Alice will go. Don't worry. We can talk about this, in the cottage. It's all been too much. We're all emotionally exhausted.'

Alice took steps backwards, quickly. Mac inched closer to Finn.

Finn looked over his shoulder. Looked down to the rocks and waves below. To where he'd nearly died the day before. Alice wanted to scream. She forced it in. Forcing herself to be silent. Not to startle him. To do nothing that might prompt him to do something stupid. Mac moved closer. Was he close enough? Alice couldn't tell in the blinking dark.

Finn looked back at her.

'I love you,' he said.

And turned.

It went black.

FIFTY-SEVEN

There was movement. A dash. Confusing flashes in the dark. A scream. Alice didn't know if it was hers or Vivienne's.

And then, from far below.

A splash.

The smack of something hitting the water.

This time Alice knew the scream that split the night air was hers. Erupting from the depths of her soul.

'Noooooo!'

She fell to her knees.

'It's okay! It's okay! I have him,' Mac's cracked voice rang out. 'We dislodged a rock, that's all. I have him.'

With each pulse of light, Alice made sense of the scene. Mac and Finn a tangled heap on the ground, Mac's head close to Finn's shoulder as he restrained him in an embrace. Vivienne falling forward, dropped to them, grabbing hold of Finn, even though he was safe now. Vivienne's head then beside Mac's, and Finn's, a three-headed creature. Vivienne sobbed. She lifted an arm and thumped Finn on the shoulder.

'Don't you dare do that! Don't you dare.'

Alice, apart, wept.

. . .

From a tray, Mac handed Alice a mug of tea. He then picked something small from it and held out his hand to her. From the armchair Alice reached up and accepted his offering.

'Paracetamol. It's not much but all I could find in the cupboards here. I think – that eye, your head – you need them.'

'Thank you, Mac. And not just... not just...' A choked-up Alice clasped her hand around the little white pills. Mac laid a hand for a moment on her head, then moved over to the sofa, distributing hot drinks to everyone.

They had walked a dazed and shaken Finn inside, compliant as a child. But the divide between them remained. Finn, Vivienne and Mac on the sofa. Alice at a distance, on the armchair.

Mac took a sip of his coffee and looked around the room.

'I think perhaps it is time, Alice, to tell us what you've been doing.' They'd filled in the gaps that Alice had missed when David had her trapped, as they'd lit the fire and covered Finn in blankets. Explained what David had done to manipulate them and what he'd planned to do. What Finn had done long ago. And what Vivienne had nearly done today.

'You know all our secrets now. In all their grubby, painful glory. None of us here is free from regret, shame. A wish that we'd been better or done things differently. We all have blame to shoulder. We'll listen to you, give you space to explain.'

Alice nodded, grateful. She gathered her thoughts.

She took a deep breath, but her voice still shook as she began.

'I wanted to ruin you, Finn.'

Despite what Mac had said, she hung her head. The shame was too heavy. This was too hard. She couldn't look at Finn. But she pushed on. Mac was right, they had shared their unvarnished failings. She had to too.

'I wanted to destroy your life.' She forced herself to look up, to look in Finn's shaken, pale, beautiful eyes. Watch the devastation as it unfolded. 'If you check your phone, you'll see pictures of me, sleeping in your bed, hidden in the recently deleted folder. I've used your phone to send emails to myself, purporting to be from you. If everything had gone to plan and we hadn't all been sent in different directions today, a photographer would have captured covert photographs of us together. Those calls I made were to a journalist, Ted Shaw, who has been writing a damning article about you, with information supplied by me, which would have highlighted your abuse of position in dating me. How you'd essentially lied about our relationship to HR and the board by hiding it. HR would have found my photos on your work phone. I'd have shown them the emails "you" sent, promising me promotions if I came away with you. Threatening me if I didn't. I collected receipts, to slip into your expenses, proving you did all this on the company dime.

'By the time I was done you'd have breached so many company policies that it wouldn't have mattered that it was you who'd enacted those policies in the first place. In this political climate, you'd have had to resign in disgrace. I was going to make that my one life's goal. If I'd been angry enough to perjure myself, you might have ended up facing charges, jail time. And I was very, very angry. I was going to do everything I could to try and ruin you.'

From across the room, Finn, wan and shaky, managed one word.

'Why?'

Alice forced herself to look him in the eye. Not to break his gaze.

'Why? I wanted to ruin your life. Because you ruined mine first. You ruined it when I was only a baby.'

The already still air in the room slowed even further.

Vivienne, as if controlled by an independent force, stood. Her eyes wide and stunned. Her breath was coming in raggy bursts.

She stepped into the centre of the room.

Breathless, she looked down at Alice in the armchair.

'I can't believe it... it just can't be...' She shot a look back at Mac and Finn, then looked back at Alice.

She reached out a hand.

'Hannah?'

FIFTY-EIGHT

Alice looked up at the desperate hope in Vivienne's eyes. And died a little more inside.

She shook her head.

'Oh God, Vivienne. I'm so sorry. I'm not Hannah.'

'Oh,' said Vivienne, her voice reduced. Small, as if far away. She covered her mouth with her hand, her eyes now cluttered with fresh tears. 'I, oh, I thought. You're the same age as she would be... You just said he ruined your life when you were a baby...'

Mac stood up and gently eased Vivienne back onto the sofa. Finn, though reeling himself, turned to his friend.

'Viv, I have money. I'll put an investigator on this. We'll find her for you. I promise... And I have something for her too. I was going to look for her anyway, in time. I've been putting money into a trust fund for her. For twenty years. Since I started earning. I felt so wretched that my actions had taken her from you, I wanted to do something to make up for it. I know money is no substitute...'

Vivienne took her friend's hand and squeezed it. Tears rolling down her devastated face.

'We'll find her,' Finn whispered.

They all looked back at Alice.

Mac, borrowing Finn's line from earlier, but uttered now in his soft, gentle baritone.

'Alice, who are you?'

Alice stood and retrieved her handbag from across the room. She then slumped back into her chair. She cracked the bag open, dipping her hand into the secret pocket inside. She took out the driver's licence, key and gate fob from within and placed them on the coffee table. She pointed at her picture on the plastic rectangle.

'My name is Alice *Kennedy*-Armstrong. My mother is Molly Kennedy. Is, not was, Finn. She's not dead. That's the key to the flat where she lives.' She nodded at the keys. 'I dropped the Kennedy just in case you remembered her. Made myself younger, too. Muddying all the waters, just in case. In the small chance you somehow made the connection. I didn't want to take even the slightest risk that you would remember and put two and two together.'

'Molly Kennedy,' Finn repeated.

'Yes, D—'

'Doctor Molly Kennedy?' Finn interrupted her.

Alice nodded.

'Doctor Kennedy,' said Finn once again. 'Christ. I never forgot her. She was the junior doctor who helped me. Lost her job because of it.'

'Lost her *career*. And then she spiralled. Drank too much. Suffered such serious mental health issues. My father had left her when I was a baby. Never met me. We had no safety net. So, when her life was ruined, so was mine. I know she made her own choices, she should never have taken that money from you, but she was desperate. She'd so many debts, I was only six months old. I wanted to ruin your career, just like you ruined hers. And ruin your life, just like you ruined hers and mine.'

'I never forgot her,' Finn repeated. 'I never let that guilt go.'

'I believe you. Now that I know more. And David has his share of the blame in her career destruction. He tried to bring himself back to life and triggered the investigation that ruined her career, though I don't think she realised that. So it wasn't just you.

'I'm so sorry, Finn. I was only seven or eight when I decided this was what I was going to do with my life. When Molly was drunk, she'd ramble on. Talk about the guy who ruined her life. How he'd wrecked her career. I was too young to understand, but I could understand enough to know that my mother, the doctor, was now a penniless, neglectful drunk because of some nameless, faceless guy out there. My tummy rumbled, I blamed you. When the kids laughed at me in school because I smelled, because of the lice in my hair, when my clothes didn't fit, I blamed you and hated you. The bogeyman whose fault this all was.

'When I was older, I made more sense of what Molly had said about it all. I did some research. I found out some of the story that she was too far gone to explain. By the time I was in my teens she was too addled from addiction and mental health issues to remember the specifics, no matter how hard I tried to get her to dig up the memories.

'I couldn't quite discover what she'd done, a lot was confidential. But I felt, from what I'd found, that maybe it was prescriptions, falsified ones, that had got her into trouble. I knew it was documentation of some sort and they made sense. Good little earner if you were willing to do it. I never knew it was a false death certificate. And I only discovered it was you when my mother saw that profile of you. You were right about that. She came home, brought a copy of the paper with her, she was gibbering unintelligibly. I finally got her to calm down, and I understood. It was you. And that was my final piece. I knew then who'd destroyed her career. I was going to destroy yours. I knew who'd destroyed my life. I hoped I'd be able to return the favour.'

Alice looked at Finn.

'I never realised meeting you would do the opposite. That you'd take my life and give it actual meaning. Build it up into something worth living for. I never had to pretend for a single moment. It was all real. I love you. I've no right to say that. Not after what I tried to do. But it's true and I want you to know that despite all the lies, I never lied about that.'

Finn stood up.

'What I did to your mother was the worst part of what I did.' He ran his hands through his hair, his mouth a straight line. 'I... I was a scattergun of misery, the cause of so much pain. But with everyone else I at least thought I was helping. Not with your mother, I knew it was wrong. I bribed her and pretended it didn't matter. You don't have to apologise to me. Everything is completely my fault.'

Alice shook her head. 'No...'

'My fault. No argument. But... I'm not actually sorry.'

'What?'

'Okay, sorry, that sounds all wrong. What I mean is... if it hadn't happened, I wouldn't have met you. And that is something I could never regret. You're smart, beautiful – tenacious. You see the real me and love me. I wish so much suffering hadn't preceded our meeting, and I am going to do everything in my power to fix what can be fixed... but let's... let's do it together?'

He looked back at Vivienne and Mac as well with these last words.

Finn put out his hand to Alice. She took a step towards him. She put her hand out too. Finn took it and pulled her into him. He wrapped his arms around her. Kissed her head. Alice buried her face in his warm, strong chest. Heard his heart beat.

'Together,' she whispered.

EPILOGUE

Vivienne climbed into the limo, pulling the door shut behind her.

'How do I look?' She wriggled and vibrated like a child in line to see Santa. 'Do I look okay? Are we still sure this was the right outfit?' She spread her hands down her cream shirt and skinny jeans. With her hair recently done, her blonde waves bounced and shone.

The car moved off, into traffic.

'You look amazing,' said Alice, sitting across from her. She reached over and tucked a straying strand of hair behind Vivienne's ear. 'It's exactly right.'

Alice thought of that Saturday afternoon when she'd asked a doom-filled Mac why they were at the lighthouse and he'd murmured an ominous 'closure'. The irony was they'd gotten that resolution. All of them. The ghosts that had plagued them, everyone, had been exorcised.

Alice's phone vibrated. Finn, sitting beside her, looked down at the device on her lap. He raised an eyebrow as she unlocked it. Some things hadn't changed. But they were getting better.

'Molly?' he asked.

Alice nodded as she read the text. 'Just checking in.'

'Things any easier?'

Alice shrugged. 'She understands that no one made her do the things she did, you know? But I guess decades of blaming you are hard to let go of. I think she's trying.'

'I hope so,' said Finn. 'For your sake, not mine.'

'We'll get there. Don't worry.'

Finn squeezed her hand.

'And Ted has definitely stopped bothering her? I can get my legal people on it again if he hasn't.'

Alice gave Finn's hand a squeeze back. 'I've told you already, you can stop worrying about him. He's moved on. Yeah, he got a sniff at it all, he was definitely getting close to what really happened back then. But David taking all the responsibility for the faked death at trial, that finished it. He lost interest.'

'You know I was ready to take responsibility for my actions, David didn't have to do that,' said Finn.

'I know, hon,' said Alice.

'Really, don't be concerned, Finn,' said Vivienne. 'David knows Hannah's trust fund is safer if you're not ruined or in prison. He was going down for so many crimes, claiming he'd been the one to bribe Molly and all of that, it was a drop in the ocean of his sentence.'

'And maybe a little financial help in the future from his daughter will be a drop in the ocean of her trust fund,' muttered Alice.

Vivienne looked at her. 'I hope not. I want to believe David has finally stepped up for his daughter, that he's doing it for the right reasons,' said Vivienne.

'I hope so too,' said Alice.

'Have you seen him recently?' asked Finn.

'I've visited a couple of times. It's better to forgive it all... it's a lot healthier.'

Finn looked out the window then tapped on the divide between them and his driver.

'Stop here,' he called.

The car slowed and pulled into the kerb. The car door opened and Mac hopped in.

'Hey, all,' he beamed at them.

'Hey, Mac,' they chorused back.

'How was it?' asked Alice.

'Same as usual.'

'What step are you up to now?'

'About five hundred and fifty, I think.' He laughed. 'It's all good. How was the first day at the new job? The other kids play nice?'

'Ah yeah, it was fine. Everyone was lovely. Not as much fun as TobinTech.' Alice looked at Finn and they both blushed a little. 'But I get a nice celebratory dinner out of it tonight, so that's nice.'

'It deserves celebrating,' said Finn. 'I'm proud of you.'

Alice leaned over and kissed Finn on the cheek, beaming at him.

The car wove its way through the afternoon traffic.

'What was the final choice of destination?' Mac asked.

'Stephen's Green,' Finn replied.

'Well, it's a lovely day for it.' They all looked out the tinted windows at the sun-dappled streets. The summer sun solar-powering the crowds, who laughed and joked, ate ice creams as they enjoyed the beautiful day.

The car drove up Kildare Street and turned left. It pulled up and stopped outside the Shelbourne Hotel. A doorman approached and opened the door. Vivienne smiled up at him. She looked at the others.

'I guess this is it, then.'

'Yep! Good luck, we'll be dying to hear,' said Alice.

Mac grabbed Vivienne into a bear hug. Finn leaned over and squeezed her knee.

'Thanks, guys.'

With a deep breath, Vivienne got out of the car. They all turned and looked out the right side window. They watched as she skipped across the road, not waiting for the green man. She stopped on the other side, by the Wolfe Tone statue guarding the far entrance to the green. At the same time, approaching from around the corner, came a young woman, tall and slim with wavy blonde hair. The pair stopped and looked at each other. Identical wide shy smiles spread across their faces. Alice saw Vivienne's lips move. *Hannah?* The girl nodded. They turned, already chatting, into the park.

Finn, Alice and Mac sat back down, away from the window.

'Oh, I hope it goes well,' said Alice.

'It will. I know it will,' reassured Finn.

The confused doorman peered in, an eyebrow raised.

'This is you, I think?' said Mac.

'Yes, dinner reservation,' said Finn, as if suddenly remembering. 'Tell James to drop you wherever you need.'

'Thanks, Finn. Enjoy your evening.'

'We will,' Finn replied, and got out of the car. The glorious sun shone down on him, to Alice's eyes making him practically glow. As if he had a spotlight on him. His dark curls shone, and his pale blue eyes sparkled. She felt her breath catch. He leaned back in, putting a hand out for her. She hesitated a moment. This feeling of freedom, to be seen together, was still taking time to get used to. Even now.

'Come on then.' He smiled at her.

Alice reached out and took his hand. She stepped out, joining him in the sun.

A LETTER FROM TRÍONA

Dear Reader,

I want to say a huge thank you for choosing to read *The Other Couple*. It really means so much to me that you did. If you enjoyed it, and want to keep up to date with all my latest releases, just sign up at the following link. Your email address will never be shared and you can unsubscribe at any time.

www.bookouture.com/triona-walsh

Like a lot of fiction, this story was inspired by a grain of truth! A few years ago, when checking into a B&B, the host murmured something about hoping the other people who booked the accommodation didn't show up. It turned out a website glitch had let someone else book the cottage, and no matter how hard she'd tried to contact them, she never reached them. I will never forget the dread of that night, staying in the middle of the wild, west of Ireland countryside, waiting for a knock at the door and strangers to be on our doorstep. Thankfully, they never showed up. I don't know what happened to them! (Perhaps that's another story altogether.) But the memory of that anxiety, to be faced with the arrival of strangers with nowhere else to go, never left me. And, being a crime writer, when I used this moment in my own life as inspiration, it all got very sinister very quickly.

As with all my books, the setting – the lighthouse at Fanad –

is a real place. Stunning, wild and beautiful. And that sunken WWI ship? It's real too... as is the missing gold.

I hope you loved *The Other Couple*, and if you did I would be very grateful if you could write a review. I'd love to hear what you think, and it makes such a difference helping new readers to discover one of my books for the first time.

I love hearing from you – get in touch through my social media or my website.

Thanks,

Tríona

www.trionawalsh.com

 facebook.com/TrionaWalshAuthor
 x.com/thetrionawalsh
 instagram.com/trionawalsh

ACKNOWLEDGEMENTS

To Jayne Osbourne who was there when the idea for this book emerged and provided such wise guidance as it decided what kind of book it was going to be.

And to Ruth Jones, my editor, who jumped onboard as the first words were written and who has been a fantastic partner in bringing this story to fruition.

To all the team at Bookouture, from my copyeditor and proofreader (thanks DeAndra and Liz!) to the publishing executives and the unfailingly enthusiastic publicity team. And all the other talented members of the team whose hard work makes this all happen. Thank you.

As always I must thank my wonderful parents, still my poor, tortured first readers. You get the first glimpse at new words and your insightful feedback is always gratefully received!

To those brothers of mine – Ciarán, Dara and Garry. Always enthusiastic and supportive of their writer sister and her murdery books. It means so much to me. Thank you, I love you all, you're the best.

A special mention goes to Ciarán and my sister-in-law Rachel, in whose house so much of this book was written. Thank you for accommodating us in your gorgeous home while ours was being ripped apart. I wrote sitting in the upstairs bay window, taking breaks to watching the world go by. From the people during the day to the eerie silent ambulances at night, blue lights flashing but no sirens, off to nearby James's without waking up the neighbourhood, they all kept me company as I created this book. (And a special side thank you to Bread Man Walking – the microbakery we discovered around the corner in Dublin 8. Those Basque cheesecakes and beignets kept me going!)

Thank you to all my friends who are always so encouraging and interested, in particular Lisa, without whose wisdom and kindness I'd be lost.

To the Hurts Like A Pain Writers – Cait, Joe and Niamh. I've thanked you before and I'm going to thank you again because you deserve all the acknowledgement in the world. You are legends! I am so grateful to know such a talented bunch of writers who are also the kindest, most generous, most supportive souls ever. There's a little piece of all of you in everything I write.

And to those kids of mine, to whom this book is dedicated. As I said in the dedication, you four will always be my very best creations. You're funny, wise, loud, messy, and occasionally quite incomprehensible. (But always in a charming way.) I love you more than can be put into words. And that's saying something 'cause I'm a writer.

And my husband Dan, you deserve a medal. All the medals. It's a cliché to say I couldn't do it without you, but it's true.

To all my readers, thank you, you're why I do this tricky but wonderful job. Thank you to everyone who has taken time to drop me a message to tell me how much you've enjoyed my books. I don't think you'll ever understand how much that means to this writer, and what a boost it gives me.

And, as ever, I sign off thanking those feline MVPs, Bob, Maggie and Zuzu, my constant companions. We still don't have that cat flap, and I know you're just as annoyed about it as me. But it means we get to hang out more as I write my books. And yes, I think you really do want to go outside this time.

PUBLISHING TEAM

Turning a manuscript into a book requires the efforts of many people. The publishing team at Bookouture would like to acknowledge everyone who contributed to this publication.

Commercial
Lauren Morrissette
Hannah Richmond
Imogen Allport

Data and analysis
Mark Alder
Mohamed Bussuri

Editorial
Ruth Jones
Sinead O'Connor

Copyeditor
DeAndra Lupu

Proofreader
Liz Hatherell

Marketing
Alex Crow
Melanie Price
Occy Carr
Ciara Rosney
Martyna Młynarska

Operations and distribution
Marina Valles
Stephanie Straub
Joe Morris

Production
Hannah Snetsinger
Mandy Kullar
Jen Shannon
Ria Clare

Publicity
Kim Nash
Noelle Holten
Jess Readett
Sarah Hardy

Rights and contracts
Peta Nightingale
Richard King
Saidah Graham

Made in United States
Orlando, FL
26 October 2024

53113755R00193